I0612648

Quarantine Stories

25 Short Love Stories set During the 2020 Quarantine

By: Jacqueline Thomas

Copyright © 2020 Jacqueline Thomas

ISBN: 978-1-7358006-0-8 (Paperback)
ISBN: 978-1-7358006-1-5 (eBook)

First paperback edition: September 2020.

Edited by: Linda A. Dickey

Published by JST Publishing
https://jacquelinecthomas.com/

Quarantine Stories

25 Short Love Stories set During the 2020 Quarantine

Jacqueline Thomas

To my quarantine mates, thank you for putting up with my insufferable ass.

I want to dedicate this book to all of the frontline workers who kept the world moving in our darkest hours. Thank you for your sacrifice and service.

Table of Contents

Table of Contents

Introduction

In late February, 2019, as my husband and I walked down the beach in Malibu, California, passing celebrity homes the first spark of an idea came to mind. At the time, I was on the West coast for a business trip. That morning as I got ready for the day, scenes of COVID ravaging Italy was all over the news. Cases had begun to pop up in New York, and on the West Coast. COVID. During our trip there was a feeling that something big was coming but I didn't know what.

In the span two weeks between walking on the beach in Malibu, and full quarantine, everyone's lives changed. In that span of time I had also started a new job in a major American city. I remember sitting on the commuter train, watching less and less people get on each day. I was on the train the night that the President Trump addressed the nation, watching in disbelief on my phone like my fellow passengers. I looked up and saw a couple sitting across the car, reassuring each other that everything would be okay.

Soon stories and examples of people were preparing, adapting and adjusting to what life would become were apparent in my own life and in the headlines. When everyone was sent home to work, and the lockdown started, I wondered what a love story would look like in this time. How would people meet, let alone fall in love?

During the early days of quarantine, we also saw frontline workers become everyday heroes, grocery workers, truck drivers, nurses, doctors and so many more brave individuals that kept our society and economy running. I tried to capture the bravery, loneliness, love, and connections that were prevalent during this time. I started the project in April of 2020, the during the height of the lockdown. I went through many of the difficulties my characters faced, from job furloughs, to the fear for loved ones, and a further respect for those who acted so bravely during these dark days. My only rule for these stories that was that the characters must be stuck together in quarantine. So without further ado, I present, Quarantine stories, a twenty-five short love stories set during the pandemic and quarantine of 2020.

Mia & Luke: A Beach Story

Mia stepped into the elevator with a weak cup of coffee from the sad pot in her hotel room in hand. She'd get proper coffee after the meeting. Her stomach flipped nervously as the elevator descended. She said a small silent prayer that it would not stop at Luke's floor. Last night had been awkward; she had almost slept with him. The elevator bell rang as the door opened and Luke stepped in. Mia looked down nervously and tucked a strand of hair behind her ear.

"Morning," Luke said lightly.

"Good morning," Mia replied.

"Ready for this meeting?"

"Mm-hmm," Mia said, praying this would be the end of the forced conversation.

Luke turned towards her.

"Mia, about last night."

No, not here, I don't want to talk about this now, she thought. The elevator bell dinged as they reached the ground floor. Mia had never been so grateful to be out of the elevator. She stepped out, and

Luke followed. They had the pitch of their career to one of their firm's largest clients in Santa Monica. The plan had been to fly in and out quickly before travel for the country shut down. A virus was spreading rapidly across the globe, and there was talk of a travel shutdown. The company needed this pitch to go well. Mia and Luke were the top two performers for the company, so they had been sent out on a Hail Mary.

Mia stepped out of the hotel, expecting the air to be warm, but the ocean breeze was still chilly. It sure beat the snow back in Chicago, she thought. The doorman recognized her and went to get the rental car. Luke took advantage of the moment.

"Mia, about last night, I just wanted to apologize."

"There's no need. We had a nice time, and things just got out of hand, no need to apologize."

Please let this be the end of this, Mia thought to herself. She couldn't deal with this and bring her A-game to the pitch. The car came around, and Mia walked to the driver's side before Luke could. The passive-aggressive move of power was noticed. As Mia took the key, the driver asked, "Are you folks leaving today before the shutdown?"

"Hopefully," Mia said as she got into the car.

Luke, who had already gotten in the car, leaned towards the driver's side. "Any word on anything official? The news was saying maybe by 5 pm tonight?"

"I haven't heard anything official. I just know most everyone is checking out this morning."

Three hours later, Mia and Luke walked out of the Plaza Building, closed deal in hand. Mia had worked her entire career to get to this point, and now, she had just accomplished something that was sure to put her in line for a significant promotion, possibly partner in the firm. As Luke drove back to the hotel, they had both noticed that traffic seemed a bit lighter.

"Should we have a drink to celebrate," Luke asked as they pulled up to the hotel?

"Maybe a drink at the airport might be better. With everyone so jittery about a shutdown, it creeps me out. I'll feel better once we are on the plane back home.

"You're right. It's a weird feeling, isn't it? Let's pack up and head for the airport early then?"

"Sounds good to me. I'll meet you down in the lobby in twenty?"

"Sure."

They dropped the car with the valet again and went up to their rooms. Mia changed out of her suit and heels and into jeans and a soft navy sweater and a pair of loafers for the flight. She packed up the last of her toiletries and checked her appearance in the mirror. Her engagement ring caught the sunlight as she straightened her hair. She stopped and looked down at it, and thought of Landon, her finance. They had been friends first, then lovers, and now even though they were engaged, they sat in some sort of a grey area. She loved him, but the passion was gone. When she had accepted the ring, she had meant it. She and Landon had been engaged for almost five years, yet neither felt that they needed to set a date.

Mia met Luke down in the lobby, and they walked out and waited for the car to be brought around again. Mia noticed Luke's grey sweater seemed to match his eyes, as his auburn hair, with its natural golden highlights, shone in the California sunshine.

"You look nervous," Luke said.

"Me? No, not really. I just want to get home."

"Will Landon be home?"

"No, he called last night. He's going to wait it out in Singapore."

"He's still over there with that merger?"

"Yeah, he wants to be there as soon as life resumes to help push it through."

Luke nodded, and Mia knew it was a silent judgment. She resented it and felt embarrassed for what looked like Landon's lack of concern for her. The car came around, and Mia let Luke drive. She was grateful for the pause in conversation as she looked out the window. Twenty minutes down the road, both Mia and Luke's phone buzzed. Mia pulled her phone out to see that the flight home to Chicago had been canceled. Luke's said the same thing. Luke pulled off the highway and pulled into a Starbucks parking lot.

"Okay, plan B," Luke said.

"No plan B," Mia replied, "All air traffic has been halted. We're stuck. We can try and drive. I mean, we have a rental car." She didn't look up from her phone.

"If this virus is serious enough to halt air traffic, I doubt that we'll make it driving cross country to Chicago."

Mia turned and looked at Luke, hoping he couldn't see how

11

terrified she was.

"I don't know anyone out here to stay with. I guess we can go back to the hotel?"

"I have an idea. It's nuts, but it's an idea."

Mia took a deep breath.

"My Uncle owns a little cottage further up the coast, near Cambria. I could call and see if it's free, and we could wait this out up there?"

Mia looked out the window as she weighed Luke's suggestion. Who knew how long they were going to be trapped.

"Mia, do you want me to call and see?"

Mia nodded, "Okay, it's better than staying back at the hotel. The logistics of that are a nightmare."

Mia stepped out of the car as Luke placed his call. She pulled out her phone and leaned up against the vehicle. She wanted to let Landon know what was going on. It was early there, but she didn't want him to worry. Her hands shook as she texted him:

Hi babe, sorry to text so early. So, I'm stuck in California. I don't know how long I'll be here. Luke from work has a cottage up the coast where we're going to try to stay near Cambria. Hope you're safe.

She dropped her phone and reached down to pick it up. Luke knocked on the window as she wiped the grit from the parking lot off her phone. She turned around and opened the car door.

"The cottage is ours. We can order some groceries to be dropped off if we order quickly. My Uncle Dan said the place is pretty well stocked now. They were going to try to come down but didn't make it before the shutdown. Do you want to go?"

Mia got into the car.

"Thank you. I think that's the best idea, at least until we know more. Your Uncle won't mind you bringing me along?"

"No. It will just be us. As I said, they got stuck up in Washington state, where they live. Actually, had I known they had planned to come down, I would've just planned to go there anyway. The cottage is in a pretty spot."

"Thanks for letting me come along. Please make sure to thank your Uncle for me."

"I will, but we'd better get going; it's a bit of a drive. Will you look up the number to Dub's Grocery Store in Cambria City? We'll need to order groceries."

"By phone? Don't they have a website?"

"I'm sure they do, but my uncle said to talk to Dub directly."

"Ah, let me find the number here."

Four hours later, just as the sun was beginning to set, they pulled off the Pacific Coast Highway onto a dirt track towards the ocean. The drive had been so incredibly beautiful, and during normal circumstances, Mia would have insisted on stopping several times to get pictures and explore the neat little towns they passed through. The car crept over the bumpy track as they descended towards the shore. Around a bank of large trees stood a small white cottage. It reminded Mia of something out of an English garden more than the California coast. Luke pulled the car up to the covered porch and spotted the two boxes of groceries that said Dub's General Store- Cambria City, CA. on the side.

Mia stepped out of the car as the wind whipped off the ocean. Streaks of red, orange, purple, and magenta streaked across the sky as the sun made its final descent towards the horizon. Even in these circumstances, it was so beautiful that one could not help but stop and take in the splendor of it. She shut the car door and walked towards the edge of the small cliff where the cottage sat. The sandy beach was accessible through a well-worn path. She walked to the edge and looked down, thinking there had to be a good twenty feet between her and the shore. She backed a few steps back and curled her hands around herself as the wind battered her. It's so beautiful here, it's worth being cold, she thought to herself. She heard Luke approach from behind and turned to see him walk up with a wool blanket.

"Here, I thought you might want this. It's never really hot here, and always windy." He held out the blanket for her.

"Thank you," she said over the roar of the wind.

She pulled the blanket around her and took a deep breath. The wool seemed to be an impenetrable force for the cold wind. It warmed her quickly.

"You enjoy it. I'll bring our bags in." Luke said.

Snapping out of the trance-like state from the sunset, she turned and faced Luke, remembering she was a guest and had been incredibly rude.

"Oh, let me help. Sorry, I was just so struck by the beauty of this."

"No, stay. Enjoy it. It is beautiful."

Mia smiled and turned back towards the view. She heard Luke walk back towards the car and took a moment to recheck her phone. Landon had not texted back, and it was now morning. He had to have seen the text by now, Mia thought. She looked at her phone, no texts, and no missed calls. Wondering if her phone was not working properly, she turned it off and back on again. Turning back to the sunset, she checked the phone screen occasionally as it rebooted. Once fully up and running, the status had stayed the same. She tried not to be concerned.

As the last sliver of fiery orange dipped below the horizon, Mia turned back towards the cottage. It was quaint with its wood siding and turquoise blue shutters. She walked back and saw a white wicker swing partially covered, sitting on the porch waiting to be hung. On the other side, there was a small bistro table and two chairs. She knocked as she opened the front door, not sure what the polite thing was to do. The front of the cottage had been recently redone, as everything looked more modern than the structure itself. There was a large open plan kitchen that shared the space with a smaller living room and a stone fireplace off to one side. The other side of the room was flanked by French doors that looked out to the ocean.

"Come in," Luke said, standing behind the kitchen island. "I'm just putting the groceries away."

Mia slung the blanket over the back of the couch and walked towards the kitchen.

"I'm sorry I should've helped. I don't think I've ever seen a sunset so beautiful in all of my life. What a beautiful spot."

"Don't worry. It happens to the best of us. I used to spend summers here when I was a kid. The whole world seems to stop when the sun sets like that here. When I was a kid, my parents, aunts, and uncles, grandparents, they'd all have cocktails out there for sunset."

"Really," Mia said as she sat at one of the stools at the kitchen island. "That is very neat. I've never asked where you're from."

"My family is from New York, and we're spread all over the country. I grew up in New York state, though."

"Hmmm, I've never picked up your accent."

"Oh, this accent?" Luke said in a thick New York accent.

"That'd be the one," Mia laughed.

"I kind of lost it over the years."

"So summers on one coast, and the rest of the year on the other. Nice."

"Would you like a glass of wine? Uncle Dan always keeps a stocked cellar. We can help ourselves to anything but the wine on the red racks."

"Sure, where's the cellar?"

"Here, I'll show you."

Mia got up and followed Luke to the wall behind the kitchen, where a fully stocked wine cellar stood. She followed him into the small space in awe of how many bottles there were. She would have never thought from the outside that the inside of the cottage would have such lovely amenities. Luke reached around her and grabbed a bottle of Malbec. Mia caught a whiff of his scent, leather, sandalwood, and something citrusy that she couldn't place. She had first noticed on the flight out.

She and Luke had worked together for the past two years, but both traveled for work and rarely spent time in the office together for more than a week at a time. She liked him. He had always been friendly to her and competent at his job. They had gone out to a few social occasions at work, and he had met Landon. Luke had a wife, who ran off with her personal trainer, shortly after Mia had met Luke.

As they walked out of the cellar, Mia found the bathroom. She stepped in front of the mirror and took in her windswept look. Her cheeks were pink from the wind still, and her normally smooth brown locks were sticking out in every which way. She smoothed her hair down, running her fingers through it, as the noise of the ocean pulled her towards the window. She looked out of the small bathroom window towards the ocean. It was now dark outside, but she knew it was there. She could smell it and hear it.

After a dinner of grilled steaks and a bottle of wine, they sat in front of the massive stone fireplace with a small fire going. There was something so comfortable about the cottage that felt instantly like home to Mia, and for some reason, that put her slightly on edge. With its overstuffed cushions, the large white sofa felt like a cloud to sit on as Luke sat in the leather chair opposite. They had talked about the merger and toasted to their success at dinner. Mia wasn't trying to be rude; she just wasn't very talkative. Landon's absence had unsettled her. She'd try and call him when she settled in for the night.

As if Luke read her mind, he asked, "Have you heard from Landon?"

Mia sat up further on the couch.

"I haven't. Normally, I'd say he was in a meeting, but it's a Saturday morning, afternoon now. I wish he'd text, something, so I know he's okay."

"It won't bother me if you want to call him."

"I tried earlier. I'll try again at bedtime."

"I'm sure there's an explanation for his absence. Why don't I show you to your room? That way, you can call or have time to yourself when you want to?"

"Thank you," Mia nodded as she said it, although she wasn't sure if it was Luke's subtle way of asking for the living room for himself.

Luke stood, and Mia followed him past the kitchen and bathroom towards the back of the cottage.

He stopped at the last door of the hallway.

"I'm going to give you the master. You'll have your own bathroom and private deck, kind of your own space. It also has the best views in the cottage."

"Oh? You don't have to give me the best room."

"Believe me, you'll want it when you see the view in the morning," Luke said as he opened the door and switched on the light. There was a large bed with plush white linens and a tall tan upholstered headboard. The furniture in the room was in various shades of white, light tan, and the palest baby blue to look like the ocean. The far side of the room was a series of French doors that overlooked the view, and where the private deck was. The room looked like a luxury, boutique hotel room. Luke and Mia stepped into the room entirely, and he turned around.

"The bathroom is in there. There is a clawfoot tub in there large enough to swim in."

"Luke, this is generous. Are you sure?"

"Absolutely. When you wake up in the morning, look to your left out those doors. You will not be disappointed."

"Where are you staying, I mean, which room?"

"First door on the left, down the hall. It's always been my room here. Don't worry, all of the rooms are really nice. There's your suitcase," he pointed to it sitting next to the dresser, "please feel free to use anything you'd like or need. I'll let you get settled in. Think of

16

the cottage as your's too."

"Luke, thank you so much, and if you talk to your Uncle, please tell him thank you too. This is so generous and so beautiful."

Mia reached out and hugged Luke, and he hugged her back. The hug was filled with gratitude, but there was something more there, Mia felt it, and she knew Luke did too. There was something about being in his arms that she found intoxicating. The hug lasted a second longer then it should have; when she pulled away, his lips brushed over the top of her head. She wasn't sure if it was intentional or not, but her stomach fluttered. She stepped out of his embrace, both unsure and slightly embarrassed.

Luke left the room, and Mia settled in. She walked into the bathroom and turned on the light to see the tub Luke had mentioned. It was beautiful. She opted for a shower instead, saving a soak in the big tub for another night. She was grateful that the cottage had been well-stocked, not just with food, but quality toiletries as well. She slipped into her pajamas, a soft pink colored silk slip, with champagne-colored lace. She had spotted it in a window of a lingerie boutique on Oak Street in Chicago. The slip was ridiculously expensive, but she splurged and bought it anyway. Tonight the luxurious weight of the silk felt softer against her skin. She pulled the throw pillows off the bed and sat them in one of the chairs in the room. Pulling back the blankets, she climbed into the bed, sinking into the lushness of it. The bed linens were of the highest quality, and the mattress seemed to hug her body. She picked up her phone from the nightstand and called Landon again. This time she left a more serious voicemail asking him to call no matter the hour.

The next morning Mia woke early before Luke. She pulled her robe around her and set out to make coffee in the kitchen. Once the pot had brewed, she poured herself a cup and took it back to her room. She had intended to drink it in bed, but the view of the ocean from the deck lulled her outside. With the way that the deck had been built, and the cottage situated on the plot, the wind from yesterday did not batter her. It was still chilly, and she pulled her robe closed further as she sipped her coffee. She checked her phone and tried to call Landon again as she dressed for the day, but still did not get an answer. Her annoyance had begun to turn to worry.

Over the next few days, Mia and Luke passed the time by

working, reading, and playing old board games. Mia had not heard from Landon, and she was sick with worry. At the same time, she found herself falling hard for Luke. There was something in the air between them that felt like pressure building. Mia knew what the release was, but she wouldn't let herself think about it for too long. Luke took a business call from his room, while Mia worked from the kitchen island when her phone buzzed. She reached over and saw that it said she had missed a call from Landon. The phone had not rung. She picked it up and ran back to her room, calling him again. This time he finally picked up after four days of silence.

"Lan, are you okay?"

"Hi, I'm all right. How is California?"

"What? Where have you been?"

"I'm sorry I haven't answered your calls and texts. I.."

"Are you okay? Why didn't you answer me? Landon, I've been worried sick."

There was an eerie silence on the phone that put Mia on edge.

"I'm sorry I worried you. I just wasn't ready to have this conversation."

"What conversation? What are you talking about?"

"Mia, I met someone. I know there isn't a good time to do this, and my timing sucks. She lives here in Singapore."

"What, Landon? What are you talking about?"

"Mia, I'm sorry. I love you, but not the wife kind of love, more like a friend kind of love. I know I should've told you before now, I'm sorry."

This time Mia was silent. She didn't know what to say.

"Lee and I got married over the weekend. I'm not telling you this to hurt you. I just want you to know that I have fully committed to my new life here. We're going to have a baby. Mia, I'm sorry to hurt you."

Mia pulled the phone away from her ear in disbelief as she heard Landon call out her name. She pushed the red button on her screen and dropped her phone to make the pain spewing from it stop. She opened the French doors and walked off the patio, down to the beach. She sat for a long time deep in thought, how did I miss that? I know we've grown apart, but a whole other life! The more she thought about it, she wasn't sad that Landon wasn't marrying her. It was the betrayal that hurt most of all. When she looked deep down and was honest with herself, she knew it would not have worked with Landon.

The sun had shifted towards the horizon. She had sat for so long down on the shore. She was deep in her own thoughts that when Luke put his hand on her shoulder, he scared her.

"Sorry, I didn't mean to scare you. Is everything all right? You haven't moved from that spot for two hours. I thought maybe you'd gotten some bad news. Do you want company?"

Mia nodded, and Luke sat down next to her. He just sat and did not try to pull information out of her, knowing she'd talk when she was ready. Mia was grateful.

"Landon called. He got married yesterday, and has a baby on the way in Singapore."

Mia looked at him as her bottom lip quivered.

"Holy shit. Mia, I'm so sorry. That's awful."

"Is it strange that part of me thought it was coming? I mean, not exactly like this, but there was something in me that just knew something wasn't right. I was a coward. I should have left him. I... I.."

Luke reached over and pulled Mia's lips to his before she could finish her statement. His touch was gentle. He looked her in the eye, and she nodded slightly, giving permission before he brought his mouth down over hers. Suddenly Mia could feel that pressure between them begin to ease somewhat. She realized at that moment that the man she truly wanted. was kissing her in the most beautiful place she had ever been. She wrapped her arm around his neck and leaned into him, committing to the kiss. The shift in balance caused him to topple backward as he held her. He landed with a soft thud on the sand, and Mia pulled away enough to see his face. She felt his laugh before she heard it, and it put her at ease.

"I've wanted to do that for the past two years," Luke confessed.

"Only that," Mia asked with a playful tone in her voice?

Luke smiled slyly.

"We could go back up to the cottage and..." Mia said as she got off, Luke and stood.

He stood, and followed Mia, their walk, turning to a jog and then an all-out sprint by the time they reached the cottage. Mia turned around just as they entered the cottage and pulled Luke's body in close to hers. He kissed her with such passion that she felt it in her knees. The stood in the middle of the living room, shedding clothes, breathless.

"Mia, wait, stop," Luke said, each word coming out as a gasp. "I really want this, are you sure you want this?"

Mia removed her bra and let it fall to her feet.

"Mia, you're gorgeous."

"I want this more than I've ever wanted anything before." She reached up and pulled her mouth to his, kissing him without abandon.

Katie & Ken: A Complicated Affair

My phone buzzed again; shit, I knew it was him. As the woman wasn't, I was supposed to be the overly attached one in this scenario. I stood in my perfect kitchen, in my perfect house, baking cookies during quarantine, playing perfect wife and mother to the life I had built. Well, quarantine life was not what I had built, but like the entire world, I was making the best of it. We were in week three, and both my husband and I had moved our lives from outside to inside. We both traveled a lot for work, separately, of course. All that time apart left a human need for intimacy, so, on occasion, I took care of it, sometimes alone, sometimes with company. My husband, Ken, and I never discussed it, but I knew that he had done the same. My actions of infidelity weren't weaponized; they just filled a basic need, nothing more.

I remember sitting in a cab in Prague when one of Ken's flings called me. She was angry that he had broken off whatever arrangement they had. I had my suspicions that he was sleeping around, but I had not been confronted with them until then. In the back of that taxicab, his actions slapped me hard. The woman on the other end of the phone was hysterical, and something inside me told me that I was not going to play the victim, that I would handle this on my terms. I told the woman on the phone, "that's what happens when you sleep with a married man. Never call me again," and hung up the phone. When I got back to the hotel, I walked up to my room and changed into clothes to go out, like I was on autopilot. That night I got blindingly drunk and took some random man back to my room. Honestly, I don't even remember his name. The next morning, with the worst hangover of my life, I kept waiting for the feeling of guilt, but it wasn't there. I didn't run home and tell Ken what I had done; I kept it to myself.

From that night on, when I wanted company, I found it, and although Ken and I never discussed it directly, I felt that he understood and was relieved. When Ken and I both happened to be home at the same time, it now took the pressure off both of us. My actions were like a relief valve on a pressure cooker between us; it just worked. After my first night in Prague, I did set some ground rules which I had never broken until recently.

Rule 1: I never used my real name.

Rule 2: We always got a room. I didn't bring men back to the hotel where I was staying, nor did I go to their place.

Rule 3: The guy had to be a local

Rule 4: No contact information, exchanging of phone numbers, emails, etc.

Rule 5: Never sleep with the same guy twice, no matter how good the sex was.

Paolo had not just caused me to break my own rules, but smash them entirely. I met him one night in Seattle out at a bar. I was there on business, and he was too. We struck up a conversation at the bar. He was in town for a musician's conference and expo. He made bespoke guitars out of his loft on the West side of Chicago, the same city where I lived. Rule 1- broken. He had this indie rocker vibe going on, the night we met, with his chocolate brown hair resting on his shoulders, and a wool beanie on his head. He wore a beard, thick, and normally that was turn off for me, but that night it was working. The first night we slept together, I made a mistake and broke my second rule; we went back to my room. When we got in, I popped into the bathroom to freshen up and didn't think anything of it. Paolo spotted my papers that I had left out on the desk, seeing my real name, Katie Morgan, not Jenny Anderson, my fake name. This was rule 3 broken. That first night with Paolo, I didn't know it was possible to feel that much pleasure. It was the best sex of my life. The next morning when I woke, Paolo was gone, but he had left his card on top of my papers on the desk in the room. I went on with life, often thinking about him and that night, wondering if it had been my imagination or if the sex had really been that good. I wanted to see him again and challenge my own perceptions of that night. Ken had a birthday coming up and had always dabbled with the guitar. I decided to buy him a new bespoke guitar, and I knew who to buy it from. I called Paolo to see about ordering a guitar for Ken and was surprised when he remembered me. We arranged a time when I could come to the warehouse and pick out the elements for Ken's birthday gift.

Two weeks later, I drove over to the warehouse on the west side of the city. It didn't look like much from the outside. I knocked on the nondescript green metal door, hoping that someone would hear me. I had butterflies in my stomach the entire drive over. I knew this was a bad idea, but I had not been able to help myself. The door jerked open, and there Paolo stood in the daylight, in the same city I lived in, knowing my actual name, and he was just as handsome as he was on the night we had met. He smiled as he invited me in. The warehouse smelled of wood, as various workstations had been abandoned for a lunch break. There were numerous guitars in various states of construction. Paolo showed me around the shop floor. I noticed his hands, how he moved, it all felt like a mating dance. I picked out the materials for Ken's guitar, feeling the whole scene was surreal as he backed me up against the brick wall in the shop. We barely made it to his office before we were ripping clothes off of each other. He fucked me on his desk; it was the most erotic moment of my life.

Sleeping with Paolo soon became a regular occurrence when I was home, and that unnerved me. I only stepped out of my marriage while traveling, and when the need arose, not at home in the city, I lived with my husband. Paolo could do things to my body that I didn't even know it could do, and I found myself addicted to his touch. I felt untethered to reality when I was with him like I wasn't in control of anything, and that scared me. One night as we lay in his bed, in his apartment in the top floor of the warehouse, I mentioned that I had to go to London for work for the next two weeks and that it would be a while before I could see him again. It was my way of putting some distance between us, this arrangement was turning into something else quickly, and it scared me.

Two days after I arrived in London, on a Friday night, I came back to the hotel to find Paolo standing out front. Seeing him there scared me even more; this was turning into a relationship. I kept my feelings to myself. We did not leave the room for the entire weekend; neither of us able to satisfy the need for each other's bodies long enough to consider leaving. That Monday, when I went off to work, as I walked down the wet sidewalk, I knew I was in trouble with Paolo. This felt like an affair, not something transactional, satisfying a need. I knew I needed to end it. I told myself when I got back to the hotel that evening, I would. That night I fell into bed with him again and didn't end it.

We flew back home to Chicago early, due to the virus that was spreading, as there was a rumor that the borders would be closed. As we sat on the flight together, and it was clear to me that he had fallen in love with me. I had feelings for him too, but mine did not match. I still loved my husband, having made it very clear from the beginning of the tryst that I was married and had no intention of leaving my husband. I went back to the warehouse with Paolo that night and ended things; I had to, the situation was swallowing me up whole.

The next week was a blur, with quarantine lockdown coming into effect. Ken and I both had our jobs move from out in the world to inside our own home. Our three school-aged sons were home too. I found it odd how easily I slid into the life of devoted mother and wife, but I felt like a fraud. Paolo had called and texted, begging me to come back to him. I knew as I looked at my phone buzzing on the edge of the counter, it was him calling. I transferred the hot chocolate chip cookies off the baking tray onto a cooling rack, trying to ignore the call. I felt a pang of guilt that I had cut him out of my life so swiftly, as I sent the call to voicemail.

That evening, as I made dinner, my phone rang and rang. I eventually had to turn it off. Ken and I watched a movie after we put the kids to bed. I poured myself another glass of wine as Ken announced he was going upstairs to bed. It was not until the house was quiet that I was brave enough to turn my phone back on. I sipped my wine as I listened to Paolo's voicemails. His voice was raspy as he said he had come down with a cold. He professed his love for me over and over. I was so tempted to text him; I felt terrible; I had not intended for things to get so complicated. I stared down at my phone, taking one last drink of the wine in my glass. I typed, "I'm sorry." I stared at it, trying to think through what my actions would cause. I had unintentionally done enough damage. I erased my text and went up to bed.

That night I slept poorly. I dreamt of Paolo and me together. I was happy in my dream. I woke the next morning feeling unrested and conflicted. I dug into my work for the day, as Paolo kept calling. I found that part of me wanted to pick up the phone and talk to him to make it right, but deep down, I knew I couldn't. I wasn't going to leave Ken. I loved my husband and had always made that clear. The whole world seemed so surreal, with everyone at home, sheltering in place from the virus, and me going through a breakup. I debated whether to tell Ken. We had the sort of marriage where I knew I could tell him anything, but during a quarantine was not the best timing, I thought to myself. Over the next two weeks, the Paolo stopped calling, and I was relieved.

I was making dinner one evening about a month later, watching the kids play in the back yard through the kitchen window when Ken came in. He came up next to me and kissed me on the cheek, putting his arms around me. It felt wonderful, right, to be in my husband's arms. I stirred the chili, and I hugged his arms across my chest. I could hear our children laughing out in the back yard. There was something in Ken's body language that was off. I took the spoon out of the chili and set it on the spoon rest as I turned around. Ken walked over to the small bar in the family room and poured us each a drink. He brought the two glasses over and set them on the kitchen table.

"We need to talk," he said.

My stomach sank as I knew Paolo had to have contacted my husband. I tried not to tremble as I walked across the kitchen and sat down next to him. He slid my glass over to me.

"I have something I need to tell you, and I am not sure how you're going to react."

I stared at him blankly, trying to give him my best poker face.

"Paolo passed away."

I sat there still, unsure how to react.

"His family asked that you get this letter he wrote to you," Ken said as he took it out of his back pocket and slid it across the table.

My hand shook as I reached out for it.

"Did you read it," I asked as my voice cracked?

"No, but I did know about him, that you two had a fling."

"You knew?"

"Yes, one of the kids scratched the guitar you gave me. I took it back to him to have it fixed. I walked into his office, and it smelled like you; your perfume was still in the air. I asked him outright if he was sleeping with you. He didn't hide from it, he answered that he was and that he was in love with you."

Ken took a sip of his whiskey.

"I didn't say anything because I wasn't sure if you felt the same for him."

"I didn't. I'm sorry, this mess is my fault. What happened?"

"He died from the virus."

I felt the tears on my cheeks before I even realized I was crying.

"Did you love him?"

"N..no, not like I love you."

"He called me a few weeks back when you got back from London and told me he was going to ask you to marry him."

"What? No, he never asked, I wouldn't have let him. Why didn't you say anything to me about this?"

"I wanted you to be free to make your own decision. I love you, but I wasn't going to make you stay with me."

I picked up the glass that he had set in front of me and drank the whole pour in one massive gulp.

"Do you want to stay with me?"

"Katie, I love you, and I am not going anywhere. This time together with all of us home and put things in a different light. I am not going to sit here and pretend to be the model husband. I know you know about my own infidelity. It just seemed when things were so busy that it was just the way things needed to be. I realize now, being together like this, that maybe it isn't worth it, this life we've chosen."

"What do you mean?"

"I mean, I want you, all of you. I want us to be together. I want to reevaluate things. What are we doing? We're never here for our kids, each other… What, so we can have a membership to the country club we never go to? I want things to change, this time has given us a glimpse of what life can be like if we choose it."

I sat silently as I wondered when our priorities had changed so drastically.

"Will you read the letter? I don't think I can?"

I slid it back across the table, and Ken picked it up. I watched him open the envelope, and he unfolded the letter. I scanned his face for any emotion as he read it. He finished reading and folded, putting it back into the envelope.

"He saw what an amazing person you are too. He really loved you."

I wiped the tears from my cheeks, as Ken put his and over my hand that rested on the table. Our kids burst through the back door and ran through the kitchen as our son, Trevor, stopped, noticing I was crying.

"What's wrong with Mom," he asked?

"A friend of her's passed away. Go play."

"I'm sorry about your friend, Mom," he said as he walked out of the kitchen after his brothers.

I stood up, and Ken rose too. I wrapped my hands around him, and there was a split second where I wondered if he'd reciprocate; when he did, I was filled with relief. He kissed the top of my head.

"Let's change some things. You're right; this isn't the life either of us willingly signed up for. We've been walking these paths in our careers, not looking at the true cost. I want to fix this. You are the most amazing man I've ever met. How you can stand here holding me right now after all of this…"

"I love you, Katie."

"I love you too."

Peter & Molly: A Trucker's Story

I chose this life, one on the road. My two older brothers became doctors. I became a truck driver. I wanted to travel, be unattached, and see the country. Over the past ten years, I had crisscrossed the country more times than I could count. I knew the best routes to avoid traffic, the comfiest beds at the little roadside motels, and where to stop for a delicious meal. I loved what I did for a living. I mostly hauled regular cargo, nothing refrigerated, and no livestock. I had made that mistake once, hauling cattle, never again. It was more trouble than it was worth.

No matter where I went in the country, I always made it a point to stop at Molly Lane's place in Corn Crib, Nebraska. The roadside restaurant had stood there for almost 100 years, feeding weary travelers. When the interstate came through, the town shuttered, but Molly Lane's had managed to stay open, mostly due to its loyal following. The same family had owned the restaurant the entire time, the Lane family. I stopped every chance I got, and over the past ten years, I got to know the Lanes. They were good people. Last year, mom and pop Lane were killed in a car accident. The restaurant was left to their grown children, Daniel, and Molly, who had grown up in the restaurant.

Not much changed after mom and pop died. The decor stayed, which was somewhere between roadside diner and a family's living room. There were pictures of generations of the families on the wall. I liked that, even after 100 years, if you went for breakfast, there was always a linen tablecloth and fresh flowers on the table. It gave me the feeling of home. Daniel had taken his father's place cooking, and Molly ran the front of the restaurant. She always had a smile on her face. Her pale skin and bright copper hair complemented her icy-blue eyes, which were set off by her naturally pink lips and beautiful smile. Each time I walked in, she always welcomed me like I was family, throwing her arms around me.

"Peter," she'd say, "Welcome back. We missed you. Where are you on the road to today?"

One day I stopped for a late lunch; the restaurant was slow. Molly stopped what she was doing and sat with me while I ate. I had the chicken fried steak, mashed potatoes, and green beans, smothered in gravy. I could go on forever about the gravy. Ask anyone who has ever had it, about the gravy at Molly Lane's; they'll rave. Molly sat across from me, sipping her coffee. From that time on, no matter how busy the restaurant was, she always stopped what she was doing and sat with me.

We'd talk and talk, and I'd forget to eat, I'd be so enthralled with her. She'd ask if the food was okay. Embarrassed, I'd smile and resume eating. I soon found myself making sure that my routes took me by Molly's place. We watched the news in early February as news of a virus spread. I had fellow drivers start to tell me about the East coast, that things were getting bad. I looked across the table at Molly, the steam from my hot pancakes rising between us. The tv that sat on the lunch counter showed news of the utter devastation in Europe from the virus, then showed the number of rising cases in the U.S. Molly twisted her paper napkin in her hand, rolling it into a tight ribbon. She bit at her bottom lip nervously. I reached across the table and placed my hand over hers. It was the first time I had ever intentionally touched her, other than her welcome hug. Her attention snapped back towards me, and I instantly felt that I needed to remove my hand, but before I could, she put her's over mine.

"Peter, this is really scary. I'm scared." Her blue eyes were filled with fear and pain, that I would give anything to take away.

"It's going to be okay, we'll get through this."

"What about you? You're out there on the road. I don't know what I'd do if.." She trailed off.

It realized that she really cared about me. I caressed her hand.

"The country is going to need us truckers, we move the economy."

"That doesn't make me feel any better. You could go home, and sit this out or stay here, I mean if you wanted to?"

Looking her in the eye, it was clear that she meant it. She had just invited me to stay with her through the pandemic. I had dreamt about this woman, making a life with her. She was the highpoint in any journey, and here she was asking me to stay, the one time in my life when I knew I couldn't.

"It was just an idea," she said, pulling her hand away.

"I'll be careful, Mol, I drive alone. I can sleep in the cab. I'll be safe. I'm needed right now, just like you are. You have a fleet to feed. We'll each kept doing our jobs, and we'll get our country through this and each other."

She nodded in agreement.

I finished my breakfast as snow gently fell outside. In my gut, something churned, a feeling to stay with Molly, but I knew I couldn't. I had a load full of freight due for San Diego in the next 48 hours. Molly cleared my plate as I sopped up the last of the syrup on my plate. I waited for her to come back down and sit, but she didn't. In fact, as the minutes ticked by, I noticed she had not come back out of the kitchen. The restaurant was pretty empty for a snowy Tuesday morning in February. I stood up and craned my neck through the passthrough window between the breakfast counter and the kitchen. A waitress I did not recognize refilled coffees to those sitting at the counter.

"Excuse me, do you know where Molly went," I asked the brunette behind the cash register.

"You must be Peter. It's nice to meet you; I'm Nancy. She's in the kitchen. You can go on back if you want." She said as she popped the gum in her mouth and the end of her sentence.

"Thanks."

I pushed the swinging door into the kitchen and spotted Daniel grilling hash browns and a slew of other breakfast foods. Our eyes met, and he nodded towards the back of the kitchen. I came around the wall where the large dishwashing station was. I stood silently as I watched Molly. Her back was to me as she washed dishes. I could tell by her movements she was upset.

"Mol," I said gently.

She turned, wiping her eyes on her sleeves, the yellow rubber gloves she wore to wash dishes still on her hands. She was crying. Was crying over me? Was she as scared as she had seemed? Everyone was scared right now. The sight of tear stains down her cheeks broke my heart. I took the three paces between us and pulled her into my arms. She buried her head and cried gently. Neither of us said anything; we just stood there in each other's arms.

When she seemed to calm, I looked down at her, and her eyes met mine. It was like a punch to the gut; she looked at me with love in her eyes, I had been so blind up to now. All she was asking was for me to stay during a national crisis, and I couldn't. I leaned down and brushed my lips over hers. She kissed me back as her body pulled in closer into mine.

She pulled her lips from mine, "Please don't go, Peter, I.. I.."

"I promise you, Molly, I will come back to you. I have to deliver the load on the truck in San Diego, and then I'll be back, I promise. Look, I'm going to leave you my cell. You call me anytime. I mean it."

"I know you have to go. I'd just hate myself if I didn't at least try to get you to stay. Peter, I know how crazy this sounds, but I like you. I know we haven't been on dates but, I hope every day, I'll see you walk in, and when you do, I am so sad to see you go."

She looked so small and vulnerable in my arms. The truth was, I didn't want to let go.

"I really like you too. Truth be told, I drove 100 miles out of my way today, just to see you."

"Really? Not just eat our delicious food?"

"The food is delicious, but the company is the best part," I said before I leaned down and kissed her again. Her lips felt like home, like that feeling you get after being away for so long and curling up in your own bed.

I promised I would be back in a few days, as it took every ounce of willpower to leave her. I got on the road and headed west, covering as much ground as I was legally able to. That night when I pulled over, I called her. We talked for hours. The next day I pulled into San Diego and dropped off the haul. While I was in town, a friend of mine said that a company that made medical supplies was desperate for haulers to take medical supplies to New York. I had family in New York. Both of my brothers were doctors in New York, and I knew that these supplies were desperately needed. That night I called Molly and explained the situation. Right away, she insisted that I take the job, even though it meant I'd still be on the road.

My route did not take me through Nebraska on my way back. A blizzard in the Rockies pushed my route south. I knew the supplies were desperately needed as the news out of New York worsened. I thought of my brothers, and how the supplies on my rig could save their lives and the other medical professionals on the front line. Each night, as I pulled over, I'd reach for my phone and call Molly. The country was changing quickly as the virus was spreading. Molly's regular customers had fallen away, and she mostly saw truck traffic, fellow haulers desperate for a warm meal.

I pulled over in rural Pennsylvania, already two hours past my driving limit for the day. I was pushing hard to get the supplies to those who needed them. I talked to Molly and turned in. That night I was jolted awake as the alarm went off for the lock on the back of the bed of the truck. Someone was trying to break in. I grabbed my handgun and got out of the truck. I came around the back and startled the burglar. He swung a crowbar, and I weaved to miss the blow but was unsuccessful. I felt it crack just above my eyebrow, as warmth flowed over my face. I pulled my gun, and the burglar froze before he took off on foot and into a waiting car. The driver peeled from the empty lot. I stumbled back to the cab and assessed the damage once inside. The thief had split my eyebrow open. I cleaned and bandaged it as best I could, but I knew I'd need stitches. I'd call my brother, Eric when I got into town. I still had a few more hours to rest before I could drive again. I laid back down, knowing that the thief would not be back. I had similar incidents like this before, but there was something about this episode that had rattled me. I thought of Molly and me not coming back to her. I picked up my phone. It was 4 am eastern, 3 am central time. I wondered if she was awake. I resisted the urge to call her. I didn't want to worry her or wake her.

Later that morning, I delivered my load, and the supplier begged me to do another trip. I thought of Molly; I needed to get back to her. My brother had stitched my brow and had commended me on bringing the desperately needed supplies to the area. The virus was squeezing the East coast hard. I knew I had to do another trip. The materials I was hauling was saving lives. I called Molly that night and told her. She once again insisted that I take the job.

On my way back to San Diego, I made sure to stop for lunch; Daniel had made chili. As soon as word got out, Molly Lane's would have a busy few days. Daniel's chili was legendary, it had won numerous cook-off awards, but he was always humble about it. Before I was even out of my truck, I saw Molly step out of the restaurant. It had been almost three weeks since I had seen her last. The wind whipped, and her copper curls rode the wind. She ran across the parking lot, and I pulled her into my arms. I turned with, so my back faced the wind, protecting her from it. She fit perfectly in my arms, like two interlocking puzzle pieces.

She nuzzled her head deep into my chest. I buried my head in her soft curls on the top of her head and inhaled. She smelled like cinnamon and apples. I loved it. She looked up at me and lent up, placing her lips against my ear.

"Let's sit in your cab for a bit," she whispered.

I reached around her and opened the door. She climbed up into the cab. Her small frame looked tiny in my giant rig. I followed her in as she climbed into the passenger seat. I pulled the door shut, and the wind howled around the truck.

"So, this is where you live," she said, as before she noticed the dark bruising on my brow. "Peter," she said as she reached to touch the bruise, "what happened?"

I had not told her. I didn't want to worry her any more than I already had. I lied and told her one of the doors on the back had hit me when the wind caught it. I hated lying to beautiful, sweet Molly, but I didn't want to worry her. She climbed into the back of the cab and stretched out across my bunk. I wanted her desperately, but I also loved her. It struck me like the blow to the head I had gotten from the thief, but this time it struck my heart. I loved her, really loved her. I joined her on my bunk, as she ran her fingers through my hair. She leaned up and kissed me, and I knew if we didn't stop, I was going to have to make love to her right here. She deserved our first time to be in a real bed, with candles, dinner, and music. I stopped, telling her this, and she smiled.

"No, here. I want to sleep with you here, so no matter where you go across the country, you know our love lives here. It's like taking a piece of me with you."

I couldn't argue with her point. We made love in the back of my cab for the better part of the afternoon, and it was love. We emerged from the cab, famished, and I followed Molly into the restaurant. We ate a late lunch together, Daniel's famous chili. I couldn't take my eyes off of her as I ate. She glowed with beauty and happiness.

As afternoon quickly turned to evening, I had to get back on the road. It was painful to leave her side. This time I asked her to join me. I knew she couldn't, but I asked anyway. She, of course, declined, saying she had a job to do too. That night, as I pulled away, I felt like I left a piece of me behind with her.

I crossed the country two more times, bringing medical supplies to hospitals desperately in need. The country shut down, as the lockdown took effect. It was soon difficult to find open truck stops to shower and eat. I needed to be with Molly. We talked each night while I was away, she never missed our calls.

One night I called at our usual time, parked for the night just outside Flagstaff. She didn't answer. It worried me. The next day I tried her several times and did not get an answer. I even tried the restaurant, without success. One day turned into two; by the third day, I was terrified. I declined to do another cross country haul and opted to take supplies to Denver instead; it would be on my way back to Molly.

I made the trip in record and slightly illegal time. I pulled into Corn Crib, and the town looked deserted as night began to fall. As I pulled up to Molly Lane's, there were boards on the windows. My stomach churned. I got out of my rig and walked up to the door to read the sign. It said, "Sorry, closed due to illness. Call 555-555-5555 if you need a meal." Terrified, I ran back to my truck and grabbed my phone. I dialed the number frantically. I feared Molly was ill, and that's why she had not been in contact.

"Hello," the voice said on the line.

"Hello, I'm Peter. I'm looking for Molly."

"Peter, it's Nancy.

She's at Newton County Hospital; Daniel is sick. She'd been with him for days."

I hung up the phone and got in my truck. I put the location of the hospital into my phone and drove across the county. I parked my rig in a McDonald's parking lot that was closed for lockdown and walked briskly across the street, into the small county hospital. The lady sitting at the front reception desk looked up.

"Can you please tell me what room Daniel Lane is in?"

"Are you family, sir?"

"Yes," I lied, "his cousin."

The woman typed Daniel's name into the computer. "I'm sorry, sir, you can't seem him. He's in the red wing. All patients in the red wing aren't allowed to have visitors, he's too contagious."

"His sister is with him."

"Not in his room, or in the wing, she isn't. She might be in the waiting room outside of the wing. But I can promise you, she hasn't seen him."

"Where is that?"

"Second floor make a left when you exit the elevator. You'll need a visitor's pass. Here," she said, handing a sticker to me.

I stuck it on my chest and signed in before I headed towards the elevators. My heart pounded as the elevator brought me to the second floor. I followed the directions from the desk clerk. As I came around the corner, I saw Molly curled up, lying across three waiting room chairs as she slept. She wore a cream sweater and a pair of jeans, her copper curls draped down around her. She was all by herself. I walked in quietly and knelt down at her side. She slept peacefully. I flagged a nurse and asked for a blanket. I took it back into the waiting room and laid it over her gently. She stirred but did not wake. I sat down on the floor in front of where she slept. I turned and gently caressed the side of her face. Her perfect, soft porcelain skin felt like velvet under my fingertips. Even in this terrible movement, she was perfection.

She woke to my touch and opened her eyes.

"Peter," she whispered.

"It's me. I've been so worried about you."

"You came."

"Of course, I came; I love you."

"I love you too."

She brought her arms around me, and I knelt up to embrace her.

She was home. I was home.

Alley & Lex: The End of The Friendship

S o, you're staying here then," Ally asked?

"Yeah, I guess, better than going back to my place. If I have to spend the next God knows how long listening to my upstairs neighbor practice for whatever theatre show she's hoping to be in, I'm going to blow my brains out." Lex made a gun gesture, pointing it to his head.

"Fine, but you get the couch."

"The couch? Ouch."

The silence between them lingered a second longer than was comfortable.

Allie threw a couch pillow at Lex and giggled. He loved it when she smiled, and her laugh melted his heart. He wondered how he was going to quarantine with a woman he was madly in love with, as he deflected the flying pillow coming towards him.

"I'll grab blankets and clear some space for you so you can unpack your bag. I'll set up a space for your things in my room for now." Allie got up and walked into her bedroom to fetch blankets.

Lex picked up the pillow and silently screamed into it. Ugh, why can't I just grow a pair and tell her? I love you, Allie, see simple.

Ahhhhh, he thought to himself. He pulled the pillow quickly as he heard her footsteps coming closer.

"You know, I'm kind of glad you came to stay. Who knows how long this is going to last? I don't think we've spent more than two days apart since we met," Allie said as she set the blankets on the coffee table and began to make the couch into a bed. "We both know we would have gone crazy, not being able to hang out. I don't know what…" she trailed off.

"What don't you know," he asked?

"Nothing, nevermind. Here you are." Allie gestured to the makeshift bed on the couch. "I'm going to turn in." Allie stood, tucking a long, brown, curly lock behind her ear.

Lex couldn't be sure, but he felt that she had lingered a moment longer than was normal. Is she sending me signals here, and I keep missing it? Dude, this is Allie, your best friend, he thought to himself. Allie took a step towards him and wrapped her arms around him; he embraced her. Before she let go, she placed a quick kiss on his cheek. Her lips on his skin felt like an electrical current through his body.

"I'm really glad you decided to stay. Good night Lex," Allie said, still standing in his arms. She pulled away and walked into her bedroom, shutting the door behind her. Lex took off his sweatshirt, pants, and socks, staying in his boxers and t-shirt. He had spent plenty of nights on Allie's couch, through illness and break-ups. Lex climbed into the bed on the couch and stared up at the ceiling, the yellow streetlamp cast a warm glow through the living room. It made him crazy that just on the other side of the door, Allie laid in bed alone. He wanted to hold her in his arms and listen to her, breathe softly as she slept.

Lex thought back to the night Allie had literally stumbled into his life. She tripped and fell off of the last step of the large porch at a college party. He had helped her to her feet; as Allie looked up to say thank you, she vomited all over him. Despite that, he helped her back to her dorm and left her with her mousey roommate, Ellen. Allie had utterly forgotten about Lex until she sat next to him in a public speaking course two days later. Lex had been cool about it and laughed it off. From that point on, the two of them had been inseparable but only as friends, Nothing more. Both of them had been okay with that arrangement until recently. Lex found his feelings had grown into something more, but he was terrified to tell Allie. He worried about what would happen if she felt differently.

After graduation, Allie took a job in Seattle, and Lex followed her. His parents died in a car accident during his senior year of high school. As an only child, he was left without a family, so she became his family. Allie promised to stay in his life. They had spent their twenties building careers, and their friendship had been enough for both of them. Sure, there had been romantic relationships for both of them, but the relationships never lasted.

Lex finally fell asleep on the couch in the early hours of the morning. He woke to the smell of brewing coffee and the smell of Allie's shampoo. He opened his eyes, registering it was morning, but he was still tired from the lack of a full night's sleep.

"Here, coffee." Allie held out a cup for him.

He propped up and grabbed the hot mug of coffee.

"Thanks," he mumbled groggily.

"So how do you want to do this? I know we both have to work. I can take the bedroom, and you can use the kitchen table or the desk over there? I know you have to work too. I have a conference call here in a few minutes. Then maybe we can do lunch together? I have a veggie curry that I have been dying to make."

Lex sat there, not quite awake. "It's your call. I mean, put me where you want me. Curry sounds yummy. Lunch at noon then?"

"Sounds like a plan. Do you have any calls for work? Open plan living is great until it isn't. Must remember this for the next place, it must be quarantine approved." Allie joked.

Without thinking, Lex reached up and grabbed her hand gently. She looked down at him.

"Thanks again for letting me quarantine with you," he said.

Allie's thumb rubbed over the back of his hand; it was a slight gesture, but on that, his body registered.

"Of course."

She let go of his hand and turned back towards the kitchen. If he had not known her better, he could've sworn he saw a hint of embarrassment on her face. He shrugged it off and picked up his phone and saw he didn't have to start work for an hour.

"Why do you start out here? I'm going to grab a shower, and then I can log-on to work from the bedroom if that's cool," Lex asked as before he took a sip of the hot coffee.

"That will work."

Lex stood up and set the coffee down on the table. He began to fold up the blankets from the bed on the couch when he noticed Allie staring at him.

"Just leave'em. There's no use in putting it all away unless you really want to."

"Are you sure? I don't want to leave a mess in your living room."

"You mean your bedroom." Allie smiled.

He smiled back as he made his way to the master bathroom; the other bathroom in the apartment was only a powder room. He shut Allie's bedroom door and walked into her bathroom. Turning on the water, he held out his hand to test the temperature. There was something intimate about being her private space that Lex tried to push out of his head as he washed. He stepped out of the shower and dried himself, hanging the towel on the back of the bathroom door. She had left his bag just inside the door of her room, so it wasn't in the way. He stepped into the bedroom to see Allie standing in the bedroom with tears in her eyes and a look of surprise on her face.

"Oh, sorry, I thought you were still in the shower," she said as she turned around quickly.

They had been close enough to see each other in various states of undress, but neither had seen each other completely naked until now. Lex darted back behind the bathroom door and grabbed the towel from the back, pulling it around his waist before he reemerged. In that quick moment, Allie had made her way out of the bedroom. He dug a t-shirt out from the top of his bag, a pair of boxers and a pair of jeans, and threw them on quickly. Lex walked out into the open-plan living, dining, kitchen area. Allie stood at the kitchen counter with her back to him.

He walked up to her softly, asking, "Hey, Al, are you okay?"

She turned to look at him, his initial read of her face correct. She wiped a tear from her cheek. "Sorry, I thought you were still in the shower. I was looking for the employee handbook for my company. I've been fired. No warning, just done. Four years with them, and now I'm out on my ass. Lex, what am I going to do?'

"It will be okay. You're a brilliant grant writer, and if this whole quarantine and economic depression are going to be as bad as they're saying, babe, your brilliance is going to be in high demand. We'll get through this together."

Allie turned and hugged him tightly. There was something different about this hug than the many others they had shared before, although Lex couldn't put his finger on it. He held her as she cried, reassuring her again that everything would be alright. She stayed tightly cradled in his arms.

"Al, you're my best friend, I've got you if you need it. You will land on your feet; I know you will."

"Thanks, but, Lex, you've got responsibilities too. You cannot support me."

"Al, my parents left me a mountain of money."

"No! No way are you spending your inheritance to support me! No way, I mean it!"

"I make enough from my job alone to support both of us. Look at me," he tipped her chin up, something he had never done before as he still held her in his arms. Her teary blue eyes and soft pink lips took his next statement out of his mind. All he could focus on were those eyes. Without warning, she leaned up and kissed him. A real kiss, her tongue brushing over his lips gently.

He felt her push out of his arms as she backed away.

"I.. I'm sorry. I shouldn't have done that…" she said, embarrassed.

Lex stepped forward and pulled her back into his arm, this time kissing her. He searched her body for any sign of resistance but found none. In fact, the deeper he kissed her, the more her body seemed to melt into his. Breathless, they stepped away from each other.

"Whoa, where did that come from," Allie asked with an embarrassed smile on her face.

Panicked that he had misread the situation, he wasn't sure what to say.

"I.. Al.. I.. Are you mad?"

She tucked a curl behind her ear as she stared at him.

"What was that," she asked?

Tell her you coward, tell her you love her, his inner voice screamed.

"It was... Why?" he replied, not making sense.

"Because baby, this changes everything," Allie said as she wiped a new tear from her cheek. "I've wanted you to do that for so long."

Without waiting for her next word, he pulled her back into his embrace and kissed her again like he had crossed the desert, and her mouth was a cool spring. Almost fifteen years of pent up passion lived behind their lips. He never wanted to stop kissing Allie, ever again, but he knew he had to tell her. He stopped and pulled his lips away from hers, still keeping her in his arms.

"I love you, Allie Brookman. I have for so long. We don't know what the future holds with this quarantine, but I am by your side. Where you go, I go. I love you."

Her face lit up as she smiled at him, her smile sly with a hint of mischief. He looked at her quizzically.

"I love you too. This quarantine is going to be fun. Come on," she said as she grabbed his hand, leading him into her bedroom.

Julie & Luke: Divorced in Quarantine

My husband of the past eleven years, and I would be officially divorced by midnight tonight. I stood in what had once been our kitchen as I looked over the paperwork. The house that I had painstakingly redone, going room by room, was now his. I considered it a painful price for my freedom. Don't get me wrong, Luke wasn't a bad husband; there was just too much baggage for both of us to carry. I walked away to save us both from destroying each other any further. We had agreed that I could stay one last night in the house. I was off to California in the morning. I spent the evening packing the last of my belongings and making my way through the house, saying goodbye to all of the spots where I had put my love, the dining room where I had learned to hang wallpaper, the upstairs bathroom where I had laid each tile by hand, and the guest bedroom with its newly refinished floor. The house held so many memories, most of them so happy. I paused as I reached the bedroom at the end of the hall. We always kept the door closed. It was just too painful to open, with the cheery wallpaper of teddy bears and nursery furniture. I put my hand on the doorknob, but I couldn't bring myself to walk into the room and say goodbye. It was still too painful two years later. I put my hand on the wooden door and leaned my head against it.

"Bye, sweetie," I whispered.

I knew the child that was meant to be in there couldn't hear me, yet I needed to say it vocally. I walked away from the door and down to the wine fridge, deciding that I would spend the last night in my home, blindingly drunk. Walking away was just too painful to do sober. I knew it wouldn't take much; I had always been terrible at holding my liquor. I made dinner as sipped my red wine. I made sure to leave the dishes in the sink; it felt like one last fuck you to Luke. By the time my pasta carbonara was done, I had a pretty good buzz. After dinner, I took a soak in the claw-footed tub in the master bath. I had bought it at an estate auction. When I dragged it home, Luke thought I was nuts, I was thrilled. I giggled at the memory of us, hauling up the stairs together, huffing and puffing. I still cannot believe we managed to do it. I climbed into the bed I had shared with Luke for one last time, passing out more than falling asleep.

"Julie, wake up. Big surprise; you left your phone downstairs. You have a ton of missed calls." Luke said, with annoyance thick in his voice.

"I have the house until 11 am. That was the agreement, remember," I croaked.

I sat up, and the crushing pain from my head caused me to almost vomit. I instantly regretted drinking the night before.

"Nice, Jules, hungover, are we?"

"What do you care? Why are you here?"

"You clearly haven't seen the news, have you? Typical you," he said as he reached over for the remote and clicked on the television.

The headline on the morning show said National Lockdown. I sat up and tried to focus on what the newscaster was saying, but my stomach was rolling.

"Effective immediately, all residents in the state are locked down until further notice. You should remain in your home and leave only for essential items. Please use extreme caution in venturing out. All flights from Regional Airport have been grounded until further notice," the perky blonde said on the television screen.

I looked over at the clock. It was 8 am. I was supposed to be on a noon flight. The movers were due an hour ago, but I imagined if I checked my phone, there was a message saying they weren't coming.

Luke stood, watching the news with me. As the realization hit that I was now stuck, I couldn't hold back the need to be sick. I ran from the bed, shutting the bathroom door behind me. I felt a little better after I vomited, and I knew a shower would help. I could count on one hand the number of times I'd been properly drunk enough to be hungover. I climbed into the shower and emerged thirty minutes later, feeling much better. I came out wearing only my towel. I instinctively walked over to my dresser, remembering my clothes were no longer in there. I pulled out a pair of blue jeans and a cream sweater out of my suitcase and dressed. I walked downstairs as the smell of coffee wafted upstairs.

The sunny kitchen, which I had always loved, was exceptionally bright this morning as I pushed open the swinging door between the kitchen and dining room. Luke stood with his back to me as I walked in. He was pouring himself a cup of coffee, and as he heard me enter, he poured one for me. I sat down at the marble island, remembering the day we had went to pick out the perfect piece of marble for the kitchen island. That had been such a fun day, and one of the last, that I think we were both truly happy. He turned around and slid my cup towards me.

"The moving company called the house line while you were in the shower. They're not coming. They didn't give a reschedule date either before you ask."

"Thank you for the message," I said as I looked at all the missed calls on my phone from the moving company, the airlines, my new job it looked like, and my sister.

"Jules, what are we going to do here?"

"What do you mean," I asked, putting my phone back down.

"Well, you clearly aren't moving today, and I can't keep staying in a hotel. We're going to have to stay here together."

"Oh no, we aren't. You can't stay."

"It would be me who would be letting you stay, remember? The house is mine."

"Don't remind me," I said quietly as I took a sip of my coffee.

Luke may have had his faults, but he had always made a great cup of coffee.

"I'll get what I can, and I'll go stay in a hotel, or see if there's a place I can rent until this all blows over," I said as I sipped my coffee.

"I think you've missed the memo, babe. The whole country is on lockdown. This isn't going to blow over. Where have you been? Don't you watch the news?"

"I've been trying to put my life back together."

I picked up my coffee and walked out onto the front porch. I sat on the swing and pulled my knees up to my chest. It was chilly, and as the swing moved, I realized the swing was a bad choice. I had paid attention to the news. I just thought there was more time before things really got bad. I had hoped to be in my new place before the bottom fell out. I had family I could stay with, but I didn't want a daily forensic examination of how my marriage failed. My best friend in town, Blair, had three kids under the age of four, so quarantining there was not an option either. I wondered if I could just drive to California, but I ruled that out as soon as I thought of it. I was stuck at the mercy of my now ex-husband. I held my coffee close as hoping it would warm me. Overwhelmed with the feeling of now being stuck, I began to cry. This was not how the first day of my new life was supposed to go. I was supposed to be on a plane, starting a new life that I wanted. I wiped my tears away with the sleeve of my sweater. The cold was starting to really bite at me, but I couldn't bring myself to go back into the house, Luke's house. Why had I signed away the house, I wondered to myself again, for the freedom I wasn't experiencing at the moment?

Luke knocked on the door, jamb before he walked onto the porch.

"Look, I'm not going to throw you out during a global pandemic, I'm not that cruel. You can stay. Do me a favor though, can we please try and be civil to each other? There's no point in us both holding up here, only to kill each other."

I refused to look in his direction. I didn't want him to see me crying.

"Jules, look at me. Can you please be civil? It's the only thing I ask."

I nodded, but still did not look at him.

"Julie, seriously, you aren't even going to fucking look at me? Unreal."

"I don't want to," I said quietly.

"Why?"

"Because," I turned towards him, "I didn't want you to see me so upset."

"Why do you think I'm out here? I knew you would be. Hell, everyone is right now. Everyone woke up to a different world today. Do you want to stay?"

I bit my tongue not to reply that I'd love to stay in my own house, but the only thing Luke had asked for was civility. "Yes, please," I replied.

"Okay, you can stay until the lockdown is over. Since you are still in the master, I'll take the guest room."

"You can have the master if you want, it's your house."

"No, you keep it, for now. I have to log into work, so I am going to take the office too."

I nodded and watched him walked back into the house. I finished my coffee and walked back in the house to warm up and grab another cup. I listened to my messages as I poured another cup of coffee. The first two were from the moving company. I took another sip of the coffee, as the fresh hot coffee warmed me from the inside out. The next message was from my new company. The message said,

"Hello, Ms. Harris. We hope you are well. As you know, the entire country is locking down due to the Covid-19 virus. As a result, our business will begin feeling the effects quickly and severely. I am so sorry, but we are going to have to rescind our job offer to you at this time. Please know that if things improve, we are still interested in you as a potential candidate. I have sent a letter to your email inbox as well with this message. I am so sorry, Ms. Harris."

My life felt like it was imploding in one day. I left my coffee and walked back upstairs and climbed into bed. Today was too hard. I slept most of the day away, grateful for the respite of sleep. I woke in the late afternoon, and my stomach pulled me downstairs. I had not eaten since the night before. I made myself a quick peanut butter sandwich and then went in search of my treadmill. Thankfully, it had not been disassembled yet for the move. I put my ear pods in and began my run. An hour later, I felt much better, and I came up from the basement, feeling more like myself. Luke stood in the kitchen and had begun to prepare dinner.

"I wondered where you go off to. Are you feeling alright? You slept most of the day."

I nodded that I was okay.

"Do you want dinner? I was going to grill steak; I could throw one on for you if you want?"

I thought about the offer. Normally, I'd say something snide, but his request of civility reverberated through my head.

"Yes, please. Thank you for the offer. Do you want any help?"

"Do you want to do the veggies? You know I always burn them."

I smiled, knowing it was true.

"Sure," I said as I walked over to the fridge and pulled out the fresh asparagus and mushrooms caps.

We prepared our food in silence, and I was grateful for the respite in conversation. This situation was awkward enough, I thought to myself. As if he had read my mind, Luke spoke up.

"In a way, I am glad you are here. I know it's not what you wanted, but I know you are safe, at least."

I did my best to put on my polite smile as the word civility ran through my head. I held my tongue as I cleaned the mushrooms. Luke took the steaks out to the grill, and I went in search of the bottle of wine from the night before. I poured myself a tiny glass, anything to take the edge off tonight. Luke came back in and put the empty plate he had carried the steaks out on into the sink. He reached over the bottle and poured himself a glass.

"Let me know when we are ten minutes out, and I'll do the veggies," I said, trying to be helpful.

Luke nodded, and I got up and began to set the table in the kitchen for dinner.

Thirty minutes later, dinner was on the table, and we both sat down. There was a surreal feeling to eating dinner in my ex-kitchen with my ex-husband that almost felt comical if it wasn't so sad.

"Did you get a chance to call your new job to let them know you've been detained?"

I put down my cutlery, "I didn't have to, they rescinded the job offer this morning."

"Jules, I'm sorry, I didn't know. Will you be okay, money-wise?"

"Yes."

I didn't say that I had his of the bye-out from our house in my account; it felt like salt in a very open wound. I was grateful for the silence through the rest of dinner.

Our first week of quarantine seemed to pass as we settled into a new routine, making sure to give each other a wide berth. Luke did his best to keep his feelings to himself, but it was clear to me that he was still in love with me. I had chosen the divorce, and he had fought me on it, not wanting to throw in the towel. One night, a few weeks into the quarantine, I woke from a noise from downstairs. I crept down to the living room, seeing the lights from the television on. I walked into the living room and saw Luke sleeping on the couch; it was his turn to drink more than his fair share. I bent down, pulled the half-empty bottle of Jack Daniels from his hand, and set it on the coffee table. I pulled the blanket from the back of the couch and pulled it over him. I couldn't help but stare, he looked like the man I had married, so young, innocent, optimistic. My guilt gnawed away at me. I reached above him to switch off the lamp next to him when I saw his eyes open. His gaze was kind.

"I still love you, you know," he said softly with a drunken slur. "I just want you to know."

I stood back and bit down hard on my bottom lip. It had been me that had taken the final blow to our marriage, and I still don't completely understand why I had done what I did. I reached down and brushed his sandy-brown hair off of his brow.

"I know you shouldn't," I whispered back.

He rolled towards the back of the couch and away from me. I walked upstairs, feeling more like a piece of human trash than I had in a while. I climbed back into bed and laid awake for most of the night. I finally drifted off to sleep in the early hours of the morning. By the time I woke up, Luke had already shut himself in the office, working. I tried to keep myself busy, but nothing seemed to keep my attention for long. I decided to make dinner, and I'd make Beef Bourguignon for dinner. It would entertain me for the afternoon, and it was a nice way to thank Luke for letting me stay. He emerged from the office at the smell of it cooking.

"Are you making Beef Bourguignon," he asked as he came into the kitchen.

"I am, I hope that's okay."

"Are you kidding? You know it's my favorite. I think you make it better than anywhere else on Earth. Remember when we went to France and I ordered it, it was awful."

"And it made you so sick," I chimed in.

"Man, that was awful. Remember, I totally ruined the back of that cab, and the cabbie was so mad."

"I thought he was going to kill you."

We both laughed as we remembered that night.

"What inspired you to make it tonight?"

"Boredom, honestly."

"I have a room that needs to be painted if you want. I'll pay you for it."

"Which room are you painting?"

"The one at the end of the hall."

His statement took the breath out of my lungs. I set my wooden spoon down on the counter and walked out. I could not believe he had said it. Luke was not a cruel man. I walked upstairs and passed the room with its closed door and into the master. I sat on the bed, taking in deep breaths, trying to calm myself. I laid back on the bed and curled up, pulling my knees up to my chest, unable to hold back the tsunami of emotion that came spilling out. I was startled by Luke's knock on the door.

"Jules?"

"Go away, Luke."

"I'm sorry, that … I don't' know why I said that. I'm sorry."

I pulled the duvet over my head. It was too much, all of it, my current situation and my past situation. I once again weighed the options of staying with friends or family, but I honestly didn't know if I could even get them or if they'd want a house guest right now. At any rate, I wasn't leaving the bedroom until I was sure Luke was asleep for the night. I laid in bed as afternoon turned to evening, just watching the sun move across the wall of the bedroom. As dusk turned to night, I could have smelled dinner cooking. It smelled like beef Bourguignon. I had not finished it before my encounter with Luke, not that there had been much left to do. I wondered if he had finished it. An hour later, Luke knocked on the door again.

"Jules, please come down. I'm really sorry. I finished dinner. Please come eat."

I remained silent. When he cracked the door, I pretended to be sleeping. He shut the door, and I rolled away. My stomach growled at the delicious smell, but I ignored it. A little later, he knocked on the door again.

"I made you a plate. I'll leave it here for you. Julie, I'm an asshole,

I'm sorry for what I said."

I heard the tray of dinner clink as he set it outside the door. I wasn't hungry enough to get out of bed, and I left it outside my door as I fell asleep for the night. The next morning, I woke, uninterested in getting out of bed. I pulled the drapes closed and climbed back into bed, and went back to sleep. Around noon I finally ventured out of the bedroom, noticing that the dinner tray had been cleared from the doorway. I made a bowl of cereal and crept back up to my room. After I finished it, I rolled back over and went back to sleep. I woke to a dark room and Luke's knock at the door again that evening.

"Jules, I'm coming in. You're scaring me up here."

He cracked the door and peeked in. I stayed still in the bed, facing away from him. I hoped he'd just close the door and leave, but he walked in. I could smell reheated Beef Bourguignon, and he set a dinner tray on the dresser. He paused, and I willed him to walk out. Instead, he came and sat on my side of the bed. He reached out his arm, resting it on my upper arm.

"Jules," he whispered. "Please eat something, and I'll go."

I laid motionless, trying to decide what I wanted to do when he clicked on the light.

"Honey, are you still in the clothes from yesterday? Julie, I'm so sorry. I don't know why I said it." He paused. "That's a lie. I said it because I was hurting, am hurting. Seeing you in our kitchen, making our favorite meal. It was a terrible thing to say to you. If I could take it back, I would."

I rolled towards him, feeling too fragile to fight.

"Look, if you eat, I'll leave you in peace."

I propped myself up, and he took the cue, grabbing the tray of food, setting it across my lap.

"I finished it last night, but it's missing something like a spice missing."

I looked down at the dish.

"It's missing thyme."

"Damnit, that's it."

I looked up at him, and I know he read the damage his words had done on my face. He sat back down and put his hand over mine. I lost my composure and buried my face in my free hand. He let go of my hand and grabbed the tray, putting it on the floor. He sat back up and pulled me into his arms. I expected to feel repulsed, but his hug was genuine, and I felt comfort in his arms. I didn't push away, but I didn't embrace him in return either. When I quieted, he grabbed the tray and set it back on my lap. I nodded, understanding the silent ask for me to eat, and he stood up and walked out, leaving me in peace. When I finished dinner, I took a bath. After I dressed in clean pajamas, I grabbed the tray to take it downstairs. I froze as I overheard Luke's voice in the living room, and I realized he had to be on the phone. I stayed frozen as I listened.

"No, it's my fault, this is all my fault, mom. I know she's lost. I had no right to say that to her. I've apologized, but I'll never be able to take it back."

There was a pause as my now ex-mother in law who I had always adored, spoke on the other end. I couldn't hear her side of the conversation. She had always been kind to me. Even when we announced, we were divorcing, but I wondered if Luke had ever told her the true catalyst for the divorce. One of the only things she had asked of me when things were truly awful between Luke and I, was not to continue to hurt each other. She didn't know how deep that hurt went and was still worried about us. I filed for divorce the next day. I wouldn't destroy her son as a person.

"I love her so much it hurts," he continued, "And I would give anything for her to see it. This is all my fault."

I heard his voice crack as he said it, and decided I'd heard enough. I walked all the way to the kitchen. I set the tray down and started to wash the bowl. I had played a bigger part in our demise than he had. The fact that he thought the entire thing was his fault left me hollowed out to the point that if I didn't talk to him, there wouldn't be anything left of me by the time this whole ordeal was over. I had planned a life across the country to avoid this conversation, and now I was stuck in the house with him, unable to escape it. I set the clean bowl down in the dish rack and dried my hands. I walked towards the living room and knocked on the doorjamb as Luke sat with his head in his hands. He looked up at my entrance.

"You're up and showered."

I could see that he had been crying, his eyes were still red, and his face splotchy. I crossed the room and bent down in front of him.

"I overheard your conversation with your mom. I need to set this straight; this is not all your fault; I share the blame."

"I pushed you into it, all of it."

"No, I had free will, we equally participated in a lot of the wrongs."

"All losses and you said you didn't want to keep trying for a family, but I kept pushing. I saw what it did to you emotionally, physically each time, what it did to us. I really believed if we kept trying, we'd get there, and a baby would make everything all better."

"I know, I did too."

"I didn't listen when you said you didn't want to try anymore after we lost Daniel. I was selfish."

"So was I. I couldn't handle being a disappointment to you anymore, not able to give you the one thing you wanted. Do you know why I had an affair, the real reason?"

Luke looked up at me as he wiped a tear from my cheek.

"I just wanted to be loved for me and not with the pressure to get pregnant each time we were intimate. I needed to still be touched as a person for me, and we couldn't do that. Each time we slept together after Daniel, I was terrified to become pregnant again, but I couldn't tell you and break your heart further. It was an awful thing to do. I'm sorry, Luke."

Luke grabbed me and pulled me in closer to him, and this time I wrapped my arms around him. We held each other for a long time, even after my legs fell asleep from kneeling in front of him. Luke pulled away first.

"I knew I was pushing too hard, but I didn't know how to stop. To be so close to being parents, and to have it ripped away, I didn't know how to process it. I pushed you away."

I leaned back into him and let him hold me. We stayed up well into the early hours of the morning talking. Finally, all cried out. I grabbed him by the hand and led him upstairs to our bed. That night I fell asleep in his arms.

The next morning, he woke first, and he trailed his index finger down the bridge of my nose.

I opened my eyes, and there he was, his deep brown eyes smiling.

"You are so beautiful; I was such a fool to let you slip away."

"Where do we go from here?"

"Wherever the road takes us if you're open to it?"

"I think I am," I said before I leaned up and kissed him.

Hailey & Adam: Starry Night

S tary, stary night," he sang to me softly in the darkness of my bedroom that had become our bedroom.

I hated that I needed him this much, but the truth was I did. His voice, soft and gentle, soothed my ragged nerves. Six months ago, my whole life was different; the child moving inside of me reminded me of that. She loved the sound of her father's voice. Six months ago, I was celebrating the biggest promotion of my career. At this rate, I thought I'd make partner before forty, a firm record. Work was my life. What was the most incredible one-night stand of my life, followed by a whole weekend in bed with the man now lying next to me, changed my entire life.

I found out I was pregnant as I rode the elevator up to my office. Someone had on a strong perfume, and the smell of it made me sick to my stomach. I fled from the elevator as it reached my floor in search of the bathroom. My best friend, Hattie, called it, as we awaited the results of the pregnancy test I had bought on my lunch break. She had come home with me, eager to see if her hunch had been correct.

That evening, I chewed at a dry cuticle on my index finger as the hourglass in the digital window of the test blinked. My life changed in a moment as the test said pregnant. I quickly ripped open a second test, which produced the same result. It's impossible, I kept saying again and again, almost in a trance. Hattie reassured me all would be okay before she left that night.

I couldn't have children, or at least that's what my gynecologist had told me. Something having to do with the angle of my uterus. The only person I had been with was Adam, that wild weekend, and then a few days later. It had been wonderful, but I didn't have the time for a relationship, and neither did he. Our arrangement suited both of us well; it was casual, just sex. We had always been careful, he had used protection, and I thought I couldn't get pregnant, so I did not bother with birth control.

I walked out of my gynecologist's office with a confirmation that the test was positive. I had been seeing her since my early twenties; I was now in my mid-thirties. She was just as surprised as I was that I had conceived. After my exam, I dressed and walked into her office, where I sat across the desk.

"Hailey, I know you mentioned that this was not planned. I just want to say, the fact that you're pregnant is a miracle. Please think about your choices. I would be remiss if I didn't mention this. My medical opinion was that you'd never be able to conceive."

"What are you saying," I asked?

"You may not have this chance again. I am not telling you this to influence your decision one way or another. I would not be upholding my oath to you if I didn't."

I thanked her and took my prescription for prenatal vitamins. I knew what she meant about choices, not that I had discussed it with her. I left the office, knowing that she was right. I knew I wanted kids someday; I just didn't think it'd be now.

Two weeks passed, and I knew what I wanted. I just had to call Adam and pray he wouldn't react too badly. My hands shook as I dialed his cell phone. I wondered where in the world he was as I listened to his phone ring and a foreign tone.

"Hi Hailey," he said in a cheery voice.

"Hi, where are you? The ring is different."

"I'm in Beijing. I'm actually getting ready to board a flight home.

The virus is really taking hold here, so my company is recalling everyone home. I'm not normally very jumpy, but this illness makes me a little nervous."

"Really?"

"Yeah, I can't really talk about it right now."

I understood the undertone of what he meant; he couldn't discuss it publicly in a communist country.

"Anyway, how are you?" He asked.

"I thought you were boarding a flight. Do you need me to let you go?"

"No, I've got about a half-hour before I'll go down and board. I'm in the lounge. It's practically empty. Everyone has been leaving for days. Guess I'm at the tail end."

"Ah, well, I have some news," I paused as I took a deep breath. I felt like my heart was going to leap out of my mouth, it was pounding so hard. I couldn't form the words. Only bits of sound came out that did not even resemble words.

"Are you all right?"

I felt the tears well and swallowed hard. Just tell him, my inner monologue screamed.

"I'm pregnant." I blurted out.

The other side of the line was silent, too silent.

"Adam, are you there," I asked softly.

"Wow, okay. Are you sure? Have you been to the doctor?"

"I have. I'm about ten weeks along. I haven't known for long. I'm sorry, I didn't call you sooner. I just needed some time to think. The baby is yours. I'm keeping it. I just wanted to say that I didn't plan this, and I was as shocked as you are now. I mean, we used protection. I..."

"Hailey," Adam said calmly.

I stopped talking.

"Can I come to see you when I get back home?"

"Of course. I know this is a lot. I'll give you some space and some time to process."

"Thanks"

"Come by, and we can talk once you get in and get settled."

"Sounds good. Get some rest; I'll be home tomorrow. We can talk about this weekend."

"Okay."

"Okay," Adam said as he hung up the phone.

The call had ended more abruptly than I had expected, but the fact that he hadn't shouted was a relief. I didn't think he'd be the sort to do something like that, but in all honestly, I really didn't know him.

The next day I slept in, early pregnancy exhaustion had set in, and I found it difficult to do much of anything aside from sleep. I was woken by the noise of my doorbell. I stumbled half-awake in a pair of sweatpants and U of C. T-shirt, a real vision. I couldn't be bothered to do better. Whoever was at the door could fuck off; I wanted to go back to bed. I opened the door, and Adam was on my doorstep with three dozen long-stem pink roses. I stood there, my mouth literally aghast. His luggage was at his feet; he had just come from the airport.

"Hello, sleepyhead," he said softly.

"Hi," I replied, not completely awake and comprehending him standing in front of me. "I thought you were coming by this weekend."

"Is it a bad time?"

"No. I just wasn't expecting you. Come in."

I moved out of the way as he handed me the roses. They smelled beautiful. He grabbed his luggage and stepped inside the entryway to my townhouse. I brought the roses to my nose and inhaled deeply. They were gorgeous.

"These are lovely. Thank you. Would you like some coffee?"

"Yes, please."

Adam followed me into the kitchen as I set the roses in the sink and started making coffee.

"How was your flight," I asked, trying to make conversation and break the tension a bit.

"Relatively empty. Have you seen the news this morning? All travel between here and China has ceased. The U.S. closed the border. This virus is going to be a bigger deal than the U.S. media is letting on."

"That's crazy; I hadn't heard. Do you think there will be an outbreak here?"

"I do, but let's talk about that later. A flight from China gives a man a lot of time to think. I've given this a lot of thought. I was married years ago in my twenties, we wanted it all, the family, minivan, white picket fence, all of that. When we divorced, I decided I didn't really want that, and I never went in search of it again."

I slid a cup of coffee across the island, along with the sugar bowl and a small pitcher of milk. He took it and took a sip, drinking it black. He set it back down on the counter and continued.

"I'm almost fifty. I didn't think I would have the chance to be someone's father, and I was okay with that until yesterday. When you called me yesterday, something changed. I know it sounds cliché, but it's true. I want to be a part of this if you'll let me?"

"Of course, this is your child too. I am happy to give you a paternity test if you want to confirm. I'm just relieved that you want a relationship with our child. I want you to know I don't want anything from you; I can provide for this child."

I put my hand over my slightly swollen abdomen, which looked like I had overindulged at the taco bar, instead of growing a child.

"I believe you. You have whatever the two of you need from me. All you ever need to do is ask. Where does that leave you and me?"

"Oh, well, I'm not sure. Friends, I guess? I don't see why anything needs to change between us. I did not expect you to show up here with a ring. In fact, I am so glad you didn't. I think a baby is enough of a life change right now, don't you?"

I watched his posture change as he took another sip of his coffee. It almost looked like disappointment if I had to guess.

Adam finished his coffee and headed home. I promised him we could talk more after he had settled in and was more well-rested.

Over the next three weeks, the world seemed to fall apart. Adam had been right; the virus had taken hold in the U.S. Our offices closed, and I was now working from home. I had stocked up the best that I could living in the city and planned to hunker down. Adam had called a few times to check on the baby and me, and I told him all was well. It felt like the whole world was going to hunker down and ride this out.

That Tuesday morning, as I sat in on our weekly staff meeting, now held virtually, I had to step away. Someone was knocking loudly on my door. I excused myself as politely as I could, wondering who the hell would knock like that. I stormed to the door to give the inconsiderate asshole who was knocking a piece of my mind. I grabbed the knob and yanked the door open. Adam stood on my porch with two suitcases and several boxes.

"What the hell?"

"Hi," he replied.

"What are you doing? Why are you here?"

"I came to stay for the quarantine. I didn't want to leave you two to fend for yourselves. I brought groceries too."

"What? No. We're fine. Thank you, but really, no thank you."

"Hailey, please. Things are going to get worse, and if you don't let me stay for you, please let me stay for me."

I didn't know what to say. Part of me felt that it was incredibly sweet, while the other half of me was annoyed. He had mentioned the idea of staying with me last week over the phone, and I had shot him down.

"What about your house? Aren't you afraid someone will rob you if things are going to get as bad as you say?"

"It doesn't matter."

He walked forward, and I stepped out of the way to let him in.

"I'm not moving in permanently. I would sleep better at night, knowing you two are safe. You have my word that I'll go home when the stay at home order is lifted. Please?"

I took a deep breath, "all right then," I relented.

Adam stayed three nights in the guest room before he joined me in my bed. I found that I actually liked having him around, and we settled into a routine. We both worked during the day from different parts of the house, and then usually, one of us would cook dinner. We spent our evenings watching tv, reading, and playing card games or Scrabble. The more time we spent together, the more it felt like a little family, and as welcoming as it was, there was a part of me that felt uneasy about it.

As the quarantine dragged on, I knew eventually our arrangement would end. I knew we were just playing house, but it felt natural. I continuously reminded myself that I intended to raise this child alone. The days passed, and I found myself becoming more anxious. I wasn't sure if it was the thought of Adam leaving, of life, returning to normal, or just the nightly news. At first, it was manageable, but I soon found myself waking in the night. One night I woke, and Adam, sensing that I wasn't sleeping, snuggled up next to me. He wrapped his hands around me, and he started to hum the tune to the song, Starry, Starry Night. I couldn't help but laugh.

The last night of quarantine, I sat outside on my back deck and sipped a cup of mint tea to quell the nausea that had stuck with me through the pregnancy. I tried not to show my sadness that Adam would be moving back home tomorrow. I wanted him to stay, but I couldn't bring myself to ask him. Although it was now May, the temperature outside was still chilly, and I had wrapped a blanket around me as I sipped my tea. The sun had begun to set, and I had not started dinner yet. Adam had a call that went long, so I had decided to wait. As I sat there and thought about him leaving, it dawned on me that I had fallen in love with him over the past ten weeks we had lived together. Even if I wasn't carrying his child, I would've still enjoyed our time together; he was kind, thoughtful, and fun to be with. The more I thought about it, the more upset I became. I had made one hell of a mess, I felt, and I did' t know how to fix it. Just tell him the truth, my inner voice told me. I dismissed it angrily, but my mind continued to think about what to do. I stood up, setting my mug down on the table next to me. I had nothing to lose, asking him to stay. I turned to walk into the house and saw Adam standing in the doorway. He startled me.

"You know, I was thinking," he said as he leaned up against the doorjamb, "what if I didn't leave tomorrow?"

My bottom lip quivered, and I bit it hard to keep from crying.

"What if this was home now, with you and our daughter?"

He stepped out onto the deck, and I stood there, and he walked towards me.

"Hailey, what do you think?"

"Marry me," I blurted out.

"Hey, that's my line," he joked.

"What?"

"I was coming out here to ask you to marry me."

"You were?"

I couldn't help but cry, and Adam took me into his arms.

"These past ten weeks have been a gift for us. It gave us time to really get to know each other. It gave me time to reinforce my original impressions of you."

"Which were?"

"That I was going to marry you. For the record, I thought that before this peanut came along," he said as he rubbed my stomach. "So, what do you say? Will you do me the honor of becoming my wife?"

"Yes," I blubbered as I buried my head in his neck.

He pulled me closer to him, as our daughter moved between us.

Lily & James: Leaving on a Jet Plane

"Hi, is this seat taken?" I asked, jokingly, as I stood at the mostly empty bar.

The one-man sitting in the terminal bar looked at me with a confused look on his face, and I laughed. He smiled, and I took a seat two places away from him. The bartender came around to our side of the bar.

"I only have drinks today." He said.

"That's fine. Can I please have a vodka and tonic, Brustros vodka, if you have it? Thanks."

The bartender nodded as he turned to grab the glass and set to making my drink. I looked around at the airport terminal. There had to be twenty-five people in the entire terminal at best. Normally, LAX was packed as the whole world passed through these halls. Now it was just me and a few strangers. Normally this bar that sat in the middle of the terminal was packed; I now had my pick of seats and prompt service.

"Flight number?" The bartender asked as he slid my drink in front of me.

"AA445," I replied, and slid my bank card towards him.

"Chicago, right?" He asked as he took it to the till attached to the counter where the alcohol stood.

"Good call."

I sipped my drink, hoping it would take the edge off. I used to be a very nervous flyer, but as work required me to fly more, the nerves fell away. However, something about seeing the world so empty and traveling during quarantine set me on edge. I hoped a good strong drink would deaden the prickly edges of my nervousness. The bartender handed me my card and walked away. A child squealed off in the distance, and it made me wonder who would bring a toddler out in this. It's not my place to judge. I'm the idiot flying across the country during a global pandemic, I thought to myself. I looked in the direction of the noise and saw a chubby toddler running full steam from his weary parents. The boy, with his straight black hair and bright eyes, wore a face mask. It was just another unsettling reminder of how much life had changed. At that thought, I took another sip of my drink.

"You're going to Chicago," the man two seats away asked.

I turned back in his direction. We were the only two patrons on this side of the oval-shaped bar. He wore the uniform of a well-traveled man, an Oxford button-down shirt, navy sport jacket, tailored jeans, and leather loafers. His leather briefcase sat on top of his expensive rolling luggage wedged between his seat and the one next to him. His icy blue eyes complemented his hair, that was almost a perfect shade of gold, with dark brown undertones. He wore it cut longer, so I could see just a hint of a natural curl to it.

"I am."

"Where are you off to," I asked? Normally, I kept to myself. I didn't make "single-serving friends," as the term was coined from the film Fight Club.

"Boston."

"Are you traveling for business or pleasure?"

"Neither, I'm going home."

"Ah," I replied, not quite sure what he meant but it, but there was something about the way he said it that made the statement feel like a loaded grenade. I left the loaded statement sit on the bar as I took a sip of my drink.

"You, are you traveling for business or pleasure?"

"Going home. I was out here for business. I flew out here before everything hit the fan. My company asked me to stay out here for an extra week. I did, and then I woke up to a pink slip this morning. No warning, no explanation. It's happening to a lot of people right now. I was just caught off guard." Take that grenade in return, I thought to myself.

"That's rough. What do you do? I mean, what did you do for a living?"

"I was a V.P. of strategic communication at March & Wakeman. You?"

"I work in entertainment out here. Sorry about your job. Companies are going to need good comms people when this is over, I'm sure you'll land on your feet."

"Let's hope," I said as I raised my glass, and he raised his in return. We both sipped our drinks. My guess was his was scotch. He looked like a scotch drinker to me. There was a pause in our conversation, and I looked around the mostly empty terminal again. I took another sip of my drink and put together what I knew of the handsome man at the end of the bar. He said home was in Boston, but he worked out here. Hmmm, mystery, but I didn't want to pry. If I was going to have a single-serving friend, I was going to be a good one.

"Flight 487 to Dallas is now boarding at Gate M13. Flight 487 To Dallas is now boarding at Gate M13." A woman's voice echoed through the terminal.

The man on the other side of the bar downed the rest of his beer, grabbed his bags, and walked over to the gate. The man next to me and I watched a total of eight people board the flight.

"Last call for flight 487 to Dallas." The airline employee said, clearly out of formality, as everyone had already boarded.

"That's an odd scene, isn't it?" The man two seats down from me asked.

"It is. This feels like a strange dream I keep expecting to wake from. Yet here I am."

"I'm James," he put his hand forward to shake mine and then pulled it away and waved instead.

"Hi James, I'm Lily."

"Nice to meet you, Lily. So, what are your plans when you get to Chicago?"

"I guess the same as everyone else, I'll hunker down and wait this thing out, look for a new job."

We watched two more flights board as the terminal emptied. We each ordered another drink; there wasn't much else to do.

"What time is your flight?"

I looked down at my ticket. "6:45, I've got an hour. I doubt they're going to start boarding soon. I wonder if I am the only person on the flight? What time is yours?"

"7:15. I think you're right. Other than those people and the bartender, I think we're the only ones in the terminal right now. What a weird experience."

I looked at the two women across the terminal who were looking out the window to the tarmac and then glanced around. James was correct. It really was just us. My stomach growled loudly. Two vodka and tonics on an already nervous stomach may not have been the best idea. I put my hand over my stomach.

"I wonder where I can get some food?"

"The bar will have food."

"Nope, the bartender said drinks only when I sat down."

"Let's ask him where to find food, I'm hungry too," he gestured towards the bartender who was on the other side of the bar, wiping it down. "Excuse me."

The bartender stood and came over. "Another round," he asked as he picked up the scotch bottle James was drinking.

"No, thanks, say, do you know where we could find some food?"

The bartender thought, "well, there's nothing in this terminal. You could try terminal J. I know there's an In and Out Burger over there that is rumored to be open. Everywhere else, you'll have to go back out through security, but, honestly, I wouldn't risk it. Your two flights are the last two tonight, and I don't know if you be able to get back through. They've been running a lean crew as it is."

James turned towards me, "Want to give terminal J a try?"

"It's better than our current options," I paused for emphasis, "nothing."

James let out a little laugh.

"Do you want anything," he turned, asking the bartender.

The small gesture struck me. It was so simple but so kind.

"Nah, I'm good. I'm almost done for the day. Thanks, though."

James stood and grabbed his luggage as I followed suit. I could feel the vodka in my system. I wasn't drunk, not even close, but I felt happy and at ease. James and I set off in search of terminal J and did not pass another soul as we walked through the empty airport.

"I expect to hear my alarm going off at any minute and wake up from this weird dream," James said as we entered terminal J, which was just as empty as ours was.

"I was just thinking the same thing. I smell French fries."

"Me too, now I'm really hungry."

I let out a little laugh as we walked through the terminal. Halfway through, the terminal opened to a circle with food options and a few tables on either side of the main hall. All of the food options were closed, and my stomach reminded me that it would be a long flight to Chicago, hungry. An employee in the In and Out Burger walked from behind the wall to the kitchen and came around to the register. The gate was down, but James and I looked at each other and walked up.

"Excuse me, do you have any food left for sale?" James asked.

"Sorry, we're closed."

"I understand. But there is nothing to eat in the airport right now, and my friend and I both have long flights. I'll pay you double."

The employee looked up at that and held up a finger signaling for us to wait as he walked behind the wall into the kitchen. I looked up at James, who shrugged. The man returned a minute later with a large white to-go bag. He walked up to the gate and opened it, handing us the bag of food.

"It's just fries, they're probably cold, but it's something."

James reached for his wallet.

"No charge, man."

"Then something for your trouble," James insisted.

"Don't worry about. Stay safe." He said as he walked back behind the gate and pulled it down.

My phone buzzed, and I reached into my back pocket to retrieve it, the bag of fries in my other hand.

"My flight's been delayed until 9. How is there a delay? No one's traveling," I asked to no one in particular.

"Maybe the plane left Chicago late?"

I nodded and looked towards the end of the terminal, where the last of the day's golden sun streaked through the windows at the end.

"I love the color of the sunlight here. It is so beautiful."

"Why don't we go sit down there then? Let you soak it all in before you return to Chicago?"

"Sure."

James and I walked to the end of the terminal and sat directly in the light of the waning sunset. We dug into the bag, which had a generous helping of French fries. It wasn't enough for a meal for both of us, but there was enough food to take the edge off of hunger. I felt like a teenager eating just fries with my single-serving friend. In the middle of a spacious airport, there was an intimate feeling between us, like we were the last two people left in the building. I knew it wasn't true. James' phone buzzed, and he pulled it from his jacket pocket.

"Huh, my flight is delayed now too."

"How long?"

"Two hours, like yours."

"That makes me nervous. I hope our flights are canceled. I don't want to go back to the hotel. I want my own bed."

"Nah, they won't cancel."

I was skeptical as James put his phone back in his pocket. He reached for another French fry as his phone began to buzz again. He pulled it out.

"Sorry, I have to take this," he said as he stood up and walked away.

I tried not to eavesdrop, but it was hard not to in the silent terminal. James had walked back towards the food court, but his voice still carried.

"Yes, I'm at the airport. Look, I don't know why we have to do this now, in the middle of a global pandemic. Isn't it enough that I am flying across the country to be there?"

I couldn't hear the other end of the call, but there was tension in James' voice, and I felt uncomfortable listening. I reached for my bag to grab my own phone as I heard him continue.

"What difference does it make? Why couldn't you just send me the papers; I don't see why I have to be there to sign them."

Was he going home to sign divorce papers, I wondered? I had not noticed a wedding ring. His annoyance turned to anger as I watched him begin to pace out of the corner of my eye.

"I am staying in the guest house. Look, I'll sign the damn papers, but then I am coming home," there was a pause as the other person on the phone talked. "You don't get to tell me where home is anymore," he said as he hung up the phone.

He brought his hand up to his head, but I couldn't see what he was doing; he stood with his back to me. I looked at my phone as I put another French fry into my mouth, trying to act like I was oblivious to the call I had just witnessed. James walked back up and sat down.

"Sorry about that."

"Huh," I said, trying to be polite.

James understood and gave a slight smile of acknowledgment.

"Would you like a magic French fry?"

James looked at me, quizzically as I picked up a French fry.

"This is not just any French fry, you see it's a magical L.A. French fry."

James laughed as I continued.

"Yes, it will make you younger, richer, healthier." I laughed and put the fry back down.

"No, keep going, you have my attention."

There was a genuine smile on his face, and for the first time, I truly noticed how handsome he was.

"Well, Sir, this magical fry," I said as I picked it back up, "it also cures all ailments and maladies. Generations of explorers have searched for this magical fry only to end up disappointed. I offer it to you, my weary traveling friend."

I held out the fry, and James laughed.

"Magic, you say? That was quite the story. You'd fit in well out here."

"I guess you doubt it's Magic? This fry will have to be all mine then."

"No, no, I don't doubt it."

I raised an eyebrow as I looked at James and laughed as he took the French fry from my hand. He popped it into his mouth and chewed slowly with emphasis and swallowed.

"Is it working? Do I look younger, healthier?" He joked, turning his face side to side.

"Whoa, you do." I laughed.

James laughed too.

"Thanks for sacrificing that magical fry for me, a weary traveler," he joked.

We both laughed as I wrapped up the paper from the fries and put all the trash into the bag. I stood up and took the empty bag, and put it into the trash can.

"What time is it," I asked, looking back at James.

"It's 6:08."

James got up and grabbed his luggage and mine as he pulled mine over to me. I took it from him as we began to walk slowly towards the terminal entrance.

"Do you want to walk to terminal D? I don't think we have to leave the security to do it." He asked.

I weight my options, the only thing that awaited us in our departure terminal was the bar, and I had my fill.

"All right."

We pulled out luggage through the empty airport towards terminal D. The sole of my leather booties echoed through the empty halls.

"I'm going back to Boston to sign divorce papers," James said.

His statement caught me off guard.

"I'm sorry to hear that."

"Me, too. My soon to be ex-wife is insisting I be there to sign in person. I think she's going to try to use our kids to get more out of me."

"That's rotten. How old are your children?"

"I have two girls, Ellie, who's 11 and Margie, who's 13. I hate that they're having to go through this. I took a job out here, and my ex, Karen, didn't want to move the girls out here."

"How long have you been working out here?"

"Five years. My wife and kids lived here up to a year ago. I couldn't understand what was so bad about living out here. Karen just hated it. She wanted to be home in Boston with her friends. She started flying home most weekends. Weekends turned into long weekends, and then weeks at a time, until one day she called and said she was done with our life out here. I think there's someone else in Boston."

"That's rough."

"I worry about my girls. I hope this doesn't destroy our relationship."

"Can I ask a question?"

"Sure."

"Did you offer to move back?"

"I did, no job is worth my family. When I told her I'd finally move back, she told me not to bother, it wouldn't make a difference."

"Ah, that makes sense why you'd be suspicions of someone else."

James nodded. Our walking slowed as I put my hand on his arm to comfort him. He put his hand over mine. The gesture felt appropriate and awkward at the same time.

"We're a barrel of fun, you and I. Me, unemployed and well, you..." I gestured.

"I guess we are. I think this is the most fun I've ever had in an airport."

"That's just sad," I joked.

"No, I mean it. I knew this trip was going to be difficult, and I didn't expect... I'm glad I met you."

"I'm glad I met you too."

We turned into terminal D, which was deserted. My heels clacked on the floor, echoing through the terminal. We walked in silence past empty gate after gate. This terminal was longer than the previous two. James stopped in the middle of the terminal, and I stopped two steps ahead of him and looked back in his direction. Letting go of his luggage, he walked up to me and slid his hand along my cheek. I could smell his cologne as he stepped towards me. His hand was soft against my cheek. He leaned down and brushed a soft kiss across my lips. I stood in awe as he pulled away.

"I'm sorry, I know I shouldn't have done that. I just wanted to know."

"Know what," I said as I licked my lips, still tasting him, and the salt from the fries.

"I wanted to know what kissing you would feel like," he said with an embarrassed look on his face, "I'm sorry, if.."

I closed the space between us and wrapped my arm around his neck as I pulled his lips to mine. This time I felt him brush his tongue across mine, and it had the same effect of striking a match as my body felt like it was in flames. I had never had an experience like this before. I didn't know if I was drunk from the booze and didn't realize it, or the current situation of being alone in an airport during a global pandemic, but something in me let go of my reserved nature. He pulled my body in tighter against his as his kiss deepened. I took my hand off my luggage and looped it around his neck as I held him with both hands.

He pulled away and looked down at me. I had not realized how much taller than me he was than me. There was something in his icy blue eyes that pierced through me.

"Wow," he whispered.

"Wow good, or wow bad?" I asked softly.

"Wow, good, very good."

In the boldest action of my life, I pulled him over to a gate, the noise of my shoes muffled on the carpet of the gate. I pulled him gently behind the wall of the desk at the gate. As soon as we stepped behind it, he pulled me back into his arms. Pinned between him and the cold wall, I felt like a teenager. He kissed me again as he slid his hand up my soft gray sweater. As his hand connected with my breast, I let out a soft moan.

I reached between us and tugged at his belt, but the fancy buckle wouldn't release. He pulled his hand away from my breast and released the clasp on his belt. As he brought his hand back to me, he pushed my sweater up. My breast sat, eager to be touched in my white demi-cupped lace bra. I reached between us, unbuttoned his pants, and pushed them down, listening to the contents of his pockets hit the carpeted floor. He reached down and unbuttoned my jeans, but they did not fall from my hips. His kisses were deep and with a feverish intensity that made me feel like we were both on the precipice of something. I helped him as I pushed my own pants down. I slid my foot out of my booties and out of one of my pant legs as he lifted me against the wall.

This is nuts, but I love it, I want it! My inner voice screamed. My body was warm against him, and everywhere he touched seemed to tingle. I felt like clay in his arms. He entered me, bringing a rush of pleasure with it. He kissed me as we had sex secretly in the middle of an empty airport terminal. My fingers dug into his back as the pleasure built. He pulled his lips away from mine, and I pulled the cool air of the terminal in greedily into my lungs, unable to keep as silent." I bit down hard on my lip to keep from screaming out as the orgasm tore through my body. James brought his mouth over mine to muffle the sound. My body shook, and my fingers and toes tingled.

He pulled his mouth from mine and whispered in my ear, "I can feel you coming, it's so fucking hot."

I brought my mouth back to his and tried to kiss him with as much intensity as he had kissed me with. It was all he needed as I felt his body lurch, and my back pressed harder against the wall. I wanted to stay pined like that forever, as my own orgasm was still in its final waning moments. We stayed like that, my body lifted in his arms, back cold against the wall, as we both breathed hard.

James set me down gently, and we both dressed silently. I could not believe that I had sex with a stranger. I watched James dress, in amazement of what had just happened, that I now know him intimately. We walked from behind the wall, hand in hand, our luggage still standing in the middle of the terminal where we had left it. Grabbing our luggage, we started walking back towards our terminal.

"I don't believe that just happened," I said out loud.

"Me neither."

We both looked at each other. I reached over and wiped a streak of my peachy colored lipstick from the side of his face.

"Lipstick," I said as I pulled my finger away to show him.

"Ah, thanks."

My phone buzzed as we reached out terminal. I pulled it out of my bag.

"My flight is boarding."

"Can I have your number, Lily from Chicago?"

"All right, James from L.A., 312-333-9380. I have to go."

"Bye, he said softly."

"Bye," I waved.

I turned back and looked at him as I got behind the one other person boarding the flight. His polished traveler facade back on. He waved again as I boarded, and I waved back one last time.

I took my seat on the flight and counted two other people on the plane, still in awe that I had just had sex with a complete stranger. As I felt the plane push back, I realized I didn't get his number in return. I wanted to leap off the plane and get it from him. I wanted to get to know him more. As we took off, I thought about him leaving L.A. shortly to go home to Boston, and I wondered if I'd ever see him again.

I returned home and began the lockdown with the rest of the city as I applied for jobs online. I thought about James a lot. My encounter with him had been the craziest thing I'd ever done. Three weeks later, on a rainy night, my phone buzzed. I looked down to see it was an

L.A. number and answered excitedly.

"Hi is this, Lily," James asked?

Ava & Aaron: An Iowa Adventure

K atie and I saw it coming, the quarantine. We work together at the corporate offices of a national insurance company. The afternoon that the quarantine closed the offices, Katie and I rode the El back up to my place. We had met on our first day and had been friends for the past ten years as we both rose within the organization. She had become the best friend I never had. As we rode north, the buildings shrunk in size through the train car windows and became more residential, Katie continued to try to convince me to come home with her to Iowa.

"The city is going to get crazy," she kept saying, "it won't be safe here. Come to Iowa with me. Come stay at the farm."

That night as I laid on my couch in my townhouse, the one I had worked so hard to buy, life just felt odd. I felt like I was abandoning my life. My mind wasn't completely even made up until Katie showed up the next morning and started to put my stuff in her car. I hated the idea of leaving the city. Deep down I knew it was a smart thing to do, but part of me felt I'd be just fine where I was. I relented and got into the car. I tried not to regret my decision as urban turned into suburban, and eventually rural through the passenger side window. I felt very out of my element without pavement beneath my feet and skyscrapers towering overhead.

I had saw pictures of Katie's family farm, an old white farmhouse that looked older than the state, and a big red barn off in the distance. She came from a long line of farmers. Katie didn't look like a farm girl from Iowa, nor did she look like a city girl either, she was a chameleon in that way. She had the ability to fit in wherever she went. I, on the other hand stuck out like a sore thumb.

As we crossed the Mississippi River, Katie's cell phone rang. She picked it up and put it to her ear, but I could still hear her mother on the other end. Eileen Bishop was everyone's mother it seemed. I had met her several times when she and Bob, Katie's dad, had visited Katie in Chicago. They were good salt-of-the-Earth Midwesterners and I liked them.

"Yeah Mom, we just crossed the Mississippi, so about two and a half hours. No, I won't speed."

I looked out the passenger window, trying not to laugh. Katie didn't know how to drive under the speed limit. I thought about my own mom. If I were having this exact conversation with her, she'd be more concerned that I brought a case good of wine, and the good ham from Jensen's Market, the best butcher in the city. "We have to eat well at this crucial time," I could hear her saying in my head. She and her newest husband had been stuck in Europe when the pandemic hit. Not that stuck is a fair word exactly, she was quarantined to her new husband's penthouse in Paris, with its breathtaking views of the Eiffel Tower. For a split second, I thought about joining her instead. When I was honest with myself, it would be fun for a few days; then I'd be stuck with my mother in a confined space for weeks on end, and whatever winner she had chosen to marry this time. No, thank you. I'd take my chances with Katie's family.

"He's coming home," Katie said, jogging my attention from the thought of my mother in her Parisian penthouse.

I prayed "he" wasn't her older brother Aaron. If it was, Katie could drop me at the nearest airport. Paris sounded like a better idea. I had met Aaron on several occasions. Met, is a kind word, it would be more apt to say fell into bed and had drunken hate sex. The truth was we couldn't stand each other. I knew this because he made sure to tell me to my face once, three whiskeys in. What did I do in return to this information, you ask? I fucked him in the bathroom. We were perfectly polite to each other when sober, but if you put a few drinks into us, we became different people. Katie knew some of the history between Aaron and I, but not all of it. Honestly, there wasn't really a history, just a string of drunken hook ups, every time we were in the same room together, followed by my self-loathing afterwards.

Katie hung up the phone and looked at me.

"Aaron is home. I'm sorry I didn't know. Mom said he was staying in Berkley and was going to ride it out there. Look, I'll make him behave. I promise. I know you, how you two feel about each other. Besides, if Daddy catches wind of Aaron's bullshit around you, he'll bring some country justice."

"Do I want to know what country justice is?" I asked.

Katie laughed. "It will be fine. I promise."

Two hours later Katie pulled off of the two-lane highway and down a long gravel driveway as the rocks hit the side of her BMW. I thought about the paint, but she didn't let her foot up as cloud of dust billowed up into the air behind the car. There was a nervous pit in my stomach as we got closer and the white farmhouse got bigger in the windshield. It looked just like the picture with the only exception being that the photo had been taken in July, when the landscape had color. In early March, everything was still dormant, the landscape was bleak. Before we even got out of the car, Bob and Eileen were standing on the porch to welcome us. I checked my make-up in the mirror behind the sun visor. I hadn't wore much, as I smudged a natural tone of peach across my lower lip. It complemented my pale skin, and set off my blue eyes. I ran my fingers through my chocolate brown hair, smoothing it.

"Ready Miss America?" Katie joked.

Her joke put me on edge. I was way out of my element and now in hostile territory with Aaron wandering around. I got out of the car, my heel hitting the gravel first. Wrong shoes for this, I thought to myself as I got out.

"Look at you two, as pretty as a picture," Eileen squealed as she came off the porch. She hugged Katie and then me. "Ava, I'm so happy you came home with Katie. I know you can take care of yourself, but it worries me, you all alone in the city with all of this craziness going on."

Bob came up and hugged Katie and then me.

"Ava, our home is your home. Please make yourself comfortable," he said.

I was touched by their warmth and generosity. They were truly kind people and I saw a lot of them in Katie.

"Come on, let's get you girls settled in. Dinner will be ready in about an hour. Ava, is there anything you don't eat? Do you have any food allergies?"

"No, Mrs. Bishop."

"Eileen. Mrs. Bishop was my mother-in-law."

I smiled as Bob and Eileen led us into the house. The interior looked like a Hollywood movie set of an old farmhouse. Dark wood floors, paneled doors, the wood staircase, even the soft yellow wallpaper. Walking in, it felt like home. Eileen led me up the stairs and into the first room at the top of the stairs, across the hall from Katie. The room was clean and cozy with its slopped ceiling and wrought-iron bed.

"The bathroom is down the hall, the second door on your left. I'm so glad you came to stay. I'll let you settle in, and I'll holler when dinner is ready," Eileen said as she started to walk out of the room.

She moved out of the way as Aaron came through the door with my four pieces of luggage in his hand. I had not asked him to bring them up, I was fully capable.

"Where do you want em'?"

"Anywhere is fine."

He took me literally and set them down where he stood. Typical asshole, I thought to myself. Eileen walked out of the room, leaving only Aaron and I. He looked at me without saying anything, it was the sort of look that I felt in my core.

"Thanks," I said, barely audible.

He turned and walked out, still silent and shut the door behind him. I sat down on the bed and took a deep breath. You do not find him attractive sober, remember? Get it together! I took another deep breath, trying to push the image of him out of my head. His sandy blonde hair, deep blue eye and sharp jawline was enough to get over, but his body was incredible. I took one more deep breath to steady myself. Katie knocked on my door, came in and laid on the bed while I unpacked.

That night we ate beef roast, mashed potatoes, gravy, and

vegetables around the dining room table. I felt like I was in a Norman Rockwell painting; it was so different from my own home, but I liked it. There was something solid, and safe about it. Over dinner we all caught up. When I though I couldn't eat anymore, Eileen brought out a chocolate cake, two tiers high. It looked amazing, but I was so full that I politely declined.

After dinner we played a game of Monopoly, and I learned the Bishop's take their Monopoly game very seriously. I watched Aaron decimate his own mother, which emboldened me to try to crush him in the game. We played until I finally beat him, much to the delight of the entire family. We all turned in for the night afterward. As I laid in bed, I thought about Aaron. It was nice to see him so pleasant. I was glad that Katie had brought me home with her so far. My thoughts drifted to the giant chocolate cake in the fridge downstairs. My mouth watered at the thought of it. Tempted, I grabbed my robe and tiptoed down the creaky wooden stairs. The house was quiet as I made my way into the kitchen. The lights were off but the small table lamp in the hallway lit the way to the fridge. I pulled the door open and looked inside for the cake.

"Looking for this?" I heard Aaron say, scaring the shit out of me.

He laughed as I turned around. I couldn't see him in the dark. He clicked on the small lamp that sat on the kitchen table.

"I think you jumped six feet, that was classic."

"You're an asshole."

"Sorry, it was too easy. Do you want a slice of cake?"

I took a deep breath, bringing my heart rate back down, but it was difficult looking at him sitting there shirtless.

"It's all right."

"Here," he said as he leaned over and pulled a drawer open and a fork out of it. "Come sit," he said as he put the fork on the table.

I knew grabbing that fork was like reaching in a lion's hungry mouth to retrieve it. I stared hard at Aaron; I wasn't going to be a shrinking violet. I stepped closer towards the table. Aaron reached out and hooked his finger in the belt loop of my bathrobe and stood as he pulled me into him. His chest was warm, I pushed away from him half-heartedly. He brought his mouth down over mine, and his mouth tasted of chocolate fudge. His kiss was powerful, and it stoked a fire deep inside of me. I knew I was in so much trouble, this was a terrible idea, but I didn't want to stop, I wasn't sure if I could.

He broke his mouth away from mine and whispered in my ear, "follow me."

He left the cake on the kitchen table and clicked off the light. I followed him upstairs, my heart pounding so hard I could feel it in my fingertips. We reached the top stair as Bob and Eileen's bedroom door opened. Quickly Aaron pulled me into my room, shutting the door silently. Behind the closed door we both remained still, as I stood in his arms. I could smell him, hear his breathing, and my resolve completely crumbled. We both listened for Eileen's footsteps. Once the bathroom door closed, Aaron reach up and took my cheek into his hand and brought my mouth back to his.

His kisses trailed down my neck as he pulled my robe open. He tugged at the collar of my nightshirt trying to kiss my collar bone. Frustrated he tugged at it and I heard the stitches in the seam tear.

"Wait," I said breathless.

I pulled the nightdress off. The soft blue moonlight flooded through bedroom lighting my pale skin. I stood before him in only my lace underwear. He licked his lips as he pulled me back into his body and crossed the room over to the bed, never taking his mouth away from mine. The bed creaked loudly as we collapsed on to it.

"Shhh," he whispered into my ear.

He brought his mouth back over mine as he reached in between us and slipped his hand into my panties. I wanted them gone. I needed any barrier between us gone. I reached down and pushed off his pajama bottoms. He tugged at my panties hard as I heard the lace seam give way, this time I didn't care. He pushed his body into mine, I cried out in pleasure, his mouth still over mine. I reached down, grasping his ass, trying to pull him into me harder and faster. The bed began to creak, and I didn't care, I couldn't care. I felt as if I was going to go up in flames. Aaron slowed his pace.

"Shhhh," he reminded me.

He slowed his pace and rather than kiss me he looked at me. I could see his face in moonlight. There was something in the way he looked at me, it was different. Something changed in that moment, I felt he saw me in a way that he had not before. He leaned down, kissed me, with affection. His movements became more deliberate. This wasn't our normal hate fuck. This was something I had never

82

experienced before, I realized he was making love to me. My orgasm tore through me as I bit down on his shoulder, not to scream out. He held me tight against his body, driving into me as my body trembled with pleasure.

"Kiss me," he said as his own orgasm took him over the edge.

He collapsed on top of me, his ragged breath the only noise I could hear. I didn't know what to make of what just happened. He brought his head up, his body still on top of mine. Our eyes met as he leaned down and kissed me again. I was sure his kiss was different; something had changed between us. He rolled off me and rather than leave, he pulled my body tight next to his. I cuddled up next to him and laid my head on his shoulder.

"I'm really glad you came home with Katie. Maybe we can give this," he gestured between us, "a real shot. I have to be honest; I compare every woman to you."

"What," I said as I looked up at him.

"It's true. I wasn't coming home until I heard Katie was bringing you home with her. I wanted the chance to see you again. I look for any chance I can to see you."

"I don't understand. You don't like me, you told me so, to my face. Our hook-ups have been sloppy, drunken hook-ups."

"I lied, to you, to myself. The alcohol, it was liquid courage."

"For what? To sleep with me?"

"All of it, to talk to you. Ava, you take my breath away each time I see you."

I put my head back down on his shoulder. I was speechless. How could I have been so blind?

"Ava," he said gently as he tipped my chin up towards his.

"I don't know what to say," I said honestly.

"Then kiss me."

I lifted my head and kissed him, as he brought his hand to the side of my cheek, caressing it as we kissed. This was a kiss of affection, love, and it swallowed me whole in that moment and for the rest of my life.

Ella & Trevor: Critical Care

Ella glanced at her watch. It was ten p.m. Her neighbor, the doctor, usually arrived home at around ten pm on the dot each night, but not recently. The rhythms of life are what she missed as a global pandemic took hold, and life slowly came to a halt around her. She had paid attention to the news when the virus first emerged and stocked up on extra groceries and supplies in her tiny apartment, just in case. She decided to ride out whatever was coming her way from home. Her cat, Oscar, was her company, and work kept her busy enough from home during the quarantine.

Ella had spent more time in the apartment in the first month of quarantine than she did for the entire two years she had lived there. In those two years, she had met a few of her neighbors, but only casually, a wave in the hall, or holding the downstairs door, leaving extra coins on the washer downstairs, that sort of thing. Last year, the doctor moved in, but they never had the chance to meet properly.

She remembered the day he moved in; he and his friends made so much noise trying to get his couch up the tight staircase in the 6-flat walk up. It was almost amusing to watch if it had not been so frustrating at the same time. That tight staircase was almost like a right of passage for the building, as each tenant had the same struggle on moving days. He and his four male friends had been good looking, but his dark curly hair, tan complexion, and deep brown eyes made butterflies fly around in her stomach when she looked at him. Ella wasn't usually shy, but there was something powerful in the way he looked at her, giving off an air of intensity that she wasn't sure she wanted to tangle with.

Ella continued to listen as the hour grew later, and the hallway outside her door remained quiet. She couldn't explain precisely why she had begun to listen for his comings and goings, but she had just the same. She dozed off on the couch with Oscar curled up next to her purring. She woke to the noise of keys hitting the wood floor in the hallway.

"Shit," a man's voice said.

He had not been loud, but the transom windows above her door did nothing to muffle outside noise from the hallway. She perked up and listened as she heard the keys drop again, followed by something substantial leaning up against the wall. A key was needed at the downstairs door to get in, so whoever was in the hallway was supposed to be there. She looked down at Oscar, her beloved white fur ball with orange, black, and gray spots. He stretched out his paws and then curled back into a ball. Ella took it as his way of saying, you're on your own with that one lady. She pried Oscar from her lap and got up to look out the peephole. She could see the doctor from across the hall fumbling with his keys. Reaching for the doorknob, she hesitated. What if he's sick, I've done a really good job staying in and helping do my part, she thought. Before she could open the door, he walked into his apartment. Ella looked down at her watch that read one am.

That night as she laid in bed, Oscar glued to her side again, she thought about the doctor across the hallway, him smiling with his friends. She found herself worrying about him. He lived alone; she never saw or heard anyone else come in or out of the apartment. She wondered how he was fairing, as the medical system was beyond stretched with resources. She wanted to help but wasn't quite sure how.

As she made dinner the next night, an idea struck, she'd make a plate for him. That night she made extra for dinner and kept a plate warm in her oven for him. She listened for him to come home as she watched the ten o'clock news, then the Late Show. She finally got up from the couch to turn the oven off when she heard feet shuffle down the hallway. She grabbed the plate with a potholder and went to open her front door.

The doctor turned around at the noise of the door opening. Ella was shocked at how tired he looked.

"Hi, I hope this isn't weird, but I made you a plate of dinner. It's a chicken breast, rice, and veggies. I know you've been keeping crazy hours, and I just thought a hot home-cooked meal might be nice with you working so hard."

His face lightened as he smiled.

"That's very nice. That sounds delicious."

Ella reached out her hand, "I'm Ella James."

The doctor pulled his hands away.

"Right, sorry, I forgot, no handshakes anymore."

"It's okay. Hi Ella, my name is Trevor. I don't think we've formally met."

"We haven't, but that's okay," Ella said as she handed him the plate. "Careful, it's hot."

"Ow, it is."

"Here, you can have the plate holder."

He took it from her and put it under the plate. There was an award pause.

"Thank you again, Ella, this is really kind."

"It's the least I can do. Thank you for serving our community. I'll let you eat in peace. Have a good night Trevor."

"You too; good night Ella."

Ella shut the door behind her and took a deep breath. She felt like she had been holding her breath the entire time she spoke to Trevor. He reminded her of a tired warrior. She felt like she had done something to help the cause in feeding Trevor. The next day she reran the scene from the night before in her head again and again. She decided to make him dinner again and waited up to give it to him hot. He stumbled in, looking more tired than the night before, about 2 am. Ella opened her door and offered him a plate of spaghetti and homemade meatballs. He took it, grateful for the hot food.

For the next two weeks, Ella had dinner waiting for Trevor each night. Giving him dinner had become the highlight in her increasingly mundane quarantine schedule. They didn't talk much when she handed him food in the wee hours of the morning, nor did she expect it. Last night he had brought her a bouquet of flowers to say thank you. They were a total surprise, and she was touched at the gesture of gratitude, not that she ever expected one. The next day she put the vase of flowers on her desk and enjoyed them immensely.

That night she cooked marinated lamb chops, couscous, and sautéed spinach. She sautéed the spinach at 10:30 pm for his portion, not wanting it to sit for hours. She waited for him to come in and felt a wave of excitement when she heard him shuffle down the hallway. She opened her door with the plate of dinner in her hand and looked at him. He had been crying, his eyes were red, and cheeks hastily dried.

"Hi," he said meekly.

"Hi," she said softly in return. "Are you okay?"

"Today was," he paused, "it was a rough day."

"I'm sorry. I really am," she said as she handed him the warm plate." Do you want to talk about it? I'm a good listener."

"Nah, thank you again for dinner. This is the highlight of my day."

"Mine too. If you change your mind, you know where to find me. Good night Trevor."

"Night, Ella."

Ella walked into her apartment and felt awful for Trevor. She could only imagine what he was living through. She had stopped watching the nightly news as the information straddled a line between informative and terrifying. Oscar jumped off the couch and wound between her ankles before he pranced off to his water bowl in the kitchen. She locked her door, turned off the lights, and climbed into bed. Seeing Trevor so distraught bothered her. She thought about the difference of him smiling and laughing with his friends on moving day to the man that stood before her earlier; it broke her heart. She rolled over, and Oscar took the action as an invitation as he curled up in the crook of her knees. She drifted off and was almost asleep when she heard a soft knock on her door. She sat up and listened, thinking her mind was playing tricks on her. She got out of bed when she heard it again. She answered her door in her pajamas, a cotton knit top, and matching pants that hugged her figure perfectly. She opened the door and saw Trevor standing there with a stack of her plates.

He had showered. She could smell his shampoo. He stood there in pajama pants and a t-shirt. His five o'clock shadow just made him more handsome, Ella thought.

"Hi, I wanted to return these. I'm sorry if I woke you."

Ella knew one didn't knock at almost 3 am just to return plates; she knew he wanted something more but wasn't exactly sure what.

"Thank you; you could have left them by the door."

"I guess I could've, but I didn't want them to get dirty, damaged, or stolen."

He handed her just about every dinner plate she owned, and the stack was heavy. Still not completely awake, the plates slipped in her grasp, and the top four plates slid from the pile and hit the floor, breaking on impact. They had both bent down to catch them, as Ella cradled the other dishes to her chest.

"I'm so sorry, Ella!"

"It's alright.

It was my fault they slipped out of my hand," She said as she turned and walked into her apartment, leaving the door open. She set the remaining plates on the kitchen counter and grabbed a broom and dustpan. When she returned to the hallway, Trevor already had a wastebasket from his apartment and was picking up the larger pieces.

"I'm sorry, can I pay to replace them, or buy a new set?"

"No need. They're old anyway."

Ella swept the grit from the porcelain into the dustpan and tipped it into Trevor's wastebasket.

"I wouldn't go barefooted out here for a while," she said as they both looked down at their bare feet and laughed.

"Would you like a cup of tea? I know it's late, but," Trevor trailed off.

"I'd love one."

"Great. It would just be nice to talk to someone who isn't behind glass or a mask. But we should probably have tea in the hallway. I don't want to risk infecting you."

"Are you sick?"

"No, but I work with virus patients every day," Trevor said as he walked into his apartment, leaving the door open.

Ella stepped forward and stopped at the doorway of his apartment. She leaned up against the door jam.

"What do you do at the hospital?"

"I only have green tea, is that okay," Ella nodded it was, "I'm an anesthesiologist at Metro."

"That must be very rewarding."

"It is, most of the time." He said, ducking below the counter.

Ella heard the rumble of pots and pans.

"What are you looking for?" She asked, craning inside.

"Sorry, I'm looking for my tea kettle."

"I have Mine on the stove. Why don't I boil the water, and we'll drink your tea?"

"Um…" She heard the pans spill out of the cabinet and hit the floor. Trevor stood up, "okay, thanks."

Ella crossed the walked back into her apartment, and Trevor came and stood in her doorway. She put the kettle on the stove and turned on. She set out two mugs, grabbed two green tea bags from her cupboard without thinking, and dropped them into the empty mugs. Trevor was supposed to contribute the tea, but he didn't say anything about it.

"So, you were saying that you're an anesthesiologist. I am sure you've been very busy. I've been reading about how people are sedated before being put on a ventilator. Have you been working with virus patients?"

"I have. Normally, I am the most welcome guy in the room. The doctor with the "good drugs," everyone usually jokes. I won't lie; my job isn't always easy. Sometimes it is sad. This virus, man, seeing what it does to the body. It's been tough."

"Is that what you were upset about earlier tonight when you got home?"

There was something about the way he looked at her after she asked that caused her to regret her choice of question. Perhaps it was too personal of a question.

"I guess I didn't hide it as well as I thought."

"It's okay. You're saving lives, that takes an emotional toll."

"It does. None of us have ever been through something like this. I see patients that I know that I am sedating that will never breathe on their own again. That's rough. I'm sorry I shouldn't be talking about this."

"I don't mind. We all need someone to talk to," she said as she pulled the kettle that had begun to whistle off of the stove and poured the hot water into each cup.

"I have my family, but they're in Colorado. I'm the only one out here. Three of my sisters are nurses. I know they'd get it, but we're all keeping such crazy hours right now; it's been hard to talk."

"So, you're one of three siblings?"

"I am actually one of eight."

"Eight? Okay, I have to ask, Mormon? Catholic?"

"Nope," he laughed, "hippie. My parents are very free spirits."

"That's pretty cool. I would have loved siblings," she said as she put his cup of tea near him on the entry table and gestured for him to take it as she backed away. "I'm an only child. I think it is why I've done so all right so far during this. I'm used to being alone; it reminds me of my childhood."

"You weren't locked away, were you?'

Ella laughed, "no, I had a happy childhood. So, back to your work and tonight? I mean, we don't have to discuss it if you don't want to."

"Ah, you remind me of my older sister Sparrow."

"Is that good?"

"Yes," he said before he sipped the tea.

He pulled away from his lips and looked down at the tea in the mug. "A colleague died today. I've worked with her for almost two years. She was alone; her husband and kids couldn't be there to say goodbye. It was so fast too. She did everything right and still got sick. I hate this virus; it's cruel; it's a killer."

"I'm so sorry, that is heartbreaking. Were you there with her?"

"I was."

Ella could see him welling up again, and it tugged at her heartstrings.

"Then she wasn't alone; she had a friend with her, you. I am sure your presence brought comfort to her, and I know it must have brought comfort to her family to know you were there."

Trevor nodded as he wiped the corner of his eye with the back of his hand. Ella brought a box of tissue from the table in the living room and set it where she had put his tea.

"I know it doesn't feel like it, but there will come a time when all of this will be in the past. You are doing such important work, Trevor, thank you. It warms my heart to know there are good people like you out there helping others. You were a good friend to your colleague until the end."

Trevor nodded, and Ella sipped her tea.

"Can I ask you a question?" He said after he regained his composure.

Ella nodded that he could as she took another sip of tea.

"Why did it take so long for us to meet? It's odd, isn't it? I keep hearing of stories like this."

"We're busy people normally with busy lives. I'm glad we met, though."

"Me too. Thank you again for the dinners. They really have been the highpoint in my days. I find myself wondering all day what you're making for dinner. I must confess, I love your cooking."

Ella laughed. "I'm glad to do it."

"What inspired you?"

"I don't know exactly. I just wanted to help out in some way. I heard you come home one night and thought you must have had a really long day. I knew you worked at the hospital as a doctor, your mail says M.D., but I didn't know exactly what you did."

Trevor finished the last of the tea in his mug as he leaned up against the doorway.

"Well, thank you. I'd hug you if I could, to say thank you."

Ella instantly wondered what it would be like to be in his arms and so much more. She bit her bottom lip to hold back an embarrassed smile from leaking out.

"I should let you get to bed," he said as he still held on to the mug.

"You don't have too if you don't want to."

"No, I should. I've kept you up late enough. Thank you for this, and for the dinners. If you don't mind, I'll take this home and wash it; it will be safer. I can return it to you in the morning in one piece."

Ella laughed softly, "Sure. Sleep well."

"You too."

Ella walked towards the door to close it behind Trevor. She could still smell his scent, and it made her tingle in all of the best ways. The next day she could not concentrate on anything other than thinking about dinner and talking to Trevor. She agonized over what to cook and eventually decided to roast a chicken. She purposely cooked it late, not starting it until eight pm. She didn't expect Trevor until well after midnight but, she'd eat before then.

The chicken finished cooking just before ten, and she pulled it out to let it rest and mashed potatoes to go with. She had roasted root vegetables alongside the chicken, and the apartment smelled delicious. She had just finished the potatoes when she heard a knock at her door. She dried her hands and went to answer it. Trevor stood in the hallway with two boxes of dishes from Crate and Barrel. Ella couldn't help but laugh.

"Hi, I wanted to replace the dishes I broke." He said from behind the boxes.

"Here," she said, moving out of the way, "set them on the dining room table. You didn't have to do that."

"I did. I broke your coffee mug this morning on my way out the door."

Ella couldn't help but laugh, "how?"

"Being stupid. My hands were too full, and I dropped it. I couldn't return another broken dish to you."

"Where did you find an open Crate and Barrel?"

"I have a confession; these are not brand new. I would have bought new ones had I been able to find an open store."

"They're still in the shrink wrap; I'm confused."

"I mean they're new. My sisters sent me a ton of stuff to set up house. These are from my storage unit. I'm sorry this sounds terrible. I'm normally a really good gift-giver."

Ella laughed harder.

"What's so funny?" Trevor stood with a confused look on his face.

"This is funny. I appreciate the gesture. Have you eaten? I roasted a chicken with all of the trimmings."

"Is that's what that heavenly smell is?"

"Would you like to join me?"

"We shouldn't be this close."

"Well, you're already here now. I can set us at different ends of the table. Or you can take it home with you if you prefer to eat alone?"

"No, it's not that at all, I just don't want to put you at risk."

"Well, you just keep your distance, and I'll keep mine, and thank you for the new dishes. I really like them. Dinner literally just finished."

"Do you normally eat so late?"

"No, but I didn't want the chicken to be dried out, so I started it later."

"I hope you didn't do it on my account?"

Ella smiled as she pulled two plates out of the cupboard.

"Do you prefer white meat or dark meat?" She asked

"I don't have a preference."

Ella smiled and put a chicken breast and leg on his plate along with veggies and a heaping mountain of mashed potatoes. She put the plate on the far side, nearest to the door on the table, and set the cutlery alongside it, before turning around to grab hers.

"Wow, this looks incredible," he said as he stood behind his chair, waiting for her to join him.

"Would you like a glass of white wine to go with?"

"Sure, as long as you're having one."

"I am," she said.

They ate the roasted chicken practically to the bone and laughed, genuinely enjoying each other's company. Ella found herself really liking Trevor, in more than a friendly way. The more she got to know him, the more there was to love. They talked well into the night, and when it was time for Trevor to go, Ella walked over towards his plate to pick it up. She noticed the hesitation in his movement to move away.

"Ella, I've had the best time tonight."

"Me too."

"I wish I could touch you. Wait that came out wrong."

Ella smiled, "I knew what you meant."

"Thank you. Good night Ella," he said as he walked towards the door.

"Good night. Thank you for joining me for dinner."

That night as Ella washed up, she had wish life had been different at that moment; she would have loved to have Trevor touch her, even if it was just a hug. To be honest, she wanted more than a hug from him, and her mind carried on with that thought as she scrubbed the roasting pan for the chicken.

The next night she couldn't wait to see him. She made a pot of veggie chili and baked cornbread to go alongside. She had a small bowl around six and would have a larger bowl with him when he came in if he was up for company. Ella waited up and eventually fell asleep on the couch. Oscar pounced on her waking her, and Ella was shocked to see that it was morning. She had slept through Trevor coming home.

She jumped up from the couch and ran to the kitchen, remembering she had left the chili cooking on the stove on low. The kitchen smelled of burnt chili. She pulled the lid from the top of the pot and looked at the black sludge at the bottom. Angry that she had wasted so much food, she turned on the garbage disposal and tipped the pot down. Once it was empty, she filled it with hot soapy water and baking soda to soak. Leaving the pan, she crossed the hallway and knocked on Trevor's door. She felt terrible that she had slept through him coming home and hoped that he didn't get the wrong idea that she had not enjoyed their dinner together.

She knocked, but Trevor didn't answer. She was mad at herself all day that she had missed him. That night she cooked pasta and made a chocolate cake to say sorry. She knew she didn't owe him an apology, but she felt like she did. She waited up again, this time until 3:30 am. When he didn't show, she finally went to bed, defeated, taking a slice of the decadent chocolate cake with her. She ate it in bed, keeping an ear out for Trevor's footsteps down the hall, but she didn't hear him.

The next day, she had a nagging feeling that something was wrong, and no matter what she tried, she could not shake it. She reheated the pasta from the night before and waited up again. Trevor did not come home again. The next morning, she woke early and knocked on his door, but he did not answer. In her gut, she knew something wasn't right.

That night she made dinner for herself and ate a more normal hour for herself. She set some dinner aside for him and put the plate in the fridge, not wanting to repeat the chili incident. She fell asleep on the couch again and was awoken by the sound of his door closing across the hall. She jumped up off the sofa as Oscar let out a sharp meow, showing his displeasure. She stopped just outside his door, as she had doubts, what if he had been purposely giving her the slip? She wondered. As she stood in front of his door, she heard his footsteps approach, and she backed away as silently and quickly as she could. She just reached the inside of her doorway and had not yet pulled the door closed when she heard his door open. She cringed with her back to him. She had been caught. Slowly she turned around and saw Trevor standing there. His cheeks were tear-stained again, and his eyes were red and swollen. He wore more than a day's worth of stubble. The sight of him caused Ella to gasp.

"Trevor, are you okay? What happened?"

"My dad died," he said as he put his hands over his face.

The virus be damned, Ella crossed the hallway and wrapped Trevor in her arms. He hugged her back tightly until he pushed out of her embrace.

"We shouldn't be this close."

"Trevor, I don't care."

"I do. If something happened to you because I was careless, I'd never forgive myself."

"It's my choice," she said as she pulled him closer again.

She wrapped her arm around his neck, and he brought his lips to hers. She kissed him gently.

"We shouldn't do this," he whispered.

"I know but, you can't be alone tonight. I couldn't bear it."

He bent down and kissed her again as he pulled her tighter to his body. She could feel his build, with her body pressed so closely to his. She wanted to sleep with him more than she wanted her next breath, but she knew like this; it wasn't right. She pulled her lips away from him, the disconnection almost pain-inducing. He looked down at her.

"Come on," she said and grabbed his hand, leading him into her apartment.

Once inside, she shut the door behind him, and she pulled him towards the bedroom. She leaned up and kissed him gently, removing his shirt over his head, and he reached for hers.

"Not yet," she whispered.

She kissed him again softly as she unbuttoned his pants and pushed them down his legs. He reached for her top again gently, and she took his hands into hers to stop him.

"Pants first," she said softly.

He understood and kicked his pants off as he stood in her apartment in only his boxer and socks. She pulled away from him and pulled the covers back. He climbed into her bed, and she climbed in next to him, still fully clothed. He pulled her body closer to his as he kissed her neck. She reached down and cupped each side of his face.

"Trevor," she said softly.

He stopped and looked up at her.

"I want this, I really want this, but I also know you are hurting. I'm not a prude, but I don't just jump into the sack either. I want this

96

if you do. I just want to make sure.."

He kissed her again and pulled his head next to her chest. She wrapped her arms around his head and cradled him close as he cried. They fell asleep in each other's arms, both knowing that this was something more than a casual fling. Ella woke to soft kisses being planted on her neck and collarbone. Trevor had spooned up behind her and held her tightly. He smelled wonderful, and she ran her hand over the dark hair on his arm as she turned to look at him.

"Hello," she said softly.

"You are beautiful in the morning light."

She turned further and kissed him, as the rest of her body rolled towards him. He pulled her in closer.

"How are you this morning?"

"I'm happy to be here in your bed with you. Thank you for last night."

He said as he continued to kiss down her neck.

"Did you go to Colorado? You haven't been home. I was worried."

He pulled his lips from her neck.

"I did. I got the call after our dinner together. I couldn't be there with him. I couldn't stay out there either; I was needed back here."

"The hospital didn't give you the time off?"

"They couldn't. But it wasn't that. I wanted you there. It was the strangest thing. Part of me felt like I had left you behind here. I know that sounds crazy. I can't explain it."

Ella kissed Trevor, pouring all the feelings she had for him into it.

"Wow," he said, "I've wondered what kissing you would be like for so long."

"And? Was it everything you'd hoped it would be?"

"It was better."

"Then kiss me."

I lifted my head and kissed him, as he brought his hand to the side of my cheek, caressing it as we kissed. This was a kiss of affection, love, and it swallowed me whole in that moment and for the rest of my life.

Heather & Ellis: The Oil Rigger's Wife

T hree dots blinking, that means he's typing. Heather thought to herself.

Heather chewed her bottom lip as she held her phone, its glow the only source of light in the dark bedroom. Her husband, Chris, slept snoring softly next to her. Heather looked away from the blinking dots on her phone at Chris as he rolled over. She examined her conscious, quickly, searching for guilt, but it wasn't there. She turned back to her phone. The three dots turned into a message that read:

"I love you too. He'll be back on the rig tomorrow. Stay strong, beautiful."

Heather read it greedily twice before she deleted it. As much as she would have loved to keep the message on her phone, she didn't want Chris to see it. She plugged her phone back onto the charger and set it screen side down on the nightstand. She sunk further down onto the bed, thinking of his hands, not her husband's hands, but his best friend's hands on her body. It felt physically painful to be sleeping next to a man she no longer loved. Trying to push it away, she thought of laying in Ellis' arms, safe and loved, as she drifted off to sleep.

The next morning Chris' alarm went off at 4am. He had an early start to get back to the oil rig that he worked in the Gulf. Heather hated that he had chosen to work away from home. Chris was well educated and could have easily worked for the company in a myriad of other ways that kept him closer to home. She roused at the sound of the shower turning on. Although they had not slept together in almost eighteen months, she kept up the role of his wife. The lack of intimacy had been a point of contention in their marriage.

As Chris showered, Heather made coffee and brought two mugs for back for them into the bedroom. She handed Chris his, as his towel hung around his hips. Heather couldn't help but stare. Her husband was built like a cover of a romance novel. His tan skin, curly chestnut hair, and muscular body was once her source of pleasure, now the sight just left her with an empty feeling.

The lack of intimacy started slowly. It started when Chris came home a little over a year ago. He was normally on the rig for six weeks and then home for three. She had grown used to not leaving their bed for the first three days he was home, neither of them able to get enough of each other, but that stopped abruptly and without warning. One day he returned from a shift, and Heather sat waiting for him, her hair done, makeup on, and sitting in new lingerie. Her face lit up as he walked in, but she could see on his face something wasn't right. He had told her he was ill, showered, and climbed into their bed. He slept for almost two days. Heather tried to nurse him back to health, even though he didn't show any symptoms of any sort of illness. As soon as he looked like he was in better spirits, Heather tried to entice her husband. It had been a long time for both of them. Chris feigned illness again. Over the next three weeks, they slept together once before he went back to the rig. The whole ordeal left Heather confused. She chalked it up to stress and didn't bring it up with him before he left.

They talked a little less than they usually did while he was away. When he returned home again, Heather pulled out all of the stops to entice him. This time upon returning, he wasn't ill. He complained of exhaustion and put off her advances, saying he was too tired. The harder she pushed, the harder he rebuffed her advances. Finally, fed up, she confronted him, wanting to understand what was happening. Pressed for an answer, he told her had changed his mind about starting a family. He wasn't ready after all. They had been trying for almost six months, but with Chris' work schedule, they both knew it could take a little longer. The news surprised her. He had led the charge to start a family. The last night he was home, she suggested they use protection, he told her he was too tired and rolled over. She laid in bed that night upset, as her tears wet her pillow. This was not the man she had married, who was kind, loving, and affectionate.

Chris went back to the rig, and Heather knew she had to find out what was going on. She couldn't go out to the rig, that was unheard of. Concerned that perhaps there was another woman, she sought out Chris' best friend, Ellis. She wondered if Chris had confided in Ellis. He had agreed to meet her at a local tavern. That night as they ate and caught up, she asked him if he had noticed anything different about Chris. Ellis said that he had not, and Heather didn't want to go into details about what was going on in her marriage. She chickened out, asking about another woman, not sure if she was ready for an answer to that question. After dinner, Ellis walked her out to her car. The orange light glow from the tavern sign lit the parking lot, and in that light, she thought Ellis looked handsome. He had always been Chris's best friend, so she had never allowed herself to look at him as she did now. There was a moment before she got into her car, where she thought he was going to kiss her.

As she drove home from the meeting, she hated that the thought of Ellis kissing her in the parking lot aroused her so much. She had never been unfaithful to Chris. Ellis called to check on her twice while Chris was away, something he hadn't done since Chris had first started the job. At first, the calls set her on edge. That next break, when Chris came home, she didn't pressure him, but intimacy had not happened either. He returned back to the rig after only a week home. Something inside Heather crumbled after he left that time. He had not touched her, kissed her, or hugged her for almost six months.

Heather continued to try to connect any way she could. She emailed him, knowing that he'd read it since he said he was too tired to talk most nights. That January, while Chris was away, a record-setting blizzard hit. Heather had prepared for it and hunkered down alone. During the storm, a coating of ice had formed before the snow hit and took a large pine tree down across the driveway. She emailed Chris to tell him, and he had actually written back saying he'd ask Ellis to come over and help with it. Ellis had continued to call and check on Heather while Chris was away, and she found that she talked to him a little longer each time he called.

The afternoon he came to cut up the tree that had fallen, Heather slept with Ellis. She had not intended for it to happen. She had hated herself for it, but her body had devoured the intimacy. That night she laid in her bed, racked with guilt and still aroused from the sex. She hated herself for being unfaithful. She cried herself to sleep as she thought of Chris and the state of her marriage.

Over the next six months, Ellis provided more than physical intimacy. Chris had returned home on his normal schedule, but never made any advances towards Heather. She still tried each time and had even suggested that they see a marriage counselor. His reply to the discussion about the counselor was to return to the rig early. She took this as Chris's intent for their marriage. He didn't care. From then on, she allowed herself to fully feel any emotion she wanted about Chris and Ellis.

The last time Chris was away, Ellis stayed most nights. She found it odd that she now dreaded Chris' return, not for seeing him, but for Ellis having to stay away. The whole time Chris was home, Heather wanted to tell him she wanted a divorce, but she couldn't bring herself to do it. There was something holding her back, even though Nothing had changed between them. Heather told herself she'd give Chris an ultimatum that they be intimate, or she'd leave. The night before he returned to the rig, she made her stand. With tears streaming down her cheeks, she pleaded with Chris to explain what was happening. Why wouldn't he sleep with her? Why wasn't he returning her calls and emails when he was on the rig. Chris grabbed his bag and left without answering. When he left, Heather called Ellis hysterical.

"Honey, I love you. I want to be with you. He doesn't deserve you. Let him go," Ellis said, trying to calm her.

That phone call changed her life. She realized he was right, Ellis loved her, and she loved him. Clearly, Chris did not want to be in a relationship any longer. They decided that she would leave Chris the next time he came home. She insisted on telling him in person that she was leaving him. She felt guilty enough for going out on her husband with his best friend, the least she could do was tell Chris the truth to his face, not email him like a coward.

She now watched Chris get ready to leave again and knew it was time to tell the truth. She had to; she had promised Ellis that she would. Besides, the secret she hid growing under her nightgown would be noticeable soon enough. She and Ellis had been careful, but apparently not careful enough. He was thrilled at the news she was pregnant, and she was happy too. This is the last hurdle she told herself, cut Chris loose. At breakfast, she told herself, at breakfast, I'll tell him.

Her hands shook as she dipped the bread in the eggy mixture for french toast. Chris brought his empty mug back in and refilled it before taking it into the living room. She could just hear the news on if she tried to listen. She flipped each piece of french toast, making sure they were golden brown. The phone rang, and the noise of it made her jump. She heard Chris answer and wondered who would be calling so early. A streak of fear ran through her wondering if Ellis was coming clean, thinking she had chickened out. Nervously, she turned down the flame on the cooking breakfast and went to grab her own phone. She took a deep breath, relieved that there weren't any texts from him.

As she walked back into the kitchen, Chris stood in the doorway.

"Who was on the phone," she asked?

"The Foreman. We're all staying landside. There's a quarantine, that stupid virus."

"A quarantine for where?"

"The whole damn country, for the next 6 to 8 weeks."

Heather felt her stomach flip as she grabbed onto the counter. Chris turned and walked back into the living room to continue watching the news. Heather picked up her phone and texted Ellis.

"I'm telling him now, and then I'm on my way to your house. He's staying landside with the quarantine. I can't stay here with him. I love you. See you soon."

Heather took the french toast out of the pan and plated it, squeezing maple syrup over it. She brought it into the living room with a glass of juice and handed Chris, who barely said thank you audibly enough to be heard. She turned and walked back to the bedroom and got dressed. She placed her bag next to the door on her way back to the living room. Chris looked up from his breakfast as she walked back into the room.

"Are you going somewhere?"

"Yes."

"You can't go out, there's a quarantine. We have to stay in."

"I am going to be staying in, just not here and not with you. I'm leaving you, Chris. I don't love you anymore."

He stared at her blankly and said Nothing. She wanted to shout at him, to provoke a reaction from him. Anything that would show that he registered what she was saying. Instead, he sat further back in his chair and put another piece of the cut-up french toast in his mouth.

"You have Nothing to say? After eight years of marriage? Chris, did you hear me? I am leaving you."

"That's your choice."

Pure rage coursed through her veins.

"I'm pregnant, the baby is Ellis'. We are getting married."

This jarred his attention, as the next bite of French toast fell off the fork. Before he could say anything, she turned and walked out of the house. She trembled the whole ride to Ellis' house. She pulled into the driveway, and before she could get out of her car, he had already come out of his house. She walked from the car, leaving the door open and into his arms.

"I am so glad you made it. They are shutting everything down. I was afraid you wouldn't make it here in time before lockdown."

"I told him. It just didn't seem to register. I am so glad that is done now."

"I am proud of you. I know how difficult that was. Did you mention me? The baby?"

"I did. When I told him I was pregnant, and the baby was yours was the only time it seemed to register with him."

"What did he say?"

"Nothing, he didn't say a word. It got his attention, though."

Ellis hugged her tightly, and she clung to him, grateful that life now showed promise. That night as she fell asleep in Ellis' arms with their child growing inside of her, she thought about how strange life was. She had never thought she would have fallen in love with her husband's best friend, let alone want to spend the rest of her life with him.

Three days after she had left, she was served with divorce papers. Both she and Ellis joked that divorce lawyers were still working. She did not contest the divorce and was eager to do what she needed to be free of Chris. Together she and Ellis settled into a quarantine routine, grateful that they could both work from home. It surprised them that

Chris had not shown up for any sort of confrontation.

As the quarantine lagged on, and their baby grew, the divorce came through. The next night over dinner, Ellis got down on one knee.

"Heather, I love you, and you have brought so much more to my life than I could have ever envisioned. I give you my solemn vow that I will always treat you with the love and respect you deserve. Will you please do me the honor of being my wife?"

With tears of happiness in her eyes, she threw her arms around Ellis and kissed him, slamming her lips so hard into his, she worried she might split one of their lips. He kissed her and pulled away.

"So that's a yes then?"

"Yes. I love you, Ellis McCarthy."

"I love you, future Mrs. Heather McCarthy."

Ellie & Henry: The Boy Next Door

I'm here by choice, I kept telling myself. You have a home to return to when this is all over. You decided to come here and look after your parents through this. You're here by choice.

My mom and dad were older when they had me, Ellie, short for Elliot, their only child. They were amazing parents, and I never gave it a second thought when the pandemic broke out, and quarantine was rumored to start, that I would go home to be with them. Janice and Dan Miller, my parents, were in their early seventies now. I called after watching a press conference about the city going on lockdown within twenty-four hours. I told them I'd be at their house before lunch tomorrow. My mother was thrilled, and I began packing as soon as I hung up the phone.

I lived in a condo in Chicago's Fulton Market district, that had a beautiful view of the river. I knew returning to suburban life would be an adjustment. I was young, single, and active; life in rural Indiana was the opposite of all of those things. I made trip after trip, packing what I thought I'd need, for how long, I didn't know, into my Volvo hatchback. The car was filled to the seams with my belongings. The next morning, I grabbed my tabby cat, Homer, turned down my thermostat, and closed the door to my condo. It felt like I was closing the door on a part of my life as well.

Homer sat curled up in his carrier on the front seat as I headed east towards the home that I grew up in. I pulled off the toll road, just over the border, and grabbed a cup of coffee through the drive-thru. I had not made coffee at my place, afraid that I'd leave the pot on or forget to clean it out before I left. I pulled into a parking space and sipped my coffee. I had also gotten a bottle of water and poured a little water for Homer into a small plastic dish. He wasn't interested. I petted him while I sipped my coffee, savoring my last few moments by myself. I pulled back onto the toll road after I had drunk half of my coffee. Homer was not thrilled to be put back in the carrier, and he made his displeasure known as he hissed at me.

Three hours later, I pulled into the small town of Murdoch, Indiana, the town that I had grown up in. The population was only about three thousand. There was Main Street and a few blocks of town, but beyond that, it was cornfields. At this time of year, everything was still dormant. Early March was always the bleakest time of year. The entire town was set in a twelve-block square. Most of the houses on Lincoln Street, where my parent's house was located, were Victorian. My mom and dad owned the house on the corner of Lincoln and 2nd Street. The large white Victorian house stood proudly as it always had. My dad had always kept the best lawn on the block, and my mother constantly gardened in the warmer months. I always thought my house was the prettiest house in town. As I pulled up, I thought the house and yard looked a little tired, even for March. I tried to push away the realization that perhaps it was all too much for my parents to care for in their later years.

I pulled my car onto the brick-paved driveway and looked over at Homer, who slept in his carrier. I knew this was the end of a time of my life and the beginning of a new part that layout ahead of me unknown. I got out of the car, and the cold wind blew past me. I had left my coat in the back seat as I scurried around to grab Homer. My dad spotted me and came out onto the porch.

"Where's your coat, pumpkin?" he asked, as I approached the front porch with its wide-planked steps.

"Hi Daddy, it's in the back seat. I didn't want to drive in it."

I wrapped my free arm around my dad and held Homer's cage in the other. He embraced me tightly.

"Your mother had been waiting for you all morning; she's already cooking."

We both laughed, and I stepped into the house ahead of my dad. That familiar smell of the home I had grown up in was still there. It smelled of old house, years of freshly baked bread and cookies, and roses. Mom always had a vase of fresh roses on the dining room table, no matter the time of year. I set Homer down in the living room and went in search of my mother, who was standing in front of the old stove. When they bought the house, there was a stove from the 1950s in the kitchen, and my dad hated it, but my mother loved it. The stove was the most modern piece in the kitchen, and she loved her farm kitchen as she called it. She turned around as she heard the swinging door move between the dining room and the kitchen.

"Hi, Mom," I said as I walked in.

The room smelled liked homemade chicken soup, one of my favorites, and baking double chocolate cookies. I looked over at her brown, stripped bowl that was about as old as her. The dishtowel laid over the top let me know she had bread rising in it. My mouth watered at the eventual meal of homemade soup and bread, with cookies for dessert.

"Hi Sweetie, how was the drive?" My mother asked, as she set down her wooden spoon on the stovetop and came over to hug me.

I wrapped my arms around her and embraced her, she was smaller, almost frail in my arms, and it concerned me. My mother had never been a big woman, but she was even smaller than I remembered.

"It was good, easy. It smells so good in here."

"Good, I am making all of your favorites. The soup should be done shortly. Once you are settled in, would you mind taking a quart next door? I made extra for the Mattesons."

"Are they ill?"

"Not with the virus, Selah is still battling breast cancer. I thought a nice hot meal would be nice."

"Sure, is she doing any better?"

"She had a mastectomy and seems to be doing a little better."

"Poor thing. Sure, I'll take it over. Let me get Homer upstairs, and the car unpacked, and I'll take it over if that's okay?"

"Sure, sweetie. Have Daddy help you. Now your kitty, he can have roam of the house. I've put litter boxes in the upstairs and downstairs bathrooms and one in the basement next to the washer. He doesn't go outside, right?"

"Mom, you didn't have to do that, I brought everything he needs."

"Well, he's family too, what's his name?"

"Homer. He can't go outside, he's an indoor cat."

"Okay, sweetie, why don't you go get him, I cooked him a piece of fish last night, and it is in the icebox."

Seeing the look on my face that she didn't have to go through the trouble, she shrugged and gave me the look not to argue. I went and grabbed Homer from his cage and spotted daddy, who had half of my car unpacked and scattered around the living room. I deposited Homer in my mother's arms and went back to help my dad unpack.

Within an hour, I was unpacked and had moved back into my childhood bedroom. My trophies from t-ball still stood on the shelf, along with all the memorabilia of my childhood. Terry, my favorite teddy bear, still sat on the shelf. I didn't go anywhere without him during my first four years of my life. Homer had found a small spot under my bed and refused to come out as I hear my mother call my name from the kitchen. I tried to coax Homer one last time and knew it would just take some time for him to get comfortable with his new surroundings.

I walked downstairs and into the kitchen. My mother had wrapped up a large container of soup for the Mattison's. I grabbed it off the counter. The warmth of it still could be felt through the ancient Tupperware.

"Here, take my sweater, it's snowing again," my mother said, as shrugged, offer her sweater before I could protest.

I put it on knowing that resistance was a waste of time.

"Thanks, sweetie," my mom said as I walked out of the kitchen.

I stepped out onto our porch and looked out as the snow fell slowly, in big white flakes. The wind gusted, and the snow fell heavier for a brief moment as I walked down the driveway to the sidewalk between our houses. I noticed an old black Jeep in their driveway with the hatch open, and I thought I spotted Mr. Matteson pulling something out of the back as I approached. The man grabbed a box, and a crate of records spilled out and onto their driveway. He turned to catch them and failed. It was not Mr. Matteson Sr., Henry Matteson stood in the driveway; his black wool coat collar pulled up around his ears. I froze with the warm soup in my hands. I had not seen Henry since the day that I left for college, broken-hearted.

Henry was my first, my first everything, and I was his. I had not stood face to face with him in almost fifteen years, and here he was. I realized as I clutched the soup harder that I was holding my breath. As he turned to pick up his records, he spotted me. I walked over and helped him pick them up. He righted the bin and set his records in it. I handed him the few that I held.

"Hi," he said, "I was wondering if you were coming home to ride this out?"

"My mom sent some soup over for your mom. Is she in?"

"Yes, she's here. Are you staying with your parents?"

"I'd better get this to her; it's cold out here."

I walked away from the open hatch of the jeep and up the steps to the porch of their house. Mary, Henry's mother, stepped out.

"Oh, Ellie, it's so good to see you! I would have come over and got that. Come in, it's so cold out here."

I didn't want to go in, I didn't want to be anywhere near Henry, I felt like I was entering enemy territory. I walked in anyway, not wanting to be rude to Mary. George, Henry's father, stood as I walked in. He had always been kind to me and was like a second father in a lot of ways. I followed Mary through the house to the kitchen, where I set the soup down on the counter. The kitchen had not changed from when I had last been in there, so many years ago.

"Would you like a cup of coffee, dear," Mary asked?

"Um."

Before I could answer, Henry walked into the kitchen.

"That's probably not a good idea, mom, we should really be keeping our distance from others right now."

"I'm sorry, Mrs. Matteson, Henry is right. I should go. But I promise, when this is all over, I'd love to come to have a cup with you."

Slightly defeated, she nodded, and I gave a wave as I walked out of the kitchen. There was barely enough room to pass through the doorway with Henry standing there, but I did anyway. I looked him in the eye as I did. I waved at George as I pulled the front door closed behind me and stepped off the porch. The snow was still falling, and I pulled the cold air into my lungs. I had not been prepared to run into Henry. So much life had passed since we had seen each other last. I walked down the sidewalk back towards my house as I thought back to the day that I had left, the last day we had been together.

"El, wait," Henry called out as he jogged down his driveway and caught up with me.

I reluctantly stopped and turned around.

"El, sorry, I wasn't trying to be rude. My mom has a compromised immune system right now. I didn't mean anything by it."

"I get it," I said as I turned and walked back towards my house.

"El, wait, I haven't seen you in more than a decade."

"I know."

"Are you mad at me, still?"

"I don't have a coat on, and it's freezing out here, literally. Bye, Henry."

I turned and walked back into my house and straight into the kitchen.

"Mom, why didn't you tell me Henry was home too?"

My mother did not turn around as she stirred the soup.

"It must have slipped my mind, sorry, sweetie."

"Mary didn't mention it to you?"

"Well, she may have, but you know, I forget things sometimes."

I knew she had not forgotten. To her, Henry would always be the one who got away. We had grown up together. He was six months older than me, and we had been best friends until high school until we became more than friends.

That night I tried not to think about the past and Henry as I ate dinner with my family. The soup and bread were delicious. After dinner, I lied about having to catch up on work and secluded myself in my room. I shut the door and collapsed on my bed, feeling like I was sixteen again. I starred up at my celling, finding my favorite crack in it. I hoped my presence would coax Homer out from underneath the bed. When he didn't come, as I called for him, I got down on all fours and looked under my bed for him. He wasn't there. I began to search the room for him, calling out his name. When I had searched my room and had not found him, I searched the entire upstairs, calling out for him. I walked down into the living room where my dad was reading a book.

"Dad, have you seen my cat? I can't find him anywhere."

"Oh, yes, I let him out after dinner."

"Let him out where? He's not supposed to go outside."

"Sorry. I'm sure he'll be fine."

I went to the coat rack, pulled my coat down, and walked out of the front door. It was now dark, and the streetlamps did very little to light the yard. I called out for him as I began searching in the bushes around the house. I prayed I'd find him, and that he wouldn't be hurt. He had never been outside before. I came around the back of the house and heard something rustling on the other side of the fence between our house and the Matteson's. I stepped up on a rock and peeked over and was startled when I saw Henry's face doing the same. I let out a small scream. Henry walked around the fence and into my backyard. He had a flashlight in his hand.

"I figured you were looking for a pet and might be in need of a flashlight."

"My dad let my cat, Homer, out. He's a tabby cat. He's never been outside before."

"Never?"

"I live in a condo in the city."

"Ah. Homer," he called out.

"I don't need your help."

"No, you don't want my help. You could use another set of eyes if you want to find him out here."

I walked off in the opposite direction, annoyed. I knew he was right. I continued to search in the bushes along the fence as Henry went off in the opposite direction. As I searched, I heard a faint meow, and I called out his name as I pushed into the bushes at the back of the yard. I shined the flashlight on my phone around, and I knew he was close as I hear him meow. Hearing the anxiety in my voice, Henry came back. I continued to search everywhere and flashed his light up in the tree.

"Found him, is that him?" Henry asked, as he pointed to poor Homer, wet and stuck up in the tree.

"Oh no, how did he get all of the way up there? Come here, buddy."

"We're going to have to go up and get him."

I looked at Henry. There was no way to climb up the tree.

"I'll call the fire department."

"No, wait, here, hold my flashlight," he said, shoving it into my hands before I could protest.

He wedged himself between the fence and the tree and began to shimmy up the tree. I watched nervously as he climbed higher and higher. As he approached Homer, my cat hissed, as if he sensed how much hurt Henry had been responsible for. Henry reached out for him, and Homer hissed again. Clutching Homer tightly, Henry began to climb down carefully. Watching them made me extremely nervous. Halfway down, and still, about thirty feet up, Homer had enough and began to struggle in Henry's arms. Henry slipped, and Homer fell. I managed to catch my cat mid-air, not believing my luck, as Henry came down too, landing in the bushes. I ran to the back door with Homer in my arms, chucked him inside, and pulled the door shut behind him as I turned and raced back to Henry. He was crawling out of the bushes, and I was relieved to see that he was at least moving.

"Are you okay?"

Henry looked up at me, wincing at the light of his flashlight.

"It wasn't the first time I've fallen out of this tree, remember?"

I thought back to the night I had caught him peeking in my bedroom window. I startled him, and he fell that night too. I couldn't help but laugh, and he looked up at me, amused. I reached down to help him up, still laughing. He got to his feet, and I pulled him into my body to steady him. He smelled the same. His touch was the same, filled with familiarity and so much hurt. I pulled away.

"Sorry," I said. "Are you hurt?"

"Only my pride."

"Thank you for your help."

"I'm glad you caught him."

"Me too."

"El, I need to tell you something. I need you to know that I never slept with Karen Lake. I never had the chance to explain. I came after you to try to fix things, and I chickened out."

"What difference does it make? That was so long ago. I don't think about it anymore," I lied.

"It makes a difference to me. El, I think about you constantly, about what could have been, had I not fucked it all up, and had more courage to set things right."

"Just forget it, that was a whole other lifetime ago."

I started to turn to walk into the house.

"Are you honestly telling me that you don't think about it, about us what we had?"

"We were kids."

He took a step closer to me, and I could smell him again, mixed with aftershave. I found the scent intoxicating.

"We aren't kids anymore. I compare every woman I've ever dated to you. Every kiss, every dance. You are it for me, El, you always will be."

Something in my hardened interior cracked, and I stood up on my toes, hooked my arm around his neck, and kissed him. He instantly pulled my body into his, and as our lips met, I no longer felt cold. His kiss felt like home, safe, and warm. I kissed him with reckless abandon and didn't want to stop like my will had been a broken dam, and all of the pent-up emotion I had for him flowed through my lips. I pulled away first as I remembered the pain of how things had ended.

As if he read my mind, he spoke up, "El, I promise you as long as I live, I will never hurt you again. I love you. I've never stopped loving you."

I leaned my head against his chest as he pulled his wool coat around both of us. We stood for a long time silent in my back yard. So much history had passed between us, and I knew right then that I had been right when I left my condo, that life would never be the same. By April, I had an engagement ring on my finger. We planned our wedding to take place in my back yard.

As my dad gave me away, I kissed him on the cheek and turned to look at Henry, who stood proudly in his dark grey suit. Our few guests watched on as we took our vows, the boy and girl from next door, now the happy couple.

Isabel & John: Room 568

"Y ou'll be fine, they assured me, just get in, close the deal, and you'll be home in no time," Andrea had said.

I was dumb enough to believe her. Ignoring the media and the risks, I got on the plane and flew to Detroit to close this deal. There was a lot of money on the table. If one of the big automakers picked up our computer programs for their automation line, it would be a big win for our company. Also, when the Vice President of the company singles you out to go, you go. At the time, my apprehension about going just seemed like paranoia. The plan was to get in and out with a signed deal. God, I was so stupid.

I have been stuck in this hotel room, quarantined for the past three weeks. When I got here, I felt a little under the weather, but I pushed on, thinking it was a cold. When I got to my meeting, most of the board members who I would meet with had declined to come due to the pandemic. A wasted trip, I thought to myself. I went back to my hotel and decided to sleep off whatever I was coming down with. It never dawned on me I had caught the virus. I woke the next morning feeling even worse. I always carried a small kit with me, a fever reducer, thermometer, antacid, etc., like a traveling medicine cabinet.

I took my temperature, which was high, 103. I took a fever reducer and went back to bed. I was so sick I didn't care to eat.

I was awoken late in the afternoon by a loud knock at my door. I got up, still feeling unwell, and answered the door.

"Miss Lannert, are you all right, you missed check out? We've been trying to reach you by phone."

I tried to piece time together. I didn't check out until the next day. I was confused.

"What day is today?"

"It's Thursday, March 15th. Are you okay, Miss Lannert?"

I had slept for almost thirty-six hours straight. I was so confused.

"I'm sorry, I'm unwell. Can I book the room for another night?"

"Of course. We have a hotel doctor; I can have him come and help you if you'd like?"

The panic on the hotel manager's face said it all, I was in trouble, health-wise. Usually, I would decline, but I simply shook my head, affirming to send the doctor, and closed the door, crawling back into the bed. I couldn't remember the last time I had been so ill.

The next time I woke, there was a man standing above me, with salt and pepper hair and a face mask on. Normally, I'd startle, but I was too sick to care. He introduced himself as a doctor for the hotel and performed a cursory exam, stating that he thought I had come down with the virus that more than half of the country had.

"I'd send you to the hospital, but they're beyond capacity. I can start an IV here, and see if a bed opens up for you at the hospital. In the meantime, we'll monitor you closely from here. I need to know if you are experiencing any shortness of breath, blurred vision, or numbness in your extremities. The gentleman next to you is ill as well. We will see which one of you goes to the hospital first. Have you been in contact with anyone who you think might have the virus?"

I shook my head that I had not. He asked more questions, which only confirmed his suspicions that I had the virus. With a lack of tests, and them being slow to provide results, neither of us pressed the issue. I scribbled my name across a consent form, and he started an iv.

Before he left, he told me a nurse would be by to help look after me and the gentleman in the room next to me, but if I had any trouble breathing, call 911. I could barely keep my eyes open and was asleep again before the doctor left my room. I woke in the late afternoon, feeling better than I had in days. My I.V. bag was almost gone, and all I could think was that the fluids had to have helped. I sat upright like I was waking from a trance. I reached over from my phone, seeing all the missed calls from my roommate, Becky, work, and my parents. I didn't want to worry anyone. I needed to think about what to say without terrifying them. I texted my roommate, then called into work, which exhausted me. I would wait to call my parents when I sounded stronger.

The next two days were a blur, as I slowly improved. I don't think the fear of my condition helped any. On the fifth day of my illness, my fever broke, much to my relief. I began eating again and slowly started to feel better. The hotel had been excellent, making sure I was cared for, and I was genuinely grateful, albeit terrified of my situation. After a week down, I finally felt well enough to get up and move around my room a little. I finally called my family and told them what was happening, as I hoped the worst had passed. I was still weak, but grateful to be on the mend.

That night as I laid in bed, the hotel seemed quieter than usual. At dinner, the nurse had come and removed my IV. I was grateful to have it out. Needles had always creeped me out. Despite being exhausted, I found sleep eluded me. I tossed and turned, longing for my own bed at home, but even if I was well enough to travel, I wouldn't have wanted to go home and infect my roommate, who was still healthy, thankfully. I heard a soft noise I couldn't quite make out, I listened again, and it seemed familiar, but I still could not name it. The noise was coming from the room next to me. I got up and listened. It was the noise was of a man crying. There was something about the noise of it that hollowed out my soul. I knew he was ill too, but I didn't know much beyond that. I wanted to help, but I wasn't sure what to do. I knocked gently on the wall. He quieted, and I hoped my intentions had not been misconstrued. I wasn't asking him to be quiet. It was my way of letting him know someone else was here. I pressed my ear against the wall and heard him still crying quietly.

The hotel was old but renovated, and it still had a door that connected our rooms. I knocked again on it, not sure if I was nuts or not.

"Are you okay?" I called out softly.

"Sorry, I didn't mean to wake you." He called out in return.

"It's okay, do you need anything?"

The question seemed absurd, I was barely out of bed myself, what could I possibly offer a complete stranger? I pushed my ear against the door, listening, but heard nothing. I waited, hearing only the sound of my battled breathing. Eventually, I climbed back into bed, but the situation left me uneasy. I rolled over and dialed 568, the room next door, never expecting it to work. The phone rang, and a man's voice croaked,

"Hello?" he asked weakly, then coughed.

I regretted my boldness. This was a mistake. The guy next door was a stranger, but I was in it now.

"Hello, hi, I'm in the room next door."

"Oh, sorry, I didn't mean to wake you."

"No, I wasn't calling for that. I couldn't sleep. I just wanted to see if you were okay?"

"It's weird, this illness, isn't it? At first, you can't sleep enough, so tired, and then you can't sleep to save your life."

I let out a small laugh. He was right.

"Yeah, I think I've reached that phase. I am on day 10. How about you?"

There was a pause, and I instantly feared I had crossed some unspoken line in our conversation.

"I am on day 11 or 12, I think; I couldn't tell you really. The days, in the beginning, are sort of a blur."

"Yeah, I have never been that sick in my whole life."

"Hey, I don't want this to come out wrong, but thank you for calling. This is so lonely being stuck in this hotel room alone, away from home, ill. It's," he paused, "It's scary, you know?"

"I do. I'm here on business."

"Me too, where from? You don't have to answer that if you don't want to."

"I'm in from California, I work for a tech company. You?"

"I'm in from New York. I think I came down with this on the plane. Had I known I was ill before I left, I would've never left."

"Same here. What do you do for a living?"

"I'm a lawyer, corporate law. Thank you for calling, it was very kind of you."

"We're all doing our best to survive this, you know?"

"I do. Tell me something good, something happy."

His breath was more labored from the conversation, and I knew he was getting tired because I was too. I didn't know what to tell a complete stranger, so I chose the only thing we both shared in common.

"My I.V. came out today."

"That is good news. I hope mine comes out tomorrow.

"You're welcome, 568."

"568?"

"It's your room number, 568. I didn't get your name."

"Ah, clever. It's John."

"It was nice to meet you, John, I am Isabell. Sleep well."

"You too, Isabell. Call if you need anything in return.

Over the next week, John and I spoke nightly. He was the only person I knew that shared this experience with me, thankfully. His voice on the phone became something I looked forward to, beyond the endless hours of television. I was well enough to work for short periods of time, but I found that I tired easily. John confirmed he was experiencing the same symptoms. We were both quarantined along with most of the 5th floor for the next month. I was desperate to return home, but I also understood that I could still be infectious and knew it was best to stay put.

We had spoken a lot about random things, and I noticed our conversation tended to stray away from the personal. I didn't mind. John was a stranger, after all. Curiosity finally got the better of me, as I looked John Hampton up on social media. His salt and pepper hair, strong jaw, and deep brown eyes were just my type. I saw that he had gone to Yale. His photos sported a string of pretty women at his side. I noticed no one was pictured more than once. I couldn't help but feel my neighbor was a bit of a player, yet over the past few weeks, I had gotten the impression that he was a decent guy. I laid on my bed and jumped when the phone on the nightstand rang. I felt like I had been caught red-handed, even though there was no way for him to know I was creeping on his Facebook page.

"Hello?"

"Hi, Isabella. I was wondering, does anyone ever call you Izzy?"

"My mom does sometimes. How are you tonight? Any new weird symptoms since you seem to be two days ahead of me?"

"Thankfully, no. Can I call you Izzy?"

"I guess. How are you feeling?"

"A little better every day. You know it surprises me, even after all of these weeks, I still tire easily. How are you feeling today," he said as cleared his throat.

"The same as you. I'm homesick today."

"Tell me, what do you miss most about home, other than the fact that it is home?"

I paused in my response as I thought.

"Well, my own bed for one, but I think I miss the ocean most of all. I really miss it."

"Do you have a favorite spot to view the ocean or a favorite beach?"

"I have lots of favorite places, but more in general, I just really miss it."

"You'll get back soon enough, I promise. So, tell me something good that happened to you today."

He asked me that every day, and I found myself thinking all day what my good thing to tell him would be.

"Well, there are new free movies on the movie system. I've never watched so much tv in my life, but I must admit my guilty pleasure, there is a new Jules Derry documentary I really want to watch about washerwomen in India."

"That is good news. I met her once on a flight from Brazil."

"Really, that's so cool. What was she like?"

"Artsy. She was nice enough. I've only seen one of her films about the women from the Inuit tribe. I remember it. It left a lasting impression on me. So, if you were at home in California, would you have gone to the theater to see it? Are you a movie snacks kind of person?"

I giggled, "Yes, and no. I usually buy my own popcorn, then sneak in Chardonnay. I know that's weird, but I really like popcorn and Chardonnay together. I always feel like such a rebel. How about you?"

I heard John laugh, and for the first time, I noticed I liked making him laugh.

"I'm the guy with the giant snack tray. I can't help it. I came from a poor family, and as a kid, I didn't get to go to the movies a whole lot. If we did, we didn't get snacks. Now, as an adult, I buy the whole counter when I go."

This time he made me laugh.

"That's funny, I can imagine you, arms full of junk food with a big grin on your face."

"Have you been online stalking me?"

I had outed myself unintentionally, I laughed nervously. "I may have looked you up."

"Well, since we are being honest, I looked you up too, it's nice to put a face with a name."

"It is."

"What did you order for dinner tonight?"

"I haven't decided. You?"

"I thought it seems like a good night for a burger and a beer."

"That does sound good. And a good documentary."

"I have a crazy idea. Feel free to decline, but would you like to eat dinner with me tonight, and then maybe we could watch that documentary if you were up for company?"

I felt my stomach flip nervously.

"Are we allowed to do that?"

"I don't see why not, we've both had the virus. We can't re-infect each other, and we aren't leaving our rooms. If you don't want to, that's okay."

"No, I'd love to. My room or yours?"

I realize how forward that sounded and cringed inside.

"Your choice."

"How about mine in a half-hour?"

"Okay. See you in a half-hour."

I hung up the phone as a wave of panic washed over me. I had not washed my hair today or put makeup on in almost a month. I tided the room and made the bed. It felt strange to be inviting a man to my room. After the room was more presentable, I put some blush on and noticed my hand shook. I realized I was nervous. I knew it was crazy to be so excited to have dinner with a man who was practically a stranger. I hadn't seen another person unless it was medical staff, and they were in full PPE when they visited. Housekeeping left clean bedding and towels outside our door, as we swapped clean for dirty that was bagged up every other day. Even room service left the food outside our doors. We were not allowed to open our doors until the room service staff had cleared the hallway. I tried to make my hair more presentable. It was naturally curly, and I normally straightened it. I pinned it back as best I could and put on lip gloss. I examined myself in the mirror. It looked like I had put in effort, maybe too much. I wiped my gloss off.

I heard a knock at the door that separated our rooms. I felt a nervous flip in my stomach. He was on the other side of the door. I put my hand on the doorknob as I unlocked the deadbolt with my other hand. I pulled the door open, and there he stood, before me, the calming voice on the other side of the phone. He had on a soft blue, button-down shirt and jeans. He had rolled his sleeve cuffs on his shirt and wore a thin beard. I couldn't believe that he was finally standing in front of me.

"Hi," I said.

"You're real," he said, vocalizing my inner thoughts. "I hope this isn't too forward, but you are more beautiful in person."

I smiled as I looked down bashfully. I had always been terrible at taking a compliment.

"Your hair is curly. On social media, your hair is straight."

"I normally straighten it. I am naturally curly. I haven't really done anything with it because.." I gestured around the room.

"It's pretty."

I found his complement sweet. I could not stop staring at him. His eyes were the color of a dark cup of coffee. I felt like I was reconnecting with an old friend, even though we had not met in person until now.

"Thank you, do you want to come in?"

I moved out of the way and gestured to the tiny couch. Having him sit on the bed just felt odd.

"Your room is the same as mine." He laughed. "I haven't ordered dinner yet. Have you?"

"No, not yet, I wasn't sure if you wanted to wait.," I said as he sat on the navy-blue couch.

"I'm starving, so I am ready whenever you are."

"Me too."

I walked over a picked up the phone, and put in our orders. I sat in the armchair in the small sitting area of my room and caught John staring at me.

"What?"

"Sorry, it's just nice to be next to another person. I didn't mean to stare."

"It's all right, I get it. It has been an odd experience, hasn't it?"

"I don't think odd is a big enough word for it. Have you seen the news today? Over fifty-thousand have been infected so far here in the U.S. Poor Italy, they are still in the trenches too."

"I had to stop watching. I just couldn't handle it. That is so many. It feels like the whole world is falling apart every time I watch it."

"I lost my job today."

I turned and looked at him, the shock of his news spread across my face.

John shrugged his shoulders, "I'll be all right. I always seem to land on my feet."

"You know things are bad when America is laying off attorneys."

I wasn't sure if he would understand that it was meant as a joke, albeit a poorly timed one. I was relieved when John let out a laugh from deep inside.

"I shouldn't have said that I'm sorry you lost your job."

"No, it's true. I'm going to have to leave soon. I can stay for a few more days, but work will not be paying for the room anymore."

"Oh, John, are you well enough to travel home?"

"I'm going to rent a car and drive. I want to reduce exposure to as few people as possible."

"That's a long drive, are you up for it?"

"It is, but I can do it in one day, a long day, but one day."

"That's actually a good idea for getting home. I was nervous about flying, even though we aren't supposed to be infectious anymore, I don't want anyone to go through what we just went through. It would be a much longer drive for me, though, and I'd have to stay at hotels along the way."

"After I leave, can I still keep in contact with you? Maybe not nightly, but you know. Just keep in touch?"

"I'd like that."

There was a knock at my door, and I knew it was our dinner. I jumped up and waited on our side of the door for the room service attendant to clear the hall before I stepped out and grabbed the trays that were stacked on top of each other. They were heavier than I had expected, and I strained at the weight of them. John came from behind me and gestured to grab them. I pressed my body up against the door, so he could pass. I could smell him for the first time, and there was something about the way he moved that I found incredibly attractive. There was a moment, just a split second, where he noticed me in the same way. The hair on my arms stood as I felt prickles on the back of my neck. John carried the trays back to the sitting area and set them on the small coffee table. I sat back down on the chair, and he sat back down on the couch. We ate our dinners, and he was right; a burger and a beer hit the spot. As we ate, I realized that something special shared between us was coming to an end, and that realization was met with sadness.

After dinner, we sat on the bed to watch the documentary. Part of me wondered if he was doing it for me, or he had a genuine interest in Jules Derry's work. I tried to concentrate on the film, but I couldn't help but wonder if he would make a move. I played and replayed my reactions to his advances time and again in my head, so much so that I found it difficult to concentrate on the documentary. I had surprised myself that I would actually welcome his advances. It was so odd; John felt like a stranger. The back of his hand brushed up against mine. I wasn't sure if it was intentional or not, but I hooked a finger of his, and he took the cue, gently grabbing my hand to hold it. I waited with bated breath for his next move, but it didn't come. The sexual tension was heavy, and he still hadn't made a move.

As the credits rolled, he turned to look at me, and my stomach did that nervous flip again.

"I know this sounds crazy, and I hope you don't take this the wrong way, but I'm really going to miss you."

"Not at all," I said softly, "I'm going to miss you too."

He leaned in to kiss me, and I knew it would stoke the 4-alarm fire going on inside me. He kissed my cheek softly and pulled away just enough to look me in the eye. Before I could make another move, he pulled away completely. I had given all of the signs for him to go ahead, but he didn't. I felt panicked. Had I misread the situation entirely? John got up off of the bed, his body language said he didn't want to leave.

"I need to go. Thank you for tonight."

Before I could respond, he turned and walked out, closing the door between our rooms behind him. I was so confused. I reached for the phone to call him and then stopped. I wondered if I had offended him somehow. I put the phone back down on the receiver and sat in silence. His room was silent, as well. After a while, I got up and took a shower. I buttoned my pajama top and looked in the mirror after my shower, still confused. I had to know. I walked over to the hotel door and knocked gently. I didn't hear any movement and wondered if he was asleep. I knocked again, deciding this would be my last attempt tonight. I heard his footsteps approach, and I took a step back so he could open the door. He opened the door and stood there bare-chested, his pajama pants hugging his hips.

"I'm sorry to disturb you, but I just have to know, did I offend you in some way?"

"No, it wasn't you. I'm sorry I left the way I did. It was rude."

"What happened?"

"I couldn't stay and not kiss you."

I stepped forward into his room and placed my hands around the back of his neck, and kissed him. I didn't hold back. I felt his arms wrap around me as he pulled me in closer to him. I kissed him right there until my lips tingled. Kissing him was so much better than I had imagined. He felt like home, and passion, and warmth, and so much more all at once. John pulled away first.

"Wow," he said in a whisper.

I leaned back in, and he pulled away a little further.

"Wait, Izzy, I really like you. I don't want to hurt you; I have a terrible track record with women. You've been someone special to me, I couldn't live with myself if I hurt you."

"Then don't."

"Isabella."

"If you aren't into me, that's okay, I'm a big girl, I can handle that. If you are afraid, then what we have been through together is all of the more reason to take a chance, isn't it?"

He moved his hands to either side of my cheeks as he brought my lips to his, kissing me, to the point that my knees wobbled. I had never been kissed like that in my life. We spent the night together in his bed. I woke the next morning in his arms, and I knew something had changed for both of us. Little did I know that it would be the first morning waking in the arms of my soul mate, my husband, the father of my children, and my best friend.

Drew & Nathan: A Photographer's Dream

S top peeking, he's going to see you." Drew said.

"So, what, he's just so weird." Anna replied, "Leave it to you, my sister, to rent the loft to the weirdest guy on the planet during a pandemic."

"Seriously, get away from the window, it's rude. Besides, I think I remember, my beloved sister, telling me that this massive mortgage on this beautiful house would be a breeze as long as I rented out the loft."

"Yeah, not to a massive weirdo, though."

"Well, I didn't know he was," Drew said, thinking of the right word, "quiet, he's quiet."

"Yeah, okay, if that's the adjective we're using today. Drew, he's odd."

Drew walked to the window at the back of the kitchen and looked out across the driveway to the small apartment above the garage. She had invited her little sister Anna to come to stay for the duration of the quarantine. Anna tugged playfully at Drew's long red locks.

Drew had inherited the old house on the shore of Lake Michigan from her great uncle. It was a grand old cedar-shingled house with vines growing up the front, original fittings and fixtures, and a mountain of debt. The house was due to be sold at auction, but Drew couldn't bear to see the house leave the family. Her great-great-grandfather had built it. Anna loved the house too, but not enough to buy it.

"What do you think he does up there all day," Anna asked?

"I don't know, as long as he isn't breaking anything, I don't care. Come on, let's go make a pitcher of mimosas and binge watch that new series on Netflix."

"Throw in facemasks and pedicures, and I'm in," Anna suggested.

The two passed much of the day having an impromptu spa day at home as they sipped their mimosas and ate a homemade pizza that Anna had made. As the last episode of the series came to a close, they laid on the couches in the massive living room, lethargic from sitting around all day.

"This strenuous day had really taken it out of me, all this day drinking and pampering. I'm going to take a nap. Don't let me sleep past dinner, okay?" Anna said as she rose from the couch.

"All right."

Drew watched Anna leave the living room and glanced at the large French doors behind them. The beach looked so inviting. She grabbed a sweater and decided to go for a walk. As she walked north along the shore, she thought about how odd it was that she hadn't seen Nathan, the man above the garage, very often. She had done a background check and credit check before he moved in. She knew he worked at the local college in the art department, but other than that, he was a mystery. He never had company, not that he could now, in the middle of quarantine.

As she walked, her thoughts turned to Anna. She was grateful that her sister had come to stay. Sometimes living in the large house alone creeped Drew out. When Anna's job furloughed her, Drew invited her to come to stay. The whole world seemed to have flipped upside down. Drew and Anna's parents lived in Europe, so the sisters knew they only had each other. Drew wondered what it would be like to have something more, more precisely, someone to go through this with. Sure, she was grateful for Anna's company but Drew craved something more. A relationship, a life with a spouse, kids.

The frigid surf lapped at her feet as she continued. After a mile or so, she turned back. She watched the dune grass blow in the breeze.

The beach was empty, with just the noise of the waves. The state had closed the beaches due to the quarantine, not that it would have been busy on a chilly April day anyway. As she got closer back towards the house, she noticed a figure hidden between a few of the smaller dunes. At first, it alarmed her, as there had not been another soul out on the beach for weeks. As she approached, she kept her distance, but it became clear that it was a man. He looked dirty and unkempt. Drew walked into the surf to give the man a wide berth. The beach had shrunk considerably due to erosion leaving only thirty feet of sand between the tree line and the shore. She watched the man, who looked to be setting up camp from the corner of her eye. Occasionally they'd get vagrants on the beach, which didn't bother Drew so much. She felt they had a right to the beach too, as long it didn't become a problem. They usually were runoff within a day or two when other locals got wind of the newest town resident.

The man seemed not to notice Drew as she walked past, and that put her at ease as she moved further down the beach. The wind direction had turned, and the temperature had dropped considerably. It was going to rain for sure. She only hoped she'd beat it by the time she got back to the house. She picked up her pace but had the unmistakable feeling that she was being watched. She looked behind her, wondering if the homeless man had followed her, but saw no one. She continued on, picking up her pace a little more.

Without warning, she felt a tug on the back of her sweater. Startled, she turned around and was hit in the head with something hard. She couldn't register what it was, as her vision went blurry. The world went black.

Drew shivered; it was the cold she felt first as she slowly opened her eyes. It was dark. She lay on the freezing, soft sand as she felt the raindrops hit her body hard,

the noise of the surf in the background. She looked around without sitting up. She wasn't sure who had attacked her and if they were still there. She lay shivering, too afraid to move, and heard something large move in the dune grass above her. She was terrified; it was the person who attacked her. She shut her eyes and tried to listen for movement. Her head ached so intensely that she felt like she was going to vomit.

"Drew?" She thought she heard her name being called out.

Something rustled in the grass and came closer. Terrified, Drew lay there, paralyzed by fear when she thought she heard her name called again. She didn't recognize the voice, and that made her wonder if she was hallucinating. The voice grew closer, calling out her name. The man who hit her came across the dune and started to drag Drew towards the tree line.

"Drew?" She heard a man's voice call out.

She didn't know who was calling, but she knew if she didn't fight now, that she would die. She tried to scream as her voice cracked. She took a deeper breath, wetted her mouth, and screamed. A hand came down hard over her mouth. Drew began to thrash around, to kick, claw, and fight with all she had in her.

"Drew?"

She felt the light of the flashlight on her face, as the man trying that was trying to drag her took off on foot.

"Help! I'm here! Help, me please!"

She looked towards the flashlight, the beam of light from it, blinding her. A man appeared next to her. She didn't recognize his voice and couldn't see his face.

"Oh my God," he said, as he set the flashlight on her chest and scooped her up into his arms.

The flashlight showed the good Samaritan's face, and she recognized him as the man who rented the apartment above the garage, Nathan. The rain pelted them as he carried her down the beach. Her entire body hurt, and she nuzzled her head against his chest. Nathan knocked on the set of doors that led to the living room. Anna opened it.

"What the hell did you do to my sister, you son of a bitch!"

"I didn't. I found her."

"Oh my God, Drew, sweetie, wake up."

Drew felt the warmth of her own home as Nathan set her on the couch. It wasn't until her body made contact with the warm, soft couch that she realized how much pain she was in.

"You son of a bitch! I'm going to fucking kill you! What the hell did you do to my sister, you fucking creep!"

"I swear I didn't touch her, I found her like this."

"Yeah, right, you weirdo, I'm calling the cops."

Drew tried to sit up to set the record straight. Anna was a pit bull and fiercely loyal. Drew knew she had to say something before Anna pulled a gun on the man.

"No, Anna, it wasn't him. Please call the police."

"I'll call," he said.

"Prove it wasn't you," Anna said.

"Anna, it wasn't, will you help me up? I'd like to wash up."

"No, stay here. I'll go get a washrag to help clean you up."

Drew heard Anna leave the room, and Nathan, on the phone, talking with the police. Drew's whole body hurt, and she tried not to cry. Nathan walked over to her and knelt next to her.

"They're on their way. You'll be all right."

"How did you find me?" How did you know I was out there?"

"I'll explain it to you later."

Two hours later, the police had left, and Drew was tucked up safely in bed. She had declined to go to the hospital with the virus raging. An EMT cleaned the cut on her head where she had been hit and put in a stitch. She had been robbed of her jewelry, but other than some minor cuts and scrapes, she'd be okay. Anna checked on her sister every twenty minutes. Drew begged Anna to go to bed, and around 3 am, she finally did. The police said they'd comb the beach for the vagrant but would probably not find him. The force had been cut by half with officers down with the virus.

Unable to sleep, Drew got out of bed. She used the ladies' room and caught a glimpse of herself in the mirror on the back of the bathroom door. She was not a pretty picture. She returned to her room and curled up into the large chair in her room where she usually read. The chair faced the beach and overlooked the garage. She noticed a light turn on in Nathan's apartment and saw the door open to the balcony. She watched Nathan step out.

His words from earlier ran through her mind, "I'll explain later." Explain what, she wondered. Whatever he had told the police, they bought the story, and so did Anna. She knew Nathan had not attacked her on the beach. Nathan had looked troubled by the events earlier in the night, just as she was. He returned inside, and Drew sat there watching. Her stomach grumbled as she realized the last thing she had eaten was lunch the day before.

She crept down to the kitchen and made two slices of toast as the sky was just beginning to lighten from black to indigo. The sun would be up soon. She spread butter and strawberry jam onto the slices, placing them on a plate. She took the plate to the breakfast nook in the large kitchen, noticing Nathan's light was still on. Curiosity got the better of her; she needed to know how he had found her on the beach. It had not been a night for a nice walk; she knew he had to have been out there looking for her.

She set down the slice of toast on her plate, walked out of the kitchen, across the driveway, and stopped at Nathan's door. It was early, what if he wasn't awake, she wondered. Impulsively, she knocked anyway, instantly regretting her decisions. She heard him walking down the stairs to the door; she backed away slightly as he opened the door in his boxers and t-shirt.

"Drew, are you all right?"

"I'm sorry. I shouldn't have knocked. I'll come back later. I'm sorry."

"I wasn't asleep. Do you want to come up?"

Drew hesitated.

"Or we can talk out here?"

Drew took a deep breath, "No, I'll come up."

Nathan opened the screen door; Drew walked up the stairs to the apartment above. She had not been in the apartment since Nathan had moved in. He had made the space cozy. The main living space had been divided into a living room and eating area. She instantly noticed the photographs of the beach on the walls.

"Did you take these?" Drew asked as she stepped closer to look at them.

"I did. Would you like some coffee? I just brewed a pot."

"Sure," Drew said as she admired Nathan's work. "These are beautiful. I never see you on the beach, though."

"I'm out there. I just usually keep to myself," he said as he handed Drew her cup and crossed into the living room area. He gestured for her to sit. She took a seat on the couch.

"Thank you for the coffee. I wanted to ask you about what you said earlier tonight."

"Ah, I thought you would."

"I know you didn't attack me. I'm certain of it, but what I don't understand is how you knew where to find me, or that I was even missing. It doesn't make sense."

"I know. Um, I saw you leave, and I saw you walking down the beach."

"Okay, but that still doesn't explain it."

"No, I know. Um, this is going to come out wrong, and I don't want to scare you."

Drew set her coffee down on the coffee table. Noticing Drew's change in posture, Nathan put his down too.

"Oh no, it's nothing bad. At least I don't think so."

"What are you talking about?"

"I've been photographing you."

"What?"

"No, it's not like it sounds. I've been photographing you as you walk down the beach. Shit, this is coming out wrong. Not like a creepy stalker. You're so beautiful, and I've done a series. The first time I saw you walking on the beach, you took my breath away. I snapped your photo, and it was gorgeous." Nathan stopped, as the expression on Drew's face cautioned him to tread lightly.

"Hold on."

Nathan got up, walking to the desk at the far corner of the room. He reached between the wall and the desk, lifting a portfolio case. He brought it to Drew and handed her the case.

"Here, you can have them. I didn't mean any harm by it. I knew you were out on the beach because I photographed you leaving. I usually wait for you to come back. When it got dark, and you didn't, I was concerned. I came looking for you to make sure you were okay. "

Drew took the case from Nathan.

"Please just look at them, you'll see, there's nothing bad."

Drew turned around with the case in hand and walked out of Nathan's apartment. She crossed the driveway and entered her kitchen, locking the door behind her.

"What's that?" Anna asked, sitting on a stool at the kitchen island, with her hair wrapped up in a towel.

"Pictures of me, apparently."

"What? From where? Oh, don't tell me, the creeper from upstairs."

"He told me I could have them," Drew said as she set the portfolio case on the kitchen island.

"Did you look at them?"

"No. It's how he knew I was down on the beach last night. He photographs me when I walk."

"Did you know he was taking your picture?"

"Of course not. It's creepy."

"Uh yeah! Let's look at them."

"No way, I've been creeped out enough over the past twenty-four hours."

"Well, I want to see them," Anna said as she pulled the case closer and unzipped it.

Drew walked to the coffee pot and pretended not to care but glanced at them from the corner of her eye.

"Drew, these are gorgeous," Anna said as she flipped through them.

Drew went and sat next to Anna as she flipped through the prints. They were beautiful. Most of them were of Drew off in the distance down the shore. There were a few that were framed through her beautiful red hair, with the beach in the background. As the two sisters went through them, both were in awe. Nathan had been right; they were not creepy. They were stunning art.

"He's in love with you," Anna said as she looked at the last photo, the only one of Drew's face. He had snapped a picture of her looking out over the lake.

"That's ridiculous," Drew said as she stood up.

"No, it makes sense now. I thought he looked afraid when he brought you in last night. That's why I thought he was the one who had hit you. He was afraid for you."

"You're nuts, no more Women's Network afternoon movies for you," Drew said, trying to brush off the comment.

"Why were you at his apartment before dawn?"

"I saw that he was awake and wanted to ask him about last night."

"Uh-huh. And?"

"He said he, never mind, it doesn't matter."

Anna stood up and walked over to her sister. "Look, I know last night was terrifying, but there was something about the way he held you like you were precious, almost fragile. I read it wrong. After seeing the pictures, I get it."

"How are you not creeped out by this?"

"Are you?"

"I don't know, a little. He never asked for my consent."

"If you knew you were being photographed, it would change the picture. If he had not told you that it was you in most of those pictures, would you have known you were the subject? Except for the last one of your face, it could've been any redhead."

"Wait, you're saying he's suddenly not creepy?"

"No, I'm just saying we don't really know him."

"Exactly."

Over the next few weeks, the quarantine carried on. Nathan kept to himself, and Drew felt conflicted. She knew her sister was right. Nathan had feelings for her. His affection and longing for her oozed from the photographs. She didn't remember a whole lot from the attack, but she often woke, thinking about the feeling of being safe in Nathan's arms, his strength, the smell of him. She wanted to ask him about all of it but couldn't bring herself to ask.

Lying awake, another sleepless night since the attack, she saw the light in Nathan's apartment come on. The soft yellow glow of his lamp light lit the ceiling of her room through her windows. She got out of bed and walked over to see him sitting out on the balcony. She found herself wondering what he was thinking about, and the memory of being in his arms surfaced again. Without thinking, she grabbed the portfolio of pictures he had given her and walked out of the house with them. She crossed the driveway and knocked on his door. Butterflies danced around in her stomach as she heard him descend the stairs to his front door. He opened the door, once again in his boxers and his t-shirt, this time Drew noticed his body. He was muscular, but not like he worked at it.

"Hi, um. I wanted to bring these back to you." She said, feeling stupid for returning the photos at 2 am. "I saw your light on."

"They're yours to keep. I wanted to.." he shifted on his feet, "do you want to come up? I've wanted to talk to you, but I wanted to give you space too. I…"

"All right," Drew interrupted.

He opened the screen door, and Drew walked up into the apartment again. She noticed the photos had been taken down, and it looked like he was packing up.

"Are you moving out?"

"Yes, when the quarantine is over. I don't want to make you feel uncomfortable," he said as he walked into the living room behind Drew.

"You don't have to leave."

"I think I do. I'm sorry about the photographs. I should have asked you. I deleted the originals. Those are the only copies," he said, pointing to the case in her hand.

"Why? They're gorgeous. I think they are the most beautiful pictures that have ever been taken of me. They're artistic, and," Drew paused, searching for the right words. "They convey so much emotion. I love them."

"You do?"

Drew nodded.

"Please don't leave on my account. I like having you here. I keep thinking of the night of the attack. I am so grateful you found me. I don't want to think about what would've happened had you not found me."

"Me, either."

"Can I ask you something," Drew said, setting the case on the couch.

"Sure."

"My sister says that these photographs depict affection, admiration, longing. I know that sounds nuts, but I wanted to ask."

Nathan looked down at the floor as he rubbed the back of his neck.

"I feel like an idiot, up here at two in the morning, asking you this, but if I don't ask it now, I'll never have the nerve."

"Your sister is a smart woman."

"But you don't even know me."

"I know you are kind, you see the beauty in nature," he said as he took a step closer towards her.

"I keep thinking about that night. The look in your eyes when we got back here, so much concern, care. Am I off base here?"

Nathan stepped close enough that Drew could smell his body, that same calm, strong, manly smell that had brought her so much comfort on that terrible night. She could almost feel his breath on her. He reached up and lightly touched her cheek as he brought his lips to hers. His kiss was gentle as it brushed her lips softly.

"Guess not," Drew whispered before kissing Nathan back.

He pulled her in close; she was once again wrapped in his strong arms. They kissed as they stumbled their way around boxes to the bedroom. He backed her up to his bed, easing her down. He lay over

138

her, his body heavy, but wonderful.

"Please don't leave," she said softly. "I don't want this to be over before it's begun."

He kissed her again with a kiss that set her entire body aflame.

"You are so beautiful. I have wondered for so long what it would be like to hold you. If you want me to stay, I will."

Nathan made love to Drew, and it was love. They stayed in his bed, in each other's arms as they watched the sunrise. Drew smiled as she looked out at the lake; she was happy, and at the beginning of the greatest love story of her life.

Sam & Lindsay: Second Chances

My body shook. It was too much emotion all at once, and it seemed to ooze out through my body physically as I trembled.

"Get out. I never want to see you again!" I shouted.

Sam just stood there dumbfounded, in disbelief that I was kicking him out.

"Linds, please let me explain, it's not what it looks like. I mean, it is, but I am so sorry I would do anything to take it back."

My anger had shifted to heartbreak again, and my tears flowed again. The harder I tried to hold them back, the fuller and faster they fell.

"Just leave," I said softly as I stood in the middle of our living room. The living room we had just pained in our new house.

"Linds, please."

Rage surged again inside me.

"Get out of my house!"

"Our house," Sam said quietly.

I knew he was right, but that was an argument for another time.

We had only just moved in two months ago. We had bought this house as our first starter home, and I imagined us starting a family in it. Now that dream was gone. Sam looked at me, the remorse coming off of him in waves. I said nothing and stared at him hard. He turned around, grabbing his bag and keys out of the dish on the table by the door. He stepped out and closed the door quietly behind him.

I stood in the middle of our living room of the life we had begun to build in shock. I didn't know what to do. What does one do when her finance sleeps with the exotic dancer at his bachelor party? Our cat Oliver wound around my legs, his tail stroking my calf. I took a deep breath and headed for the kitchen. I grabbed the bottle of white wine from the fridge, the bag of spicy potato chips, and headed for my bed. I didn't bother with a glass; I intended to finish the whole bottle. I climbed into bed as Oliver curled up alongside me. I could smell Sam's scent on his side of the bed. Angry, I pushed his pillow off the bed. Oliver seemed unfazed and was more interested in the bag of potato chips.

I woke the next morning with a blinding headache and a mouth so dry it felt like I had crossed a desert in the night. I sat up slowly and looked around the bedroom. Our bedroom that was now my bedroom, I wondered? I noticed that Oliver wasn't in bed with me, and I thought it was odd. I got up and slowly made my way to the bathroom, passing the living room on the way. As I used the bathroom, it dawned on me, Sam sleeping on the couch in our living room when I went past. I hadn't heard him come back in during the night, but then I doubt I would've heard anything after an entire bottle of wine. I walked back into the living room, and sure enough, he was fast asleep on our couch.

"Wake up," I said firmly, then lowered my voice. It hurt my head to be any louder. "Sam, wake up."

He opened his eyes, sprung up, and stumbled. He braced himself against the couch.

"I know, I'm not supposed to be here. You asked me to go, and I did."

"Why are you here now," I asked, cutting him off?

"I have nowhere to go."

"Go home to your parents, or Duane's."

"I never want to see him again. I can't go to my parents, all flights have been grounded, and nonessential travel canceled."

"What are you talking about?"

"That virus, the entire country is on lockdown. I went to rent a hotel room last night, and they wouldn't let me check-in. There's a statewide order that started at midnight. I got pulled over on my way home last night for violating it. I didn't even know the damn thing was going on. Here," he said as he reached for the remote and turned on the television.

I watched the crawl at the bottom of the screen, trying to gain as much understanding as I could grasp as quickly as I could. With the lead up to our wedding, and then this bombshell with Sam, I had been out of touch. Apparently much more out of touch than I had realized. I sat on the edge of our coffee table and watched.

"I'll make some coffee," Sam said as he left me watching tv.

I watched in disbelief at the reality I had woken up to. My cell phone rang, and I answered without looking at who was calling.

"Lindsey, are you okay? Is Sam okay? We've been so worried about you two," my mother said. "You didn't answer your phone last night, neither did Sam, we've been so afraid for you both."

"I'm sorry, mom. I didn't mean to scare you. I took a sleeping pill," I lied, "and went to bed."

"Oh, are you ill? Why are you taking a sleeping pill? Is it wedding jitters?"

"No, mom," I said as Sam walked back into the living room with a cup of coffee in his hand for me. He sat down next to me and handed me my cup. I nodded as my mother went on.

"Yes, mom, he's here. We're both safe and here, together." I tried not to look at Sam as I said it. Taking a deep breath, I searched for a way to get off the phone. I felt Sam pull the phone away from me gently.

"Hi, Mrs. Windsor, I mean mom, yes, we're safe." Sam stood up and walked over to the window as he took the "mom" bullet for me.

I grabbed my coffee and walked out of the room. I needed a shower, I smelled of stale wine, and if I was honest, I needed a minute to think about my next move. I started the shower and made it as hot as I could tolerate. I took two Tylenol from the medicine cabinet and washed them down with my coffee before I stepped into the shower.

As I walked out of the bathroom, my towel wrapped around me, I could smell breakfast cooking. I listened for Sam's voice, wondering if he was still stuck on the phone with my mother, but I only heard the noise of him cooking. I walked into our bedroom and dressed before I made the bed. I found Sam in the kitchen sitting at the table with Oliver spread out next to the plate of pancakes.

"I'm sorry about this, Linds; I'll be on my way as soon as I can. I just need to find a place."

The kitchen seemed sunnier than usual, this morning and the light pierced through my skull, angering my headache further. The sunlight in the morning in this kitchen was one of the things I had loved most about this house when we looked at it. Now the cheery sunshine felt odd and out of place. I rubbed my head as I walked and sat down at the table. Oliver took it as an invitation, stood up, and walked over. I hated it when Sam let him on the table while we ate. I petted Oliver's head and then put him on the floor. Sam put another forkful of pancake into his mouth and chewed quietly.

"I just don't understand," I said softly.

"Which thing?"

"You and me. It's enough for the rest of the world to fall apart, but to do it without the one person who I thought was my person. I think that is what is scariest of all."

Sam took a deep breath and put his fork down on the plate.

"I will always be your person, Linds. I know you don't believe that, but it's the truth. I never set out to hurt you. Believe me, if I could be somewhere else and spare you this pain right now, I would. At the same time, I'm glad I am here. Who knows how crazy this might get," he gestured outside. "I'll try to stay out of your way. I'll see if I can make a space for myself in the garage until I can find a new place."

I looked over at him and nodded, the whole scene so surreal.

He pushed the plate he had made for me towards me. I pushed it gently away from me.

"I know you're so angry with me, but you need to eat," he said softly.

"I can't eat this morning," I said as I stood up. "I'm going to go camp out in the bedroom and log-on to work to see what the plan is for Monday."

I curled up in my bed with my laptop but didn't bother to open it. All I wanted were things to be the way they were. I wanted to be in Sam's arms; I needed to be in his arms. I loved him, but in my gut,

I couldn't reconcile the betrayal. I fell asleep and woke in the late afternoon. Groggily, I walked from the bedroom. The house was silent as I walked through. There was a part of me that was afraid that Sam had left, that he had found somewhere else to stay. I walked out the backdoor and heard saw him hauling more junk out of the garage. When we moved it, the garage had been packed full of a lifetime of the previous occupant's junk. We had intended to clean it out but had not gotten to that point yet. Sam had built a sizable pile in the back yard that was separated into wood and metal. He stopped as he walked out his hands full, sweat on his brow, dirt on his face when he spotted me.

"Hi, I thought I'd get started. I cannot believe how much stuff is in this garage. It's crazy. I almost have a space large enough for a bed cleared." He said as he dumped an old chair into the pile of wooden items, none of which were functional. The slapped his work gloves together to shed the cobwebs that had stuck to them as he walked up to the back porch.

"I found a bed to put in here."

"You found a bed in the garage," I asked?

"No, I.. uh... Mark has an extra. He's going to drop it in the driveway in a little bit. Sorry, I just wanted to give you your space. I'll put the medal at the end of the driveway, I'm sure a scrapper will come to get it, and I'll burn this old wood in the wood stove in the garage if it gets too cold out here, or you can burn it in the fireplace in the house if you want. I'll break it down for you."

I felt a pang of guilt that he had to make a place for himself in the garage but reminded myself that he had done it to himself. I went back into the house without saying anything and spent my afternoon catching up on work. I saw our mutual friend Mark pull up with a twin mattress and box spring in the back of his pickup truck. Mark came to the front door and knocked, but Sam came around the front before I could answer it.

"I'm back here," Sam shouted so Mark would hear him.

I listened to Mark walk off the porch, and I left them to it as I went to start dinner. As I began to prepare dinner, I overheard their conversation.

"Man, what were you thinking, Linds is..." Mark said, the frustration thick in his voice.

"I don't remember doing it. I was so wasted. I could kill myself

145

for hurting Lindsey. I love her. Fucking Duane. I'm my own man, but damn it, why did he let me do that?"

"How'd Linds find out?"

"I told her."

"Why did you do that?"

"I couldn't lie to her."

"Wait, let me get this straight, you told her you slept with the dancer, but you don't even remember doing it? What the hell, man?"

"Duane said we were all over each other, I mean I woke up naked next to the girl. I mean, I honestly don't remember. I slept with someone. I just wish I could remember."

"I was there for most of the night, and you were fucked up, but not that fucked up. What did the girl say when you woke up next to her?"

"She didn't. I got up to use the bathroom, and when I came back, she was gone. Duane stood in the doorway of his room and clapped."

"Fucking Duane. If I were you, I'd find the girl. I know you, man, you'd never do that to Linds. I mean, did the two of you fool around before you went out that night?"

"Yeah."

"Well, is it possible that you didn't sleep with the dancer?"

"It's possible. Shit, I don't know. I wish I could remember. I've never drunk myself blackout drunk before."

"You weren't when I left, I mean you were pretty trashed, but you were still conscious. I left around 2am. Find the girl."

"I've tried. Duane said he hired her from an online ad but couldn't remember where. I told him to text her back, and he said she hasn't replied."

"Well, when all of this shit blows over, I'll go see if I can find her. I hate to see you two like this. I'm glad you're staying here, though. It makes me nervous, her by herself right now."

"Yeah. Thanks for the bed."

I sat at the table, my stomach rolling as I overheard their conversation. The fact that Sam had doubts that he had slept with the woman, yet still told me left me more confused. I stood to stir the pot of marinara sauce I had started when I saw Mark leave, waving to Sam. I moved on to chopping up vegetables for a salad to go along with my pasta when I heard a knock at our back door. I walked over and opened the door.

"Would it be okay if I showered before I grab some of my things," Sam asked, still standing on the other side of the screen door.

"Of course."

I moved out of the way and went back to cooking. I heard the shower start as I finished up dinner. I made myself a plate of pasta and salad, set one aside for Sam as I took mine back to my bedroom. I heard him dress and leave through the back door. I got up to see the light on in the garage. That night I laid in our bed once again, by myself. Oliver had chosen to bunk with Sam in the garage, and part of me was happy about it. Thinking about what to do preoccupied my mind, and I found it difficult to sleep deeply.

The next morning, I woke late and made my way into the kitchen. Coffee had not been made, and I wondered if Sam was awake and had not come in or had not woken yet. I made coffee and opened the back door, so he would know that I was awake. As late morning turned into early afternoon, I noticed that Sam had not emerged from the garage. Curiosity had gotten the better of me. I poured him a cup of coffee and walked to the door at the side of the garage. I knocked, and when I didn't hear anything, I peeked inside. I stepped inside and saw Sam's small living space set up inside the garage. Oliver meowed loudly as he walked in circles at the end of Sam's bed. Sam was curled up.

"Sam, I brought you coffee," I said loud enough to wake him, but he didn't rouse.

Concerned, I walked over and knelt down to wake him. He was feverish to the touch. I shook him hard, and he roused slightly. He was ill, very ill. Terrified, I put down the mug of coffee and pulled my phone out of my back pocket. I saw him shiver as I dialed for an ambulance. The virus started with a high fever, and I had never seen Sam sick with more than a sniffle in the two years since we had met. The operator answered, and I told her our address and Sam's condition. I opened the overhead door, so the EMT's would be able to grab him easily. As I waited, I sat as with him, the realization that he might actually die hit me hard. I knelt back down and set the phone on the garage floor. I reached over and ran my hand through this thick brown hair. He looked up at me as he shivered hard again.

"I love you, Sam, please hang on. Help is on its way."

He slipped his hand out from underneath the blanket, and I grabbed it and gave it a gentle squeeze as I heard the ambulance approach. The

EMT's got out and brought the gurney down the driveway. Seeing them in full protective gear terrified me. I knew the virus was contagious, and it hadn't occurred to me that I had been so close to Sam and might have contracted it. I tried to go with him, but the EMT's told me only patients were allowed at the hospital right now. I stood at the end of my driveway as I watched Sam leave in the back of an ambulance. A state trooper approached me from behind.

"Ma'am, are you that man's fiancé?"

I turned around to see the Sheriff standing six feet from me, with a mask on his face.

"Yes."

"You'll need to quarantine yourself in your home for the next fourteen days if your finance tests positive for the virus. Until we know, we are asking you to quarantine voluntarily. I will have to put a notice up on your property, so others know to stay away. I'm sorry, it's the law."

I nodded and walked into the house as if on autopilot. I sat on the couch, watching the last light of the day leave the room. I didn't want to call my parents, and Sam's lived out of town. I didn't have anything to tell anyone until I had more news. I got up to let Oliver in as he meowed loudly at the back door. I went out back and shut the garage door, and grabbed Sam's phone. I brought it in the house, making sure to disinfect it. I realize how silly that was, having been in close contact with him today. I made myself a cup of tea and set both his and my phone on the kitchen table, hoping the hospital would call. After I finished my cup, I couldn't wait for the hospital to call any longer. I needed to know how he was doing. The phone rang and rang without an answer. It felt like the life I recognized was slipping away from me. I was angry and terrified. I slammed my phone down onto the table.

Not knowing why I picked up Sam's phone and started to look through it. There were 14 unread text messages. Three were from Mark, and the rest were from Duane. I looked through them, as my stomach lurched. It had been a prank. Sam had not slept with the dancer. Duane thought it was a funny joke. I began to sob, thinking of Sam alone in the garage so sick and now alone at the hospital.

I sat up on the couch most of the night, as Oliver purred away on my lap. Finally, around 3 am, my phone rang. I jumped at the noise of it, startling Oliver, who clawed my lap. The screen said Lawndale

Hospital. My hands shook as I answered it.

"Hello, is this Lindsay Eaton?"

"Yes, how is Sam? Is he okay?"

"Hello, I'm Dr. Thompson, I'm treating your fiancé. He's stable for now, Miss Eaton."

I felt tears of relief spill down my cheeks.

"Can I talk to him?"

"He's resting now."

"Okay, when he wakes up, will you please tell him I love him, and I know the truth. Please, I know that sounds nuts, but he needs to know."

"I'll tell him. I'll call with more updates as we have them. He has texted positive for the virus. You will need to monitor your temperature and will have to self-isolate for the next fourteen days. This is very important."

"Of course. Can his family come to see him? I know I can't, but can someone be there with him?"

"I'm sorry we can't allow any visitors right now."

I bit onto my lip to keep from crying harder.

"He's responding well to the therapy so far, his prognosis is good. I will call if anything changes and will update you tomorrow morning. Take care of yourself, Miss Eaton."

The phone hung up before I could say anything more. I dialed Sam's parents and told them what I knew. Then I called my own parents. Everyone wanted to come to be with us, but with the travel ban in effect, they couldn't travel. I could also be infected, and I didn't want to pass the virus along any further. I fell asleep on our couch as the sun came up. I woke to the sound of my phone ringing in my hand. I saw that it was a number I didn't recognize. I answered right away anyway, just in case.

"Hello, this is Lindsey Eaton."

"Hold on," a man's voice said, and my phone beeped to accept a video call. I pulled it away and saw Sam. He had an oxygen mask on and looked weak.

"Linds?" Sam asked, pulling his mask away. "I love you."

"Sam, I love you too. Honey, please get better and come home to me."

"Are you sick?"

"No, so far, I feel alright."

"I'm so sorry for all of this."

"No, Sam, I'm sorry. You didn't do anything wrong. Duane tried to pull the worst practical joke ever. If I ever see him again, I'll kill him for putting us through this."

"What?"

"It doesn't matter, please just get better. When you come home, if you still want to, I want to marry you."

I watched as his eyes watered.

"We should wrap up. You need your rest," a voice from off-screen said.

"It's a date. I can't wait to marry you. I love you, Linds."

"I love you too."

I kissed the phone screen before he hung up.

Three weeks later, Sam returned home to our house, that once again held the promise of our future life together. I was lucky and never did end up getting sick. Sam made a full recovery. The following weekend after returning home, we got married in our living room, as our family and friends watched online.

Charis & Ben: Quarantine our Famlies Together

Y ou know, you could always stay with us," Ben said.

"I think this is going to be much worse than anyone is letting on. Have you seen the news out of New York?"

I shook my head that I hadn't as I wondered if Ben's offer was genuine.

"Thank you, that's very kind, but."

"The kids would love it; besides, I know I'm going to need the help."

"So, you want me to stay to look after our kids," I asked, confused.

"No, Charis, I'm sorry. I only thought that it could be easier if you and Milo came to stay with Bella and me during the quarantine. I know you're in an apartment, and you could come stay at the house, keep the bubble closed, you know? I mean, only if you wanted to. The kids could play together and keep each other company."

I looked over at Ben, searching his gorgeous face for any clue if his offer was genuine or if it was some devious plot, not that I thought he'd ever been capable of such things. Ben was handsome, a great dad, and single. All the other single mothers fawned over him. He used to be married to my best friend, Brooke. She was the mom all the other moms wanted to be, and together they made the perfect, beautiful power couple, but that felt like a long time ago. Our kids were the same age, only months apart, my son, Milo, and his daughter, Bella. Our kids had practically spent every day together. I knew the time apart during quarantine would be difficult for them. Ben's deep brown eyes, and wavy brown hair, complemented his permanent five o'clock shadow. I looked down at the sidewalk as I thought about the offer, as we waited for our kids to come tearing out of the school for dismissal. It was late February, and a cold wind blew. I was eager to get back into the warmth of my car. Bella came out first with the first group of kids, her toothless smile and perfectly braided hair, her mother would be so proud. At her request, I had spent hours teaching her and giving Ben a crash course as well. She ran up to Ben, who knelt down to embrace his charging daughter. She collided with him as his breath expelled in an "oof."

"Did you have a good day, pumpkin," he asked her?

"Is it really true that there's no school tomorrow?"

"It is, remember the virus we talked about last night?"

She nodded that she did, "Did you ask Charis and Milo that thing we were going to ask?"

Ben looked up for me, looking for a cue on how to proceed.

"Hi baby, your daddy did ask."

Milo charged up at that moment with equal enthusiasm.

"Bel, you didn't wait for me," he said, looking at Bella.

"Sorry, I forgot. My dad asked."

Clearly, I was the only one who had been left out of the secret plan I realized.

"Mom, can we please stay with Ben and Bella, please?"

Ben mouthed the word sorry to me, and I believed he truly did not mean for me to be ambushed.

"I'm going to think about it, okay, buddy?"

Milo slumped at my lack of an outright yes.

We waved goodbye to Ben and Bella as we started for the car. All night Milo begged, pleaded, and bargained with me to stay with Ben and Bella. When I thought about it, the practicality of it, the proposal did make sense. I wrestled with the idea, knowing it made sense, but I couldn't figure out if I had talked myself into it, or it actually made sense. Milo's dad and I divorced a few years back, and he lived across the country with his new wife and their twin daughters, so I knew that it wouldn't be an issue if we stayed. Around 11:30, I picked up my phone and texted Ben. The text read:

"If the offer still stands and you are sure, we will come stay. I saw the news tonight, and I would feel better knowing there are two adults looking after our kids, just in case."

I hit the send button and instantly wanted to recall it. I wanted to stay, but there was part of me that was nervous to do so. Ben had never made a move on me or anyone else for that matter after Brooke. The way their marriage ended, with her addiction, had ripped his heart out, and I couldn't blame him if he never made that sort of leap again. My divorce looked vanilla and simple, compared to what Brooke had put Ben and Bella through. I had been painful and gut-wrenching to watch. Neither Ben nor I was eager to jump into anything resembling a relationship. We were both too shell-shocked from the fallout of our first marriages. I set my phone down on my nightstand and rolled over. It buzzed right away, and I rolled over and picked it back up. Ben had written back almost instantly.

"I'm glad you both are coming to stay. You share my thoughts exactly. We should have everything all of us need. So just bring yourselves and anything else you might want. I'm going to leave it as a surprise for Bella."

I put the phone back down and rolled over, but although my body quieted and was still, my mind raced with thoughts of an unsure future. Around 1 am., I got up and began to pack anything and everything I thought we would need for an extended period of time. I had started a pile in the living room of our stuff, and all I had left was to pack Milo. I ran everything down to the car and then came up and cleaned the apartment. I made sure to empty the fridge and made sure the garbage was out.

Milo woke around 7 am, his usual time to ready himself for school. I had not slept the night before, and he read it on my face when he walked into the kitchen, in his droopy pj's and his mop of golden hair a mess.

"Are we going, Mommy," he asked, not fully awake?

"Yes, we're going."

"Yay!" he jumped. "Can we go now?"

I laughed at his excitement, glad that he was happy in all this chaos.

"We just have to get you all packed, and then we can go."

He took off for his room, and I laughed as I followed him, with my cup of coffee still in my hand. Within an hour, we were in the car and headed across town to Ben and Bella's house. Our small town seemed almost deserted as we drove through, and it set me on edge, although I tried not to let Milo see. We pulled into the driveway of Ben's house, with the perfectly laid bricks. The house sat proudly, as it had for almost one hundred years. Painted white with green shutters and flower boxes that Ben hired a gardener to care for exploded with flowers and vines in the summer months. The house always resembled the perfect home, like one would see in the movies. Before I barely had it in park, Milo bolted from the car and ran straight for the side door to the kitchen. Ben walked out with a smile on his face as I met him in the driveway.

"I cleared a spot for your car in the garage if you want," he said, walking closer to the car. "Woah, did you pack your whole place?"

I laughed nervously as I looked back at my car, packed full.

"I didn't know how long we'd be staying and what we might need, so I just brought it all. I hope that's okay."

"No, it's great. Let me help you unload."

It took us almost an hour to unpack the car, and as we did, I realized I had overpacked. Bella and Milo just about rioted when we tried to put them in separate rooms, so reluctantly, Ben said he'd put another bed in Bella's room for Milo. Ben gave me one of the guest rooms across the hall from the bathroom, and we all settled in. Over the next few days, we all found a sort of equilibrium living, working, and being together. There were pictures in the house, pictures everywhere of Brooke to remind Bella of how beautiful her mother was, and how much she had been loved. I had always admired Ben for that, but I found it slightly odd to be in my best friend's house with her husband and daughter, and she wasn't there. The guest room, Ben had put me in was painted the perfect shade of grey. I know this because Brooke and I had just about driven the painter mad, as she and I tried to describe it to him. I missed my friend as I looked at the walls of my room, remembering such fun times. I kept my sadness to myself, though.

Two weeks in, Ben announced at lunch that he had to do a late call for work, something about time zones and whatnot. I volunteered to make dinner and put the kids to bed. We had pretty much split the chores and childcare, so I didn't mind helping out. He was lending the use of his house after all. That night I made spaghetti carbonara, Milo's favorite. The kids ate dinner, had their baths, and listed to the book I read them before I turned the light out. As I went back down into the kitchen, I noticed it had begun to snow again, as soft flakes drifted past the window, seeming luminescent against the darkness of night. I had just finished filling the dishwasher when Ben walked into the kitchen. He looked stressed.

"How'd your call go," I asked as I began to reheat our portion of dinner?

"Not great, we're going to have more lay-offs. It feels awful letting people go right now, through the very worst time most people will live through."

"I'm so sorry, that's awful."

Ben sat at the island, eager to change the topic of conversation. "That smells yummy, what is it?"

"Milo's favorite, spaghetti carbonara. I made some for you too. I thought I'd wait to eat with you if that's okay, but if you'd rather have some time to yourself, I understand too."

"No, that would be great to eat together. Hold on, this dinner is missing something," he said as he got up and walked out.

He returned a minute later with a bottle of wine in hand and two wine glasses.

"Would you like a glass of wine?"

I nodded that I would, and he poured each of us a glass and set two spots at the kitchen table for us. I finished reheating the carbonara and brought it over to the table. We talked as we ate, and it had all of the hallmarks of the dinner of married people, I thought to myself. As we finished dinner, Ben helped me clean up again, and we took what was left in the bottle of wine into the living room and turned on the nightly news. We watched, saddened, and scared by the headlines. I sat next to him on the couch and sipped my wine, grateful for the little bit of relaxation it brought. A commercial came on, and Ben turned and looked at me.

"I can't help but think of Brooke right now. I pray she's safe."

There was pain in his voice, and I felt it too, fear for the person we had both loved and cared about.

"Me too."

"I called her mom today and asked. They've not seen her in six weeks," he said as his voice cracked.

I leaned up and put my arm around his shoulder, and he pulled me in closer to him, holding my body against his. He smelled wonderful. I tried to push that thought out of my mind.

We had spent so much time together, worrying and crying over Brooke that his emotions weren't out of place. I held him tightly as I waited for him to break, yet it did not come. He pulled away, and without warning, he slid his hand along my jaw and pulled my lips to his. Ben had always been my best friend's husband, strictly off-limits, and I had respected that even after Brooke had left, but now we both sat in some sort of grey-zone, both of us legally divorced.

At first, I froze when his lips made contact with mine, but I suddenly found myself kissing him back. It had been a long time since I had been kissed, I'd be the first to admit it, but this kiss was like no other I had experienced. My knees tingled, and an inferno stoked to a roar from deep inside my belly. A part of me awoke that had been lying dormant for so long. I found myself ravenous like I had crossed the desert, and Ben was that first sip of cold, clear water. As his kiss deepened, I felt that I was losing all control to pull back from the precipice of something, and it was the sheer terror where I found my strength. I pushed gently against his chest, and he stopped. He looked deeply into my eyes, and I felt like if I did not get off the couch immediately, I'd melt away in his.

"I... I'm sorry, Charis, I shouldn't have," he said.

I sat up and took a deep breath to steady myself. "No, it's not you, I'm sorry. I should go to bed."

I stood up and turned around in the doorway between the foyer and the living room. I waved as I turned back around and went towards the stairs. I felt like a moron, waving as I walked up the stairs, yelling at myself internally to go back, not to go back, and then the wave.... My head was a mess. I laid in bed, thinking about that kiss, holy hell. Brooke had always said that Ben was incredible in bed, but I thought that was one friend bragging to another. If his kissing was a metric of measurement for heat and intensity, I feared I might combust. I tossed and turned, unable to get the scene in the living room out of my mind. Deep from within me, he had awakened something primal, a need that

I had pushed away for so long. I wrestled with what Brooke would say and tried to push that entire roadblock out of the way, but it was still there.

I got up to use the bathroom and checked on the kids. They slept peacefully in one bed, although Ben had put a second bed in there for Milo. Neither Ben nor I cared that the kids preferred to sleep in the same bed. They were only seven. I turned, walked back towards my room, and ran into Ben in the hallway. He had a glass of water in his hand. He startled me, and I tried not to scream and wake the kids.

"Sorry," he whispered, "I didn't mean to scare you."

"It's alright. I was just checking on the kids."

His jawline seemed more pronounced in the soft light from the small lamp at the far end of the hallway. We both stood, frozen for a second, like some sort of game of arousal chicken. In the game, I blinked first as I leaned up on my toes and kissed him. It was an out of body experience. Pure impulse overrode the logic part of my brain. He stood still, and for a split second, I was terrified that I had misread the situation entirely. He wrapped his arms around me, sloshing the water from the glass he held onto the carpet runner that ran the length of the hall. One kiss turned into another and then another, as lust and desire took over. He pulled me away from the kid's door and pushed me against the wall where a small table sat against the hallway wall. My ass barely sat on it as his body moved closer to mine. Internally, my mind was screaming a million thoughts, all conflicting. We both froze at the noise of the doorknob from the kid's room, and then immediately scrambled. I turned around and pulled my cotton robe closed. Bella stood in the doorway, half-asleep.

"I need water, daddy."

Ben grabbed his half-empty glass of water, and walked towards her room, ushering her back to bed. I stood there, unsure of what to do. I heard his footsteps leave the kids' room and go straight into the room where I had been sleeping. I had gone to his room; it was further away from the kid's room. His pace quickened as he walked towards his room. I stood in the middle of the room, with only the moonlight to illuminate his way. He walked up to me but didn't touch me.

"Charis, I don't know how to do this."

"Is it what you want? Really what you want? There hasn't been anyone for me since Walter, and my voice quivered with excitement, fear, and anticipation.

"I promise you; I won't hurt you. Please don't hurt me either, okay," he asked as he closed the gap between us.

"I won't," I whispered before he took my lips again.

He backed me up to his bed, his lips never leaving mine as we crossed the room. For as much as heat and passion as there was packed into each kiss, his movement was gentle, deliberate. I came down on the bed and pulled him down with me. Breathless, he kissed my neck and collarbone as he pushed my robe open. He paused to strip his t-shirt from his body, launching it across the room. My cotton camisole and pajama pants were gone, in the throes of passion. I didn't know if I had taken them off or he had. I laid underneath him in only my underwear. His skin warmed mine, and his weight made me feel safe, in a way, I had completely forgotten. My tongue in his mouth made me feel like I'd burst in all of the best ways. He slid his fingers into me, and I moaned louder than I had meant to.

"I love the feel of your body," he whispered into my ear. "You are so beautiful, Charis."

I pushed at his boxers, needing him to be inside of me. He sprang forth, and I took him into my hands as I heard his breath hitch with pleasure. He looked down at me as he gently pulled my underwear off.

"I.. I.. I need to grab a condom..." he said, breathless.

He leaned over me and rummaged around in the drawer of his nightstand. There was an eagerness to his searching that made me feel wonderful. He found one, most likely the last one he had, and rolled it on quickly before he came back over me and kissed me again. He pushed into my body, and the world stopped. He looked down at me, into my eyes, and I knew that this wasn't a fast fuck for him, just like it wasn't for me. I wrapped my legs around his waist as he slowly began to move. Pressure and pleasure built with each move of his hips. I leaned up and kissed him, and his pace quickened. I didn't want the moment to end; I was in ecstasy. With one hand over my shoulder, he reached his other hand down and caressed the back of my ass. His breath quickened, and I knew he was close. He moaned in my ear, a masculine, primal noise of pleasure, and I was done for. My orgasm tore through me so violently, I saw stars and bit into his shoulder to keep from screaming out. I had never bitten anyone in bed. Ben slammed his mouth down over mind to quiet me, and his tongue moving over mine only intensified my pleasure. He pulled away when he was sure I wouldn't scream out and whispered into my ear, "that is the sexiest thing I've ever heard."

Without warning, he rolled us over, changing our position, so I sat on top of him. The moonlight lit my silhouette, long, lean, and endowed. He sat slightly as he took one of my nipples into his mouth. I cradled his head in my hands as he sucked away and felt another orgasm pulse through my body.

"Shit," he said through gritted teeth, "I can feel you... coming.."

Sensing he was barely hanging on, I tilted my head back and rode him, slowly and deliberately. His hands moved over my body and settled, holding my ass as I felt him finish, with deep grunts filled with release. I slowly came to a stop as I felt his orgasm wane. I went to move off his lap, and he held me there, his arms embracing my waist. I looked down at him, and he kissed me.

"You are so beautiful, Charis."

He pulled me down onto the bed with him, and I snuggled up against his side, resting my head on his shoulder. I spent the night sleeping in his arms. We were sure to wake before the kids were up. The next morning didn't bring any awkward conversations, and I was grateful for that. Over the next few weeks, we spent our nights in each other's arms. As intense as our physical intimacy was, for me, there was an emotional intimacy building. I feared the emotional intimacy, having been hurt before, but I put my trust in Ben and allowed myself to be open to where things would or could go.

As the quarantine continued, the weather warmed, and summer began to show up in small ways. We decided to plant a garden in the back yard with the kids in late May. That morning I had gone out and had bought the plants and had stopped at the pharmacy in the next town over. I had felt queasy over the past few days, and although we had used protection, I had a feeling that something wasn't quite right. As Ben and the kids turned over the soil in the back yard, I vomited in the bathroom at the sight of the positive pregnancy test. I had always wanted a big family, and I knew that Ben had wanted that for Bella, but not like this.

I called my doctor and was surprised when she answered her own phone. I was used to going through the phone tree of nurses and never seemed to get her on the phone. I explained my situation, and she ordered a blood test and an ultrasound. That night after the kids went to bed, I told Ben. I wasn't sure how he would react, but I was relieved to see that he was just as scared as I was.

"I don't understand, we were careful," he said in shock.

"I know. I didn't do this on purpose."

"Charis, I know you would never do anything like that. I trust you, I... I love you."

"You do?"

"Yes. Whatever comes our way, I am here right alongside you," he said as he pulled me into his arms.

"I'm scared, Ben."

"I'm right here, I'm not going anywhere. I meant what I said to you that first night, I won't hurt you."

He kissed me, and at that moment, as scared as I was, I believed him that everything was going to be okay.

The next day I went to the doctor's office and had the official test that confirmed the pregnancy. She confirmed that the pregnancy was healthy. I drove back, in shock, still not completely comprehending that Ben's child was growing inside me. I walked back into Ben's house with my prenatal vitamins, sonogram pictures, and a look of complete shock on my face. The kids were playing outside when I came in, and I was grateful, so I could talk to Ben, without our kids knowing what was happening.

"Is the baby healthy? Are you healthy?"

"So far, so good, it's early, only eight weeks, but everything looks healthy for both of us."

"That is good news. I know this wasn't planned for either of us, but I couldn't think of anyone I'd rather have a baby with. You are an excellent mother. These past few months living together have been wonderful. You've been like a light that has been turned on in my life and Bella's, I love you, and this will all be okay.

That night I sat on the couch while Ben cooked dinner and looked after the kids. I was too nauseated to be anywhere near the kitchen. After they were asleep, we laid in Ben's bed, curled up, and talked about what the future would look like. I wanted the baby, and I was relieved that Ben felt the same way too.

"Your move here could be permanent if you wanted," he said.

"How are we going to do this? How does this work?"

160

"Well," he paused, "How does this sound? You can move in here, and then later this summer, I am going to marry you, that is if you'll have me, and after that, we'll live happily ever after."

"Wait, did you just ask me to marry you?"

"Yes. I decided this morning that no matter what, you came back from the doctor and said that I was going to ask you to marry me. You're my best friend. We share so much history. Bella adores you, and you're an incredible mother to Milo. I want you in my life for my whole life, and Bella's life too, if you'll have us."

I couldn't help but cry, "yes," I blubbered, "I want to marry you too."

Monica & Owen: Leaving Paradise

M rs. Billet, I'm sorry, but unless you can pay, you must make other arrangements." The woman said, behind the desk. Her hair was pulled tightly in place, her makeup impeccable, not a single wrinkle in her blouse, she embodied the brand of the Sand Dollar Resort.

I stood in the open-air lobby as the wind wafted in, with the scent of tropical fruits and flowers. I was standing in paradise; more accurately, I was trapped in paradise.

"No, please don't call me Mrs. Billet, I've explained that was my fiancé's name, I am Miss Murphy. The airport is closed, your borders are closed, and will not permit me to leave. I cannot go home. I'm stuck like many of your other guests."

"Yes, I understand, but pandemic or not, you have not paid for the room beyond this evening. We would be happy to continue to have you and your fiancé as a guest if you'd like to book more time with us?"

"Do you see my fiancé standing here with me?" I asked as I raised my voice. I took a deep breath. This woman did not deserve my anger; we were all living through a pandemic.

"I'm sorry I don't understand the question. Will you be booking additional nights until you are able to arrange travel back home to the United States?" Her plastered smile did not wane, the smile she was paid to keep on between the hours of 8 a.m. and 5 p.m. for guests.

"Are you seriously telling me that you are going to put me and the others who are trapped here out on the street during a pandemic? You do not have incoming guests; your own borders are closed right now."

"I'm sorry, it is the policy from our corporate headquarters."

I walked away from the desk, my sandal clicking on the marble floor of the lobby. Clearly, there was no point. I had been trying to get somewhere for three days with the staff after the border closed without notice. I walked out on to the terrace that spanned the length of the hotel and pulled the fresh sea air into my lungs in big hungry gulps. This was all too much. The edge of the terrace had a beautiful rock wall. I sat and slung my feet over the side as I took in the view. I had to figure out what to do. I was trapped alone on what was supposed to be my Honeymoon in paradise. I could not believe that the hotel was not making accommodations for the dozen or so tourists that had been trapped on the island.

What a weird turn of events, I thought to myself. I was supposed to be in Ryder's arms safe, in love, and blissfully happy. I jotted at a tap on my shoulders and saw the woman from the reception desk.

"I'm not going to jump," I said dryly.

"May I sit?" She asked as she looked around.

I nodded that she could.

"I shouldn't be telling you this, so please," she looked at me for confirmation that I would not share whatever she was going to say. I confirmed that I understood with a nod. "There is a group of Americans and a French couple that are in the same situation as you. I've heard talk about them renting a house here on the island. I know housing is difficult to find here, but you may be able to rent with them off the resort. I'm truly sorry you are trapped here. Please know if it was up to the staff, we'd have all of you stay. It is cruel to turn you all out."

She patted my hand, put back on her professional persona before she got up, and walked away back to her post.

I had looked up rental properties the day after the borders closed, just in case. The island was small, and there were very few rental properties available, the ones that were for rent cost more than my first car per month. Living with strangers wasn't ideal, but neither was living on the street in a foreign country.

I returned to my room and changed for dinner. Despite the chaos of the world around us, the hotel had still kept up standards. I put on a black halter dress and swept up my blonde hair into a messy ponytail. My sun-kissed face made my freckles come out and blushed my skin. I swept mascara over my lashes and put on some lip gloss. I didn't need a lot of makeup. The sun had given me a beautiful glow. I closed my eyes and took another deep breath, and there he was, Ryder, the memory of him. He'd always come up behind me and wrap his arms around me in the morning. He'd kiss my neck or whisper something sweet into my ear. My body craved his arms, ugh to be held by him again. I pushed him out of my head, no, I wouldn't go there tonight, I couldn't. I had to find a place to live.

I walked down to the bar at the far end of the terrace. It had a grass roof and warm lighting. I scanned the room. There were a few people at the bar and two couples who had sat to have dinner at their own tables. The bar seemed like a good place to start. My plan was to find the others who were renting and see if they'd be willing to have another roommate.

I sat down and ordered a glass of chardonnay. I loved how the glass frosted, coming from the fridge, hitting the warm tropical air. I took a sip, and it tasted buttery. Ryder always made fun of me that it was my drink of choice, but it was what I liked. I swirled the wine discreetly on my tongue. It was delicious. I took another sip. Liquid courage was needed. As I did, I made eye contact with a man across the bar. He had on a white diner jacket and a pair of slacks. I could tell he was American, by the way, he wore his dinner jacket, uncomfortably. He nodded at me, and I nodded back. I took another sip of my wine, and as I set my glass down, he approached.

"Is this seat taken," he asked in his southern American drawl.

I turned and flashed my most charming smile, "It's not."

"Can I buy you another…" he hesitated, looking at the wine glass, "….Pinot Grigio?"

"Thank you, I'm fine. I'm Monica."

"Hi Monica, I'm Benson. You sound like one of ours, American? Where are you from, Monica?"

"I'm from Indiana, you?"

"Ah, I guessed it! I'm from Kentucky. Monica, we're neighbors!"

This was going well. I was just waiting for my moment.

"We are! Where in Kentucky are you from?"

"Louisville. So what brings you down here to paradise?"

Ugh, I hated this question. I was going to have to come clean, no matter how painful. You need a place to live, and you might be able to play the sympathy card. Everything I had been through had to be for something, I thought myself.

"I was supposed to be on my honeymoon, actually."

"Honeymoon? Supposed' ta? Did' ja drown him out there in the ocean?"

"Nope. I caught him and my maid of honor in our bed on the morning of our wedding."

"Yikes," he said as winced. "Are you down here hiding from the law?"

I smiled, "No, but I didn't marry him. I grabbed my bag and got an early flight here. I couldn't face everybody. It was too much, I ran."

"And he didn't come after ya?"

"He didn't. It ended before I left. He told me he was in love with my best friend and maid of honor. Like that, my life with him was over."

"Well, darlin, I think you're going to need something stronger than this wine you've got here." He turned to the barman, "Two Paradise Punches please, good sir."

I was a lousy drinker, I always had been, but I'd play along. I needed a roof over my head.

"So, Benson, where is your date on this lovely evening?"

"No date, I'm stag. I came down on a boys trip and stayed a few extra days. My buddy Henry got stuck down here with me. He'll be down soon. This is crazy all of this pandemic stuff, isn't it."

"It is. I wasn't prepared for it." I hesitated, not sure if I wanted to show my hand just yet and let Benson know I needed a place to live.

"None of us were. I cannot believe how quickly the hotel emptied, it was like overnight 300 people just up and left."

"I know it."

"Well, Monica, would you like to grab a table for dinner with me?"

"Sure, why not."

I sat down with Benson, and we ordered dinner. His friend Henry joined us as our appetizers arrived. I listened intently about their fishing adventures from earlier in the week, and the crazy night their whole gang had at a local watering hole off of the resort. Benson kept the drinks coming, and I tried to pace myself. As dessert wrapped up, Henry excused himself, in search of some fun down at the hot tub.

"Well, Monica, will you walk with me by the beach for a bit before the night finishes?" He asked.

Normally I'd stay off the beach with a stranger, but I had a bit too much to drink, and my judgment wasn't what it should have been. I would ask him down on the beach about the rental house. It was clear, but the dinner conversation that he and Henry had definitely rented a place, but I had resisted the urge to ask. I needed to be a cool customer. In prepping my ask, I talked about how I was a great cook, hoping that information would come into play in a decision to take on another roommate.

As we walked down to the beach, he regaled me with a story of his buddies and him trying to find food after the local bar, and how they ended up eating chicken that was cooked in a tent on the roadside. As we hit the sand, I stopped and slipped off my shoes. The sand was cool beneath my toes. There was some comfort in knowing that security did patrol the beach. I let my tension ease away as I looked at the moonlight glistening on the crashing waves. We continued to walk towards the shore when Benson stumbled. I reached out to help him, but he went down. I thought the fall looked odd, but I didn't trust my own judgment.

"Benson, are you alright?" I asked as I bent down.

"Yeah," he laughed, "serves me right for drinking all day in the sun."

"Do you want help up?"

"You come down here instead. We can sit and look at the ocean." He tugged at my arm, and it left an uneasy feeling in my gut, but I wasn't sure if it was all of the alcohol either. I plopped down next to him, my landing, anything but graceful. Now was my moment.

"Benson, I heard a rumor about some fellow American's renting a house here on the island. I know you don't know me, but if you and Henry have rented a place, do you have room for another roommate?"

He rubbed his jaw and looked out at the ocean.

"I am an excellent cook, too," I added to help sway the decision.

"Well, it might be possible, but I don't know you."

"Okay, that's fair. What would you like to know?"

"No, that's not what I mean. I'd like to get to know you," he said as he slid his hand up my thigh.

I put my hand over his, "Benson, I really need a place to stay. I am offering to pay my way, but I won't sleep my way into a room."

"We don't need a room," he said as he came over me.

I fell backward onto the sand, with Benson came over the top of me. He kept pulling at the bottom of my dress.

"Stop, no! Get off of me," I screamed.

He brought his hand over my mouth, and I began to panic. I felt like I couldn't breathe, and suddenly he was gone. I didn't know how or why. I sat up as I heard Benson's voice, "You son-of-a-bitch, you hit me."

"The lady said no, you piece of shit," another man said.

I turned in his direction and recognized him as another guest. He was a brit, and he wore his dinner jacket like it.

"I'm gonna kick your ass, pretty boy," Benson said as he lunged towards the other man who moved out of the way. Benson landed on the sand with an audible gasp.

"Look, Mate, the lady said no, let's just leave it at that."

I sat frozen, unable to move. I didn't know if it was fear or the realization that I could go, but I sat there watching the two men in front of me.

"Go get your own piece, this one is mine," Benson said as he got up to all fours.

"She doesn't agree. Ma'am, is that correct?"

"No, I didn't want to sleep with him, I…."

"See, so you can shove off, or we can call security, your choice."

"Fuck you, man, fuck both of you," Benson said as he stood upright, "Enjoy being homeless. You just blew it, babe."

He stormed off the beach, and I got to my own feet.

"Thank you for your help. I should've known better to come down here."

"Yes, you should've, especially with that asshole."

"You don't know me."

"Well, I did just pull him off of you. Who knows what would've happened if I had not strolled down here."

"Thank you for your help, Sir. It's been a long night."

I turned and walked back up towards the hotel. I expected him to say something in return, but he didn't.

As I got back to my suite, I caught a glimpse of myself in the mirror. I was a mess. The strap on my dress had been torn, and my hair was a mess. I looked like some sad P.S.A. about what not do, drinking with strangers on a remote tropical island. I took my dress off and threw it in the trash. Forget repairing it. I didn't need a souvenir from tonight. I took two Tylenol as I felt the headache from the alcohol already building before, I stepped into the shower.

I slept poorly that night, and I knew the next morning I was going to have to find somewhere to live. Sure, I could probably buy a few more nights if I emptied my savings account. The resort was not cheap, and the rooms were still full price despite the current circumstances. I packed my bag and put on a pair of jeans and my favorite Cubs t-shirt. As I walked down to breakfast, I stopped and stowed my luggage at the front desk.

The breakfast was set in the bar from last night. I grabbed a plate at the buffet and began to work my way down the line. Even though I wasn't hungry, I knew I needed to eat. I didn't know when I'd have the luxury to eat until I was full again. As I scooped scrambled eggs onto my plate, I heard a familiar voice.

"Monica."

I turned to see Benson standing there. Henry looked on from their table. "I owe you one hell of an apology for last night. I don't know what came over me. I am sorry. I know not to mix too much rum and too much sun. Can you ever forgive me?"

My lack of appetite had turned to nausea at the sound of his voice.

"And Henry and I wanted to talk to you about the place we rented. Will you join us for breakfast so we can talk this out, neighbor?"

I set the spoon back down into the tray of eggs and swallowed the rising bile in my throat. I had to at least hear him out. I'd be homeless in three hours or broke in three days. He went and sat as I brought my plate over. I set it on the table and sat down. My skin crawled, but I told myself to give him the benefit of the doubt. He apologized profusely again, and then Henry apologized for him as well. The topic turned to the rental house, with two bedrooms, on the Northside of the island. Henry and Benson said they'd share a room, and a French couple had rented the guest house at the back of the property. I almost had myself convinced that it could work, as I felt Benson's hand slide up my leg under the table. I shot out of my chair.

"You are a pig, and a sexual predator," I shouted so the whole bar could hear.

"Now, don't be that way, neighbor. I'm trying ta be charitable here."

I picked up my glass of freshly squeezed mango juice and threw it in his face. "I'd rather live on the streets with the rats." I slammed the glass down and walked out of the bar.

Shit, I'd blown my chance to not be homeless. But there was no way I could live with that creep. I was desperate. I would have to dig into my savings for another night, then call home and plead for help. I marched straight into the lobby and put my credit card down for another night at full price. As I turned to walk back to my new room, I spotted the Brit from the beach the night before. He was walking towards the lobby.

He was taller than I had realized on the beach, his skin was deeply tanned, and it made his blue eyes stand out. He had a layer of stubble along his jawline, the hair only slightly darker than his blond hair that was a mess atop of his head.

"Good morning," he said as we passed.

"Good morning, "I stopped as he walked on. I had been rude last night. "Excuse me,"

He stopped and stood there coolly with his linen shirt draping perfectly and his hands in his pockets. Down to his canvas loafers, he was incredibly handsome.

"I owe you an apology for last night. You did something very kind. I am sorry if I was rude to you."

"No need to apologize. Did you end up finding a place to stay?" He pointed to my suitcase in my hand.

"How did you know I was looking for somewhere to stay?"

"Well, it's pretty obvious, the hotel isn't going to stay open, they're closing next Tuesday."

"Ah, I had not heard that," I said, trying to hide my alarm. "Well, thank you again for last night. Have a great day."

I waved, and he nodded, and we went our separate ways. Once I got into my room, I finally picked up the phone and called home. Only my brother knew where I was. We discussed my almost non-existent options. If I could get off of the island, I stood a chance of maligning it back home before all travel ceased. That was easier said than done. I was trapped on a tiny, luxurious island in the middle of the Indian Ocean. Dean, my brother, promised he'd continue to try work with the United States embassy to see how to get me home.

I hung up and laid back on the king-sized bed with its crisp white linens. All I wanted to do was pull the shades and hideaway. I knew I didn't have the luxury, so I put on my one-piece suit a pair of shorts to go down to the beach. I was desperate, and I was just going to have to start asking if anyone had a room for rent. I did not want to be out on the streets. I spent the afternoon asking everyone I passed, even hotel staff. No one seemed to have anything available. I would have to buy another night and go into the tiny town, to see if there were any leads.

As the afternoon turned into evening, I finally sat down on the lounge chair on the beach. I was exhausted, sunburnt, and no closer to finding somewhere to live. I laid back as my toes dug into the sand.

"Any luck today," the Brit asked as he walked up and stood over me.

"I'm sorry, what?"

"Finding somewhere to stay."

I sat up, and he came around me and sat on the lounge chair next to me.

"No."

"I have room."

I turned to face him, "you do?"

"It's a little unorthodox, but I do."

"Unorthodox, how?"

"I own a boat. It's docked down in the harbor. There are two cabins. I thought you'd be able to find something, but I figured it wouldn't hurt to look for you when I was in town today. I come here each winter for a few weeks, and I've gotten to know the island fairly well. I can tell you, there's nothing available."

"Damn, I was going to try in town tomorrow. What kind of boat do you own?"

"A sailboat. I can show proof of who I am, where the boat is registered, all that stuff."

I looked out at the sun glistening off of the water.

"Here," he said, handing me his wallet. "My driver's license is in there, passport, boat registration card, all of it. I'll be back around eight for dinner. You take some time and give it a think."

Before I could refuse, he walked off. I sat there with his wallet in my hands. I ran my thumb over the expensive black leather. I shot up, wasting no time, and walked back to my room. I took pictures of everything and texted them all to Dean; his job at the F.B.I. was convenient right now. My phone rang a minute later as he answered, the sleep in his voice.

"I need you to check all of this out for me. I know how nuts this sounds but this guy has offered me a cabin on his boat."

"Mon, a boat, are you kidding?"

"Dean, there's nothing else here, nothing. I've spent the past few days looking. There is nothing else. Please check him out. I'm desperate."

"I know, that's what scares me. Your boat guy knows you're desperate too."

"Maybe I could get him to take me to another island or something, and I could try to get home."

"No, stay there. I don't want to think of what could happen with you and this stranger out on the open seas. Stay in the harbor. When do you need this info by?"

"Right now."

"Of course, you do." He groaned.

I hung up and looked up Owen James Smith. He lived in London and seemed like a decent enough guy. I knew that Dean would turn up anything criminal, so I looked for character. He seemed to have a lot of friends on social media. I texted Dean, the company Owen worked for, and all of his social media accounts that I could find.

Dean called me back three hours later, "he seems to check out Mon. A friend of mine is a cousin at a three-lettered organization here in the states. He ran a check on him too. The guy's clean. Nothing more than a few speeding tickets. For the record, I really do not like this."

"Thank you, big brother. Neither do I believe me."

"You call me each day. Don't make me worry about you more than

I already am. And don't try for home, just stay in the harbor."

I went down and met Owen for dinner and handed him back his wallet.

"Did I check out?"

"My brother, who works for the F.B.I., thinks so. I had him run a check. Can I ask one question," I said as I poked at a water droplet sliding down the side of my glass at the dinner table? "Why are you so nice?"

"It's a difficult thing to do. I have the room. You need a place to stay."

The next morning, I got up and met Owen outside the hotel. We took a taxi to the harbor. I had not been to town yet, as the hotel had been all-inclusive. I had arrived at night when I got to the island, so it was neat to see it all in the daylight. I followed Owen down the dock. He stopped in front of the large boat, with its deep blue hull. It was massive, I had pictured a tiny little boat, but the Victoria had to be at least fifty feet in length. Owen climbed on, and I followed as he led me through the yacht. It was luxurious and gorgeous. That afternoon I checked out of the hotel. I stopped back into town and purchased the supplies I'd need to stay.

I settled into the rhythm of life on the yacht very happily with Owen. I made sure to call Dean each day, as I had promised. Owen and I watched the news on his laptop each night as the world shut down further and further due to the virus. So far, the island we were docked at had been clear for the virus. Owen and I spent a lot of time together, and as we got to know each other, I found myself falling for him.

I'd told him about how the trip was supposed to be my Honeymoon. It turned out he had been jilted at the altar himself, and I counted myself lucky that my situation had not been as public as his was. Eventually, I trusted Owen enough that we began to go on short sailing jaunts, taking the boat out to atolls, and grilling fish that we had caught. He kissed me for the first time on one of those beautiful nameless atolls.

He taught me how to sail, and I loved it. I swam each day. I found that as messed up as the situation was, I was really happy. My favorite part of the day was laying in each other's arms on the deck under the stars. When we dropped the anchor outside of the harbor, it felt like we were the only two people on the face of the earth.

We quarantined on the Victoria for sixteen weeks, and when the borders opened, neither of us was in any hurry to return to life. On our last night on Victoria, Owen asked me to marry him. It had been incredibly fast, but I knew with every fiber of my being that he was my soulmate. I had ventured further than I had ever gone before on what was supposed to be my Honeymoon and found my soulmate.

Gemma & Mark: A Stranded Brit

G emma woke as Mark's arm pulled her body in closer to him. She opened her eyes not believing it was morning again. She surveyed the yellow walls of the studio apartment from the futon where she and Mark had spent all weekend in each other's arms. She rolled over slightly, and his eyes opened.

"You're awake," Mark asked, his voice still raspy from sleep.

"Mmm, I am. I need to get moving or I am going to miss my flight."

"Nope, I'm not letting you go, you're my prisoner," he joked.

"Well, I can be your prisoner next time I am in St. Louis. I need to go home to England.

Gemma watched Mark's playful smile with a pang of sadness. This is insanity she told herself. She followed Mark home after a wild night out and proceeded to have the wildest sexual experience of her life thus far. They only left the bed to eat and shower. They binge-watched old kung-fu movies, both finding a true fan in each other. Gemma sat up and looked for her phone. She had not checked it since Saturday morning. Her job was high stress, but she knew everything could wait for one weekend of fun.

Mark propped himself up on the pillows as he watched Gemma

walk around the small apartment naked. He found her boldness and confidence incredibly sexy. He could not pull his eyes away from her petite frame that was curvy in all of the best places. It didn't hurt either that her black hair swayed across her back as she walked towards her purse. Mark tried not to salivate at the thought of sleeping with Gemma one last time. As she dug in her purse for her phone, he got off the futon and pulled a t-shirt over his head.

"At least let me make you breakfast first," he said as he walked into the tiny kitchenette.

He began to make a pot of coffee when he realized Gemma had not answered him.

"Gemma?"

She still ignored him. He turned around and saw her standing still naked as she held the phone in one hand scrolling through her phone and her other hand over her mouth. Reading her face, Mark knew something awful had happened. He went over and stood next to her.

"Are you okay," he asked?

Hearing the concern in his voice triggered her attention.

"My flight's been cancelled. The borders have been closed. I…"

"What? Why? What happened?"

"It's this virus. All travel has been shut down. My mum and dad are back home in the UK, my auntie and friends."

"Does it say how long?"

"I don't know I haven't gotten that far yet."

"Here, let me look," Mark said as he turned around looking for his own phone.

"Turn the telly on," Gemma instructed.

Mark grabbed the remote on the nightstand and clicked it on. President Malcolm stood at the podium, in the middle of a televised speech. Gemma came over and sat next to where Mark on the edge of the futon, both transfixed by the American President declaring the borders of the United States were now closed, as globally travel was banned due to a rapidly spreading global pandemic. Gemma reached back and pulled the blanket from the futon around her. Mark wrapped his arm around her, not sure if it was to comfort her or himself. As the President concluded, Gemma looked down at her phone.

"I have to call parents, would that be okay?"

"Of course, I'll shower to give you some privacy."

Mark stood and realized he should probably call his own family. He grabbed his phone and walked into the bathroom, shutting the door behind himself. With his apartment being a true studio, the bathroom was the only enclosed room where one could find give and get privacy. He turned on the shower, hoping the noise would block out his own call home. He talked to his parents who were isolated on their farm in rural Illinois. They urged him to come to the farm; it sounded like a good idea, but he wasn't sure yet. He wasn't going to just leave Gemma in his apartment.

He showered in record time and put a towel around his waist as he walked out of the bathroom, hoping he would not disturb Gemma's call. She sat on the futon, her head in her hands. Mark walked over, sitting down next to her. She could smell the scent of his shampoo and could feel the moisture evaporating off his skin.

"Were you able to get ahold of your parents and your family?" he asked?

"Where am I going to go? Your President said that the borders are closed for the next six weeks at minimum. I've called my hotel and they are requesting guests check out. I guess they called over the weekend to alert me to this, but the one weekend I put my phone away, the world ends."

She wiped a tear from her cheek as Mark stood up.

"You're going to come home with me. My family owns a farm just across the state line in Illinois, in Berlin. It's a tiny town, but we have a big farm with plenty of room. I called them when you made your calls and they invited me, us, out."

"You told your family about me?"

"Not exactly, but you are welcome to come along."

"I'm a stranger to them."

"You're not to me. I know this really isn't the time for this, considering all that is going on but I like you, I mean, I really like you. That being said, you don't have to feel the same way about me. I know how nuts that sounds as we've only just met, but the offer still stands no matter what your feelings are for me."

Gemma wiped both of her cheeks. There was something about her curled up in his blanket, upset and afraid, that compelled him to lean down and kiss her, but he resisted the urge. She looked up at him with her piercing green eyes and tear-stained cheeks.

"I couldn't, its rude."

"Not here, I promise you. The city is going to get nuts, you have nowhere else to go. I'd offer to let you stay in the studio, but I don't have food here, and I don't think it will be safe. Please come with me?"

Gemma sat, considering her options. She hadn't said it, but she felt the same way about Mark. She chewed her bottom lip, thinking through her options, while she looked at the perfect specimen of a man standing in front of her. The night she met him she had found his dark curly mop of hair adorable, and his chocolate-brown eyes seemed to melt her insides. He was clean-shaven on the night they had met, but he now had the beginnings of a beard. His muscular build reassured her that he could protect her in the new reality they had woken up to.

"Are you sure it won't be an imposition?"

"No way, my parents would be thrilled. Here, I can give you the address; that way you can tell your family where you'll be if that helps?"

Mark bent down, looking at her squarely.

"My mother's name is Betty and my father's name is George. They've lived in Berlin their whole lives. The farm has been in my family for three generations now. I am their only son, my sister Carina lives in Florida with her husband. She is staying down there to be near her in-laws. You'll actually be doing me a favor, my parents are almost in their seventies. It would be nice to have someone my own age to talk to. I promise you, it is the safest place on the planet, there is almost a three-mile square perimeter of corn fields around the entire farm."

Mark reached up and tucked a long piece of her bangs behind her ear.

"All right. Thank you. Are you sure?"

"Absolutely. I promise you we'll be safe there."

Gemma stood up and began to look for her clothes, Friday night's club attire that she had worn to Mark's apartment. The hotel had instructed her in her voicemail that her bags had been packed and were waiting at the concierge.

"I'm sorry, but can we please go to the hotel for my bags before we leave town?"

"Of course."

Mark zipped his own suitcase that sat on the futon and pulled it on the floor, the metal wheels clicking on the wood floor. He had thrown a bag together as she dressed.

"Ready? We'd better get on the road, so we are in our shelter place by 5 pm. as the President said.

Gemma nodded that she was, as Mark pulled the suitcase behind him. He reached out his hand for hers and she took it as they walked out of the apartment into the unknown.

Meyer & Nathan: The Assistant and the Boss

"So, groceries have been ordered and should be here before four. You'll be able to reach me by phone, text, the normal. Let me think, is there anything else?" Meyer asked as she recounted her mental checklist. She stopped speaking at the sound of Nathan's phone ringing.

Meyer had taken the job as Nathan's assistant because she believed in the work he did. To say that she was overqualified for the job was an understatement but working for the Women's Collab Company had been her goal since she had first read about Nathan and the company in college. She took the position, hoping to move into a more senior role in time. She had been Nathan's personal assistant for over a year and had excelled at it. They both knew her time as his assistant was coming to an end, as Belva, their human resources director, was getting ready to move across the country. Meyer had gone to school for human resources and had a solid background in the field. She fidgeted with the tag on her designer purse as she heard Nathan in his office. The conversation sounded tense. Normally as his PA, she'd figure out was going on, and solve whatever issue had arisen on the call, or give him the pieces to do so. She felt awkward walking into his home office.

She had met him at his house to go over any last details before the city shut down for quarantine. The entire company had gone to a virtual set up, and Meyer had been helpful in getting Nathan ready. As brilliant as he was, technology was not in his wheelhouse.

She glanced down at her phone. She needed to get moving to get on the subway before it stopped. It would be running until four p.m. and then shut down for how long, no one knew. She could take a cab, but the fare would be outrageous. She stood in Nathan's living room, looking out over the city. His view took in the entire skyline as the city sprawled outside his window. Her phone said 3:15. Time was ticking, and she still had to pick up a few things before she was locked in her own apartment. No one knew what laid ahead for quarantine, but the thought of being locked in her tiny apartment for weeks did not thrill Meyer. With rent in the city so outrageous, she rented the largest apartment she could, as close to the city center as possible. Her studio apartment left just enough room between the end of the double bed and the fridge that she could just stand to take two steps into the minuscule bathroom. She thought that she'd only ever had to sleep there, so the small space didn't matter too much.

Nathan walked out of his office, and before he said anything, Meyer read his face. He was upset.

"Anabel isn't coming. She's staying in France."

Meyer couldn't say that she was exactly surprised. Nathan had been trying to patch things up with his soon to be ex-wife for most of the time she had worked for Nathan. He loved Anabel, but she had not been so committed to the relationship. She was not discrete about her extramarital affairs, and Meyer hated to see Nathan treated so poorly.

"Traveling can be rough right now. Maybe it's for the best," Meyer said as she slung her work tote over her shoulder.

"No, she's not coming home ever."

Meyer's stomach sank, she had been waiting for the bottom to fall out for Nathan, but she didn't think Anabel would be cruel enough to do it as a pandemic swept across the globe.

"Nathan, I'm," she paused as her phone buzzed in her hand, and she looked down at it briefly. The subway had closed early. "I'm so sorry, Nathan, that's awful."

Guilt ate away at her as she looked at him as he stood behind the kitchen island. He wore his company t-shirt shirt, and she looked at his muscular forearms. She had always been attracted to Nathan but never let herself even entertain the idea; it would jeopardize all that she had been working towards. He was about ten years older than she was and had started to grey at the temples, which only made him more attractive, she thought. He had deep blue eyes and a kind face that was weathered in a manly way. Everything about him screamed, compassion, kind, loving man. Women regularly threw themselves at Nathan, but he had been so committed to making things work with Anabel that he never gave them a second look.

"Thank you. Is everything okay," he asked, gesturing to her phone?

The fact that he was more concerned about her than Anabel and his own situation only reinforced what a decent human being he was.

"It's nothing. Do you want me to stay for a bit longer?"

"No, I'll be okay. Will you be okay? You're in The Heights, right?"

"I am."

"You're all set up with a work computer too? I know you've been so busy helping me get ready."

"I am. Do you need me to go over your office set up one more time?"

"No, I think I've got it. Thank you, Meyer, for coming over and setting all of this up, I don't know what I'd do without you."

"You're welcome. I should get going," she said as she walked towards the door. She felt awful leaving him after such a heartbreaking phone call.

"Wait, Meyer, I hope this isn't too forward but, are you going to be okay? I know you live alone, and the apartments in The Heights are infamous for being small. Do you have everything you need for the quarantine? You're good on food? Toilet Paper? Medicine?"

She turned around, standing in front of the door.

"I think so, thanks for asking. My place is tiny. I didn't think I'd actually be quarantining in it, but I've stocked up, and I'll be okay."

"How much can you stock up in such a small place? My friend Jason says he thinks we'll be stuck until the end of May. Will you be okay until then, that's six weeks?"

Meyer tried not to show the alarm at that thought, but Nathan had learned to read her face well. Her soft brown eyes were like a window into her soul, kind and loving. He had found her attractive in her interview, but didn't let himself be swayed by her looks when he hired her. Her sheer determination to take a job that she was over-qualified for just to work for the company had won him over. Her chestnut color hair had laid softly over her shoulders, the day he had interviewed her, but that was not what he had remembered most. Her lips, with their slight upturn and natural pinkness, he had found them irresistible. He thought about what it would be like to kiss her lips so many times, yet he never made a move. Although the spark had extinguished for Anabel, he would always care for her, and that being said, it had been one of the reasons he had never made a move for Meyer.

"May? Are you sure?"

"Well, no one is sure, but Jason works with the WHO and said all of New York is looking at a full shutdown until then. Will you be okay until May?"

"I didn't think it would be so long. I guess I could always rent a car and drive home to my brother's house."

"The brother in Michigan? Meyer, that's a terrible idea. Who knows what the roads are going to be like? Look, I have a crazy idea, and you are under no obligation to take me up on it, but you are welcome to stay here if you'd like. I have more than enough room. You can pick from one of the three guest rooms. Hell, pick two," he chuckled.

Meyer bit her bottom lip, a sign that she was thinking. Nathan loved that she did that and found it adorable.

"Please, you'd be doing me a favor. Plus, it will save you having to explain how to log into the remote portal over Facetime," he laughed.

Nathan prayed she would agree. He was legitimately worried about her all alone in her tiny apartment.

"I don't have any of my stuff here."

"I could drive you home and help you pack up if you wanted?"

There was an awkward pause as both weighed their options, hoping to make the correct choice.

"It wouldn't be an imposition?"

"Absolutely not. I would be so grateful for the company. May is still two months away, and who knows what the future holds. I'd be worried sick at the thought of you alone in your apartment."

"You'd worry about me?" Meyer asked, trying not to show her excitement that he genuinely seemed to care about her wellbeing.

"Yes. I know you don't have any family here. They're all back in the Midwest. What if you got sick or ran out of food, or there's civil unrest?" Sensing he had overplayed his hand, he rubbed the back of his neck nervously.

Meyer recognized the sign of nervousness; he always did that before he gave a speech. She wondered if the chemistry she had felt between them more recently was actually something more. The optics wouldn't be good, office wise. She didn't want people to get the wrong idea, but what Nathan said made sense. No one knew what was ahead.

"All right, I'll stay under one condition."

"Name it."

"You have to let me rent the room from you. The optics of this won't look good, but if I say I rented the room from you, it might look better."

"Always the HR manager," he laughed, "if it makes you more comfortable, then it's a deal, but please know I would never ask that of you. You can stay free of charge."

"Thank you, I know. We should get a move on if we are going to make it back to my place and back here before curfew."

"Agreed."

An hour and a half later, Meyer and Nathan had loaded up his Tesla with everything she'd thought she'd need. He had been surprised at the size of her place and had made a joke about needing to pay her more. She laughed, but the truth was she was already paid very well. The city was just incredibly expensive. Together they hauled everything into the guest room she had chosen at Nathan's. One wall of the large bedroom was all windows looking out over the park. It had its own on-suite bathroom and was practically larger than her entire apartment. The room had been decorated tastefully, in hues of tan and white. The wooden furnishings in the room had been collected from Nathan and Anabel's travels around the world. Nathan had left Meyer to settle in as he lied about some work emails he needed to catch up. Meyer knew it was a fib as she knew his inbox better than he did. None the less, she took the time to settle into the room. She felt relieved to share the quarantine with someone. In the back of her mind, she cautioned herself not to blur the lines of professionalism, no matter how attractive she found Nathan.

She emerged from her bedroom and instantly smelled something burning. Walking into the kitchen, she spotted Nathan at the stove, attempting to cook dinner. He had not noticed her presence as he pulled the frying pan off the burner and put it into the sink.

"Was that dinner?"

Nathan turned around at her voice, and his embraced smile set butterflies buzzing around her stomach. His nervous smile was his most handsome smile, she thought to herself.

"It was. Normally I am better at this, I don't know how I burnt that so terribly."

"What was it? I mean before it burst into flames," she laughed.

Nathan laughed too.

"Chicken, I think."

"You think? When was the last time you cooked for yourself?"

"I won't lie, it's been a while."

"Ah, the plot thickens, you needed someone to come stay to make sure you don't starve to death after the all of the microwavable food runs out."

They both laughed.

"No, I used to be decent at this. I'm just out of practice, I guess."

"I'll tell you what, how about you let me cook tonight as my way of saying thank you for letting me rent the room? How does that sound?"

"Okay, but I at least get to help. There are two more chicken breasts that I had not incinerated yet, in the fridge."

"All right, chicken breasts, and what did you want to go with it?"

"Um, I'm not sure," he paused, "yet."

"Do you have any pasta?"

"Fresh or dried?"

"You don't have fresh pasta in the fridge? I didn't order it?"

"No," he said as he laughed.

"Okay, dried then. How does chicken carbonara sound with mushrooms and broccolini?"

"That sounds incredible. I had the feeling you might be into cooking when I spotted your kitchen set up at your place. It was kind of intimidating."

"I love to cook. Can you chop mushrooms," she said as she set the container of fresh mushrooms in front of him.

"Yes, boss," he joked. "Would you like some wine?"

"Sure."

Nathan grabbed a bottle of wine from the bar in the living room and set a bottle of red and a bottle of white on the kitchen island.

"Ladies' choice," he said as he stood behind the two bottles.

Meyer turned and looked, "I think red. I know it's chicken, but I'm not a big fan of white if that's okay?"

"The Pinot Noir, it is then."

She watched as he took the bottle of white and put it back into the wine fridge. He grabbed two glasses and came back into the kitchen. She continued cooking as he opened the bottle, poured them each a glass, and then brought hers over to her, setting it on the counter next to her. She turned around as she took a sip. The wine was delicious. She felt a wave of heat, not sure if it was from the wine, standing in front of the stove or being alone with Nathan, cooking dinner for them. It was in that moment she knew she was in way over her head. She smiled as she watched him meticulously cut the mushrooms, trying so hard to do it perfectly.

That night they ate dinner together in Nathan's beautiful apartment, and both felt the chemistry between them more strongly than they ever had before. After dinner, they played a game of chess, where Meyer beat him and finished the evening watching the news. Both were incredibly distressed at the information; as a Nation, the pandemic had arrived, and it was taking its toll. Later that night, Meyer laid in the big bed, looking out over the beauty of the skyline. This view sure beats the view of the white wall in her apartment. She wondered if Nathan was thinking about her like she was thinking about him, or if he was still thinking about Anabel. That night she fell asleep with two king-sized pillows tucked up behind her, not to feel so alone in the giant bed.

Over the next few weeks, the quarantine dragged on. Work continued, but there was less and less to do as the whole world seemed to be grinding to a halt due to the pandemic. Meyer's family was glad that she had chosen to stay with Nathan. Meanwhile, she kept waiting for Nathan to bring up Anabel, but he didn't, nor did she see anything in his inbox from Anabel, or a divorce attorney. She wanted closure for Nathan, and partially for her own reasons. Keeping things strictly professional was becoming more difficult. Nathan was wonderful, and if she'd let herself admit it, she'd fallen for him completely. Yet, she did her best not to let her true feelings show, as Nathan did the same.

As the weather warmed, and the first sunny days of June came along, the quarantine was officially lifted. On her last night there, Nathan cooked them dinner. She had been giving him lessons all through quarantine, and he had been an excellent student. Meyer had enjoyed teaching him so much and would miss the nightly lessons when she returned to her own home. Dinner that night was awkward, and Meyer couldn't tell if it was her own perception, or there was truly something "off." Either way, she felt a pit in the bottom of her stomach all night. She didn't want to leave. The time with Nathan had been incredibly special.

After dinner, she scrapped the plates and began to wash up; she had volunteered. Nathan walked in and set the water glasses on the counter next to the sink, and she couldn't help but notice that he looked sad. He lingered next to her, she glanced up at him, their eyes meeting. Neither of them said anything, both having so much to say to each other, but both too unsure to act. Nathan walked back out of the kitchen, and Meyer began to load the dishwasher. The gnawing feeling that had been present all night couldn't be ignored any longer. She dried her hands and took a confident step towards the living room where Nathan was sitting with a book. She took a deep breath, knowing that she was taking a gamble on everything, and started walking. She walked into the living room, and Nathan stood up. It struck her as an odd gesture, but she didn't focus on it.

"Nathan, I am officially tendering my resignation effective immediately."

He stood looking at her, confused.

"What? Why?"

She walked up to him, "So I can do this." She wrapped her arms around his neck and brought her lips to his. The feeling of his lips caressing hers sent an electric charge through both of them, and he pulled her in close as he kissed her back.

"You don't have to.," he said in between kisses.

"Yes. I... do.." she replied as she reached for his belt.

An hour later, Nathan and Meyer laid in a sea of discarded clothes on the living room floor, both in awe of the best sex of their lives. Meyer curled up next to Nathan and rested her head on his shoulder as she played with the curly hair on his chest.

"I only have two regrets," he spoke up.

At the word regret, Meyer's heart sank.

"The first is that I am going to have to find another assistant, and no one will do as good a job as you do."

"And the second?"

"That we waited until the last night to do this. What a waste of a quarantine," he joked.

She let out a soft laugh.

"I have a confession to make," he said as he laced his fingers in between hers across his chest. "It has been so difficult not to tell you that I have feelings for you. I didn't want to make you uncomfortable while you've been here."

"Really? Well, if it's confession time, I have to confess that I've felt this way for a while myself."

"Ugh, we wasted so much time," he said playfully. "Don't go home tomorrow, stay with me."

Meyer popped up so she could his face, "What?"

"Move in with me. We've already been living together for the past three months. Move-in, for real."

"What about work?"

"Well, technically, you don't work for me anymore unless you want to. I had a wild idea a few weeks ago that I wanted to float by you anyway. What if instead of taking Belva's position, you come back to work as our second in command. No one knows this business better, is more committed, and would do a better job. You are highly educated, and you'd be a natural fit. What do you think of the idea?"

"Are you serious?"

"I am. I know I just threw a lot at you, and one offer is not contingent upon the other."

Meyer leaped on top of Nathan, and the air expelled from his body in a playful laugh.

"I take that as a yes, then?"

She nodded and leaned down and kissed him as he wrapped his arms back around her on the living room floor.

190

Josie & Spencer: Movie Star Romance

Not many got the opportunities Josie did, but her dad was one of the best accountants in the country. Paul Savoir, Josie's dad, helped the super-rich hide their money, and celebrities look close to destitute on the books. He was a wiz at what he did, and that afforded him some luxuries. He doted on his only daughter, Jose, so when she was accepted to Pepperdine for her undergraduate studies in pre-law, he wanted her to be comfortable. Through her undergrad years, she lived in Spencer Noah's pool house in Malibu, California. Paul had helped the mega-celebrity out of a tight spot with the IRS. In Spencer's elation that he would not go to prison, he had offered to repay the favor to Paul anytime, anywhere. Paul loved having Josie stay in the pool house, there was twenty-four-hour security, and his little girl was happy.

Paul made it very clear to Spencer that if he ever looked so much in Josie's direction, there would be hell to pay. Paul was a powerful enough man to turn the threat into a reality, leaving Spencer to give Josie a wide berth. He was rarely home, as he was often jetting around the world, filming his next blockbuster. He also liked having someone staying at the property, and it didn't hurt that Josie was easy on the eyes. She was petite with chocolate brown hair that stopped just above her waist and had an hourglass figure. But it was her emerald green eyes against her tanned skin, where freckles could be seen that truly made her beautiful. After her undergrad, she applied to the law school at Pepperdine and was accepted. She continued to stay in Spencer's guest house while she attended.

In the spring of her second year of law school, the news started to report on a virus that was circulating globally. Paul wanted his daughter home back east, but she wanted to stay and continue with her education. By the time the school closed, so did the flights. Paul scrambled to find her a private jet, but she once again declined, reassuring her father that she was safe and isolated in the guest house. Reluctantly Paul agreed, trusting that his daughter had a good head on her shoulders. After all, she wasn't a baby anymore. She was a grown woman in charge of her own life. As quarantine took effect, and the entire state locked down, Josie took the opportunity to study. The beachside estate was quiet, and she felt like she was the only person on the planet, not that she had minded.

Two weeks into the lockdown, as she read a book by the pool, a shadow came over her. She put her book down and looked up and was startled to Spencer standing above her. Normally one of his people would call and give her a warning when he was arriving as she tried to make herself scarce. It was his house, after all.

"Sorry, I didn't mean to scare you. I just wanted to come and let you know that I planned on staying here for the next few weeks. I didn't want to be up in the hills when I have a perfectly beautiful beach house sitting here empty."

Thinking it was a cue to leave the pool, Josie grabbed her book, "Oh, of course. I'll go. Sorry, no one called and told me you were coming."

"No, don't leave on my account. Yeah, I kind of snuck out. I didn't want the press to catch me out during lockdown and all, what a mess that would be."

"I'm sure."

"I'll let you get back to your book, I just didn't want to scare you if you saw me walking around."

"Thanks."

He smiled at her and walked back into the house. She picked her book back up and got lost in the love story of Annabella and Tristan in the book she was reading. A while later, Spencer came back out with a t-shirt and a pair of trunks. He plopped his towel on one of the chairs on the opposite side of the pool.

"Would you mind if I took a dip," he asked?

Josie put her book down so she could see him.

"Of course not, it's your pool."

"I just didn't want to disturb you. You seemed so engrossed in your book, is it any good?"

"Actually, it is. It's a love story."

Spencer nodded and took off his t-shirt, slinging it onto a lounge chair on top of his towel. Josie picked her book back up but could only pretend to read. Spencer's body was a work of art, muscular and toned in all the right places. He had been voted the sexiest man alive by so many magazines she'd lost count. Her friends made sure to bring it up every time a new magazine issue came out declaring it. She watched him dive into the pool as he powered through the water. He came up, shaking the water out of his dark brown hair, and then he slicked it back and ran his hand over his face, clearing the water from it.

"It's cold. Why is the pool so cold," he asked?

"Sorry, I don't ever swim, so I don't have it turned up. I usually turn it up before you get here."

"Your dad would be proud, saving me money."

She laughed as she set her book down on the lounge chair. "Would you like me to turn it up?"

"Sure, if you don't mind."

She gave a little nod and got up and walked around the pool as Spencer watched her. She turned the heater all the way up in hopes it would warm quickly for him.

"It should warm up fast, I put it all of the way up," she said as she walked back to her chair.

"Thanks. I bought the biggest one they had when it was ordered. I hate swimming in cold water, that's why I never swim down on the beach. Well, that and my fans, I'd be mobbed."

"That's too bad, the swimming down there is great, but we can't swim at the beach right now anyway."

"Says who?"

"All of the beaches in the state are closed right now."

"Right, I forgot."

"I doubt anyone is actually policing this part of the beach. You could swim if you wanted to, I wouldn't tell anyone," he said with a wink.

She let out a small laugh. As a breeze blew off the beach, she reached for her cover-up and wrapped it around herself. The late afternoon sun was quickly turning to evening, which meant the temperature had begun to drop. She picked up her things as Spencer started to do laps and hadn't noticed her preparing to make her exit. She began to walk away to the pool house at the end of the property when she heard Spencer call out her name. She turned around and walked back to the edge of the pool as Spencer swam up.

"Would you have dinner with me tonight?" He asked as he folded his arms over onto the edge of the pool.

Josie hesitated; he'd never asked before. Sensing her indecision, he spoke up.

"I know it's long overdue, and since we are both here, it wouldn't hurt to get to know each other a little better. We can eat out on the balcony up there and keep our social distance and all of that jazz."

Against her better judgment, Josie agreed.

"Awesome, it would be nice to know you more. All I hear about is the great things your dad is always saying. I'd like to get to know the real Josie. How does 8 pm sound?"

"Sure, that would be nice. See you at 8," she said as she walked back to the pool house.

Once inside, she showered and changed into a pair of jeans and her favorite t-shirt. She stood in front of the mirror and decided the t-shirt wasn't right. She grabbed a silk blouse in a bright rust color and put that on. It popped against her bright green eyes and long brown hair. She put on minimal make-up, not wanting to look like she was trying to impress him. As she continued to ready herself for dinner, she thought about how odd the whole thing had been. Spencer had not really said more than ten words to her in the time she'd lived on the property. Normally Celeste, his assistant, was who she talked to. She also thought it was odd that he had not brought his entourage with him. Without his staff, she wondered who was cooking dinner, or if the kitchen had even been stocked sufficiently for the quarantine. No one had been on the property except herself. She took one last look at herself in the mirror, her reflection said casual, friend, confident. She grabbed a bottle of red wine that her dad had given her, it had been expensive, and she had been saving it for a special occasion. Dinner with Spencer would be that occasion. She had been taught never to go to a dinner empty-handed.

With the bottle tucked under her arm, she crossed the property, walking past the pool, and knocked on the glass door at the back. The last glimmer of daylight streaked across the sky, and she turned to admire it, as Spencer opened the door. She turned back around and greeted him. She took in the sight of him in his tight t-shirt and perfectly tailored jeans. He looked causal, too, like he had not tried to put any effort in, but she knew better. His designer clothes costed more than her first car.

"Ooo, this is a nice bottle. You didn't have to do this," he said, admiring the wine she had brought.

She walked through the house following him up to the second-floor balcony, that had the best view on the property. She had been through parts of the house before, but not all of it. He led her out to the balcony where the table had been set beautifully. A linen tablecloth had been put down along with candles and stemware. Josie wondered what sort of dinner Spencer had in mind. It all looked terribly romantic.

"Wow, this is beautiful," she said.

"I wish I could take the credit. After you said you'd have dinner with me, I called a few people. Maggie, my cook, is going to stay, and Howka, my security guy, will be here too. I can assure you we've all been strictly quarantining at my other house."

"Of course." She said, shrugging off his comment. He didn't have to explain to her who was in his house. "I was wondering who was cooking tonight."

"Are you suggesting I can't cook," he asked as he gestured for her to sit as he took his own seat across the table?

"Can you?"

He broke down, laughing, "not a damn thing, I can barely boil water."

She laughed at his expense.

Maggie brought out the starter, as they got to learn more about each other. Spencer seemed genuinely interested in Josie's studies. As the main course came, Spencer talked about his most recent film project that had been paused due to the virus. Halfway through dinner, they opened a second bottle of wine. Josie had expected to be impervious to Spencer's charms. He was just another human, she had always told herself, refusing to treat him differently because he was a celebrity. She wasn't sure if it was the wine, or the loneliness of the lockdown was starting to get to her, but she found herself enthralled with him. By the time dessert came, her head was swimming. She knew if she didn't leave soon, if he made a move, she'd spend the night in his bed and detest herself for it in the morning. She was not some starstruck fangirl who hopped into bed with any celebrity for her moment of fame.

As dinner ended, she excused herself before Spencer could make a move. When she stood, the world spun. She was drunk. She clenched onto the back of the chair for stability. He stood and reached across the table to help stabilize her. She looked at him, embarrassed at her own foolishness as he came around the table to help her.

"Sorry, the wine hit me all of a sudden," she said, terribly embarrassed.

"Let me walk you home," he said with a giggle in his voice.

"Alright."

Arm in arm, they walked back through the house and back past the pool. When she got to her door, she turned so she could see him.

"Thank you for dinner," she said as she heard her voice slur ever so slightly, "and for walking me home."

Spencer laughed.

"The pleasure was all mine. Let's do it again."

"All right, you know where to find me. Good night."

"Good night Josie."

She turned and walked into the pool house, closing the door behind her. She leaned up against the back of it, not believing what had just happened. She had just eaten dinner with Spencer Noah and had a great time. Perhaps he wasn't as pompous as she had previously thought. She kicked her sandals off by the door and froze when she heard Spencer scream, and a massive splash. She opened her door and saw him in the pool, fully clothed. Concerned, she walked out.

"Are you all right?" she called out.

"I fell in," he said, laughing, "it's nice and warm now, though, like bathwater."

She couldn't help but laugh as she bent down to touch the water. In one swift movement, he came up and pulled her into the pool fully clothed. She came up, coughing and laughing.

"I can't believe you did that!" she said a word at a time, laughing hysterically.

Playfully, she jumped up and brought her hands over his head and pushed him underwater.

"That's what you get!" she screamed.

"Oh, now, you're in for it," he shouted back playfully as he went after her.

The two of them rough-housed in the water, and as she brought her elbow back to splash him again, she hit it hard on the edge of the pool and cried out. Spencer closed the distance between them as she tried to look at her elbow.

"Here, let me see," he said, pulling her closer to the pool light.

She had torn her blouse, and there was a shallow cut. He down pressed around the cut.

"Does this hurt?"

"Yes, but I don't think I've broken it."

They bobbed in the water, the distance between them more than friendly. Without warning, Spencer leaned in and kissed her, brushing his tongue softly against her lips, as if he was testing the waters. She pulled away gently, licking the taste of him off her lips.

"What was that for?"

"A kiss to make it feel better."

She smiled and reached out, caressing the side of his face. Her inner voice screamed at her that it was time to go.

"I should go wash this cut out."

Spencer moved out of the way as he watched her get out of the pool.

"Sorry if I shouldn't have done that," he said.

"Good night, Spencer."

When she got back to the safety of the pool house, she stripped her wet clothes from her body and walked naked into the bathroom. The water from the swim and the pain from her elbow had pretty much sobered her up. She cleaned the cut and bandaged it. That night as she tried to sleep, she replayed the night over and over again in her head. Spencer Noah had kissed her. The thought aroused her, to the point

197

that she needed a release, after which she fell asleep.

The next morning, she opened the door to the pool house, to let the warm sunlight in as she always did. On the front step sat a vase of white calla lilies with a card tucked inside. She pulled the card out and opened it. It said:

Josie,

Thank you for dinner last night. I don't remember the last time I had so much fun! I hope your elbow is okay.

-Spencer

There was no mention of the kiss. She brought them inside and set them on her desk. She tided her house again, trying to keep some semblance of a routine. As the afternoon approached, the sunny skies turned grey, and it began to rain. She had wanted to go back out the pool, but the rest of the afternoon was forecasted to be a washout. Bored, she found the book she had been reading from the day before and plopped onto the couch with it. The covered porch allowed her to keep the French door, her front door open. She read, listening to the sound of the rain. She turned when she heard a knock at her front door. Spencer stood in the doorway, his shirt wet from the rain.

"Hi," she said, not getting up from the couch.

"Can I come in?"

"Of course, do you want a towel? You're soaked."

"Nah, I'm good. I see that you got the flowers."

He milled around, just inside the door. Josie wondered if he was nervous. He moved like he was, she thought to herself. Nervous of what, she didn't know. She wondered if he was shy around her, and she liked that thought.

"I did, thank you. They're beautiful," she said as she gestured over to the kitchen table where she had set them."

"It's been a while since I've been in here. I like what you've done with the place. It's comfortable, beachy."

"Thank you. Do you want a cup of tea? I was just getting ready to make one for myself."

"Sure."

He watched her get up and cross the open plan living area. She filled the kettle and set it on the range.

"I actually came by," he said, stepping into the kitchen, "to see if you were okay, your elbow and all."

"That's nice, it's fine, just sore."

"That's good. I was wondering, would you like to watch a movie or something? We could watch it in my home theatre in the house if you wanted."

"Sure."

"Great," he said, turning around to leave.

"Oh, you mean right now?"

"Sorry," sorry, he laughed nervously, "yeah, I'm bored out of my mind. I am normally all work, work, work. I don't know what to do with myself."

"We can watch a movie now if you want. I'm not really doing anything myself."

She turned off the kettle and grabbed her rain jacket by the door. She put it over her head, gesturing to him that she'd share it. Together they huddled under it as they ran between the houses. They made it inside, and she hung her jacket on the back of one of the bar stools. The ground level had a polished cement floor that wouldn't be damaged if it got wet. Spencer led her deeper into the first floor, a part of the house she had never been in. He opened the door to the home theater. Inside the room, a large grey couch sat, the largest couch she had ever seen, larger than two king-sized beds pushed together. She walked into the room and looked at the screen that had to be twenty feet tall. The entire room was totally over the top, but she was still excited to watch a movie in the room.

"What do you want to watch," he asked as he walked over to a wall where all of the equipment had been built in.

"You can pick," she said.

"An old movie or a new movie? I have the new Blythe Bently drama, rumor says she's going to win an Oscar for it."

"Oh, let's watch that. I heard it was really good, too. I had wanted to go see it, but it didn't go to the theater before the lockdown."

"Make yourself comfortable. Do you want some popcorn or movie candy? I have them all?"

"All of them?"

"Sure."

"Okay, sure, do you have Raisnettes?"

"I think so, do you want popcorn?"

"Yeah, thanks, do you need any help?"

"Nope, make yourself comfy." He said as the lights dimmed, and he walked out of the room.

She turned to the massive couch and climbed onto it. There wasn't a graceful way to do it as she crawled to the back of it and sat down. She was grateful Spencer had not been here to witness it, as she felt stupid crawling like an infant, but there was no other way to get to the back of the couch. Spencer returned a few minutes later as the movie began with an arm full of snacks. She couldn't help but laugh. She crawled back over to the edge, took some of the snacks, and crawled back on her knees. He followed her, setting the snacks down between them. The movie started as they dug into the treats. She was totally captivated by the film, but she couldn't help but notice the distance between her and Spencer seemed to be closing slowly. His hand brushed up against hers, and she looked at him as their skin made contact. He leaned in and kissed her, this time not as gently as the night before. This kiss was lustful. This time she kissed him back with more intention than the night before. Neither of them was watching the movie as they kissed. Her breath ragged as desire built, and a sense of eagerness smoldered deep within her. Kissing turned into fondling, and then before she knew it, she was naked underneath Spencer Noah. She had not intended to sleep with him.

The sex was fast and had not rung her bell. She looked over at him as he lay next to her, out of breath. She put her top back on and snuggled up next to him as they finished the movie. After the film ended and the lights came up, there was an awkwardness between them, like the room's darkness hid their indiscretion. Wanting to be free of the awkwardness, she lied and said she had a call with some classmates to free herself from the forced conversation.

Over the next two days, she did her best to avoid Spencer. She felt weird, knowing that they'd slept together. As much as she had not wanted to admit it, part of her wanted to know what he was like in bed. Now that she knew, she had not been impressed. She figured he either had not cared about her pleasure or he was lousy at sex. When her best friend Nancy called, it took everything in her not to tell her what had happened. She didn't say anything more out of self-protection for herself, she didn't know what Nancy would think of her, and heaven forbid if it ever made it into the press.

That night as she laid in bed trying to sleep, she heard a knock at her door. Spencer said he couldn't sleep, and she invited him in. Before she knew it, they ended up back in her bed. The sex was better this time around, and there wasn't a strange awkwardness between them afterward like last time.

Spencer began to spend most of his nights in her bed, or with her in his. Josie wasn't sure exactly what was happening between them. It felt like a relationship, but she had told herself how crazy that would be. They spent just about every waking minute together, and they had so much fun. Josie felt like it was a giant sleepover with a best friend.

One morning as she crawled out of Spencer's bed and crept back through the house before Maggie caught her, she paused at the door, turning the knob as quietly as she could. They had done their best to hide the fact that they were spending their nights in each other's arms. Josie and Spencer knew that if word got to her father, it would not be good.

"You shouldn't be doing this," a man's voice said.

She turned around to see Howka, Spencer's security guard, standing behind the bar with a glass of fresh juice in his hand. She walked up to the bar.

"Because my father wouldn't like it?"

"No, you're a grown woman. He's not a good guy, Josie."

"What do you know about it?"

"Quite a bit." He said as he came around the bar. "I've known your dad for a long time, I consider him a good friend. I wouldn't want my daughter anywhere near Spencer. You can do so much better, Josie."

"Thanks for the unsolicited advice, but as you said, I'm a grown woman. It's just a bit of fun, nothing else," she said as she turned to walk out.

"He'll hurt you." He called after her.

She stopped and turned around, closing the distance between them.

"How?"

"Honestly?"

She nodded deliberately.

"You're entertainment, something to pass the time."

"So is he, I didn't think we were getting married."

"Of course not, you're smarter than that, but I don't want to see you get hurt. Like I said, I'm watching out for you as your dad would watch out for my son."

"Thanks for the heads up."

That afternoon she wondered what Howka had meant. Hurt her how she had to know. Josie scoured the web for anything she could find on relationships with between Spencer and other women. There were a lot of them, but none of his exes accused him of anything untoward. She wished she'd asked Howka follow-up questions, but his stealth attack had knocked her off her game. She wasn't quite sure what the arrangement between her and Spencer was if she was perfectly honest. She thought it was sat somewhere in the friends with benefits in the range of relationships. By that evening, she'd thought the situation out to the point where it was just pulp.

For the next three weeks, life continued on between them. One night as she laid in his bed, snuggled up in post-coital bliss as they listened to the waves outside. He nuzzled up behind her and pulled her in closer to his body and ran his hands through her hair gently. It was a loving, affectionate act, and the tenderness was not lost on her.

"Josie, thank you for this," he whispered in the dark.

"For what?"

"This, between us."

She'd tried to keep her feeling in check, telling her that it was all just a bit of fun. She wasn't delusional to think their arrangement would last beyond quarantine.

"It's been a long time since I was with someone real, you know., someone who checks me on my bullshit and has fun with me for me, not my celebrity status. You've become like my best friend. I haven't had that in so long." She rolled over, still staying in his arms so she could see his face as he continued. "Everyone has this expectation of me to be this playboy. All I've wanted for a long time was a normal, regular woman."

She pulled away.

"No, I don't mean that in a bad way. Shit, I'm making a mess of this. All I am trying to say is that I like you a lot."

"I like you too."

She leaned up and kissed him, and he pulled her back in closer to his body, unsure of how she felt about his little speech.

"I think this may be the beginning of more than like," he continued.

"What does that mean?"

"I'd like to keep seeing you after the lockdown has ended. Some states are opening back up, and I know we will eventually. Life will change, our quiet little secret will be much more difficult to keep."

"Are you asking me to come out publicly as your girlfriend?"

"No, but if the press catches wind of this, your picture will be everywhere, paparazzi will hound you, and all I'm trying to say is that I really like you, and I am open to seeing where this thing between us continues to go. At the same time, I want to be very honest with you about the cost of that once our little bubble is shattered here. Not to mention what your father will do to me."

"I think my dad will be the least of our worries. Can I ask you a question? There's something that has been bothering me for a few weeks now, and I haven't wanted to say anything?"

"You can ask me anything."

"You have to promise not to say anything."

"Okay," he said skeptically.

"Howka did not have glowing things to say about you, relationships, and women. I'm not telling you this to make trouble, I am just wondering why he'd say that to me."

"Because it's true. I have a terrible track record with women. I can understand why he'd try to put you off."

"Terrible, how?"

"Honestly, I'm not great at commitment, I'm not proud of it. I tend to freak out and do something stupid and mess things up as things get serious."

"Well, that's not a ringing endorsement, combined with the press coverage, my dad, yikes."

He took a deep breath, "Josie, we can keep this right here, if you don't want to continue to see me. I get it."

The conversation had taken a very serious tone, and as she thought about her future goals and what life could look like with Spencer publicly. She panicked and rolled out of his arms, sitting up on the edge of the bed. He sat up too.

"What's wrong," he asked?"

"I'm sorry. With quarantine coming to an end, we should probably end this. I don't think I want what you've very honestly put forth, with the press and all. I appreciate the honesty, but I just can't. The publicity freaks me out. I'm sorry, I just don't want that."

She got up and walked out of his room, pulling her clothes on as I walked out, crossing the property into the pool house. She wondered if Spencer would follow her. As she showered, she felt a nagging feeling like she'd just done something awful to him. She tried to sleep, but her guilt tugged away at her, giving her a restless sleep. The next morning, she stayed in the guest house as she thought about what she really wanted. Howka's words, and Spencer's admittance to them, left her feeling relieved and confused further at the same time.

As the sun began to set, she walked down to the beach and sat. She'd missed the ability to do it, during the lockdown. The wind changed, and mist blew in with the crashing waves hitting the shore. Shivering from the cold, she walked back up to the pool house and stopped when she saw Spencer standing at the door.

"Hi," she called out.

He turned in her direction, and she thought he wore hurt on his face, and she wondered if she'd put it there.

"I just came by to say goodbye. I'm going back to my other house; I thought it might make things easier."

"Easier?"

"Josie, I respect what you said, and I appreciate your honesty, but these past few weeks have been incredible with you. I really like you, like really like you, you're the whole package. I know life with me wouldn't be easy, and in light of my admission that I'm not good with commitment, I can understand why you made the choice you did. I guess it's my turn to know what this feels like. It hurts."

She realized that he wasn't just upset that she read on his face. It was heartbreak. She reached out for his hand and squeezed it as she placed a soft kiss on his cheek. He squeezed her hand in return before he let go. She stood on the porch to the guest house and watched him walk away. As she heard his car start, she knew that this was the end of something. Once he left those gates at the front of the property, things would be different. She realized she didn't want different. She had loved her time in quarantine with Spencer. It had been like their own little slice of paradise. At this realization, she took off running towards the driveway. As she rounded the comer, she saw Spencer's little blue sports car pull out of the gates.

"Spencer, stop!"

She saw the brake lights as he stopped his car in the street. Paparazzi appeared from out of the bushes across from the driveway. She knew there was no turning back now, but she still kept running towards him. He got out of his car as she reached him. Without stopping, she flung herself into his arms, and he pulled her in close to him as the camera clicks started. She leaned up and kissed him, and the clicks turned into a frenzy.

She pulled away first and whispered into his ear, "come back home."

He looked down at her and kissed her again. This time there was a roar of hoots and hollers as they kissed in the street for the whole world to see.

Lisa & Harry: Cooking For His Heart

Lisa crimped the crust tightly on the edge of the cherry pie. Since the quarantine had started, she had cooked a lot. It had been a goal to learn how. She always told herself she would learn when she had a family to cook for. The only other living being in her condo was her old English sheepdog, Rufus, who was enjoying her cooking journey as much as she was. Lisa put the small pie into the oven and opened the lid on the large pot on the stove. She had found a recipe for white bean soup online and had made it for dinner. The condo smelled of the fresh bread she had baked on her lunch break to go with the soup. The scent of rosemary and garlic wafted from the pot as stirred the soup.

In week three of quarantine, she decided, rain or shine, she would eat Dinner on her patio. She lived on the third story, and her balcony was covered by the balcony above her. Two weeks had passed of dinners out on the balcony, and she now had it down to a science. She had even strung up white Christmas lights to lights in an attempt to make the space feel more intimate. It brought her outside each night, and she found it raised her spirits.

Lisa put the cheery yellow tablecloth on the small dinner table outside. She returned with a bowl and cutlery and set them out on the table. She finally put half of the soup in a tureen that she had impulsively bought after deciding to learn how to make soup during the quarantine. The last thing she brought out to the table after the soup was a few slices of the hearty, fresh bread. Lisa sat and spread the cloth napkin across her lap as Rufus let out a pathetic whine from inside the apartment. Lisa rolled her eyes before she stood up and let Rufus out onto the patio with her.

Sitting back down, she ladled a bowl of soup into her bowl. The steam came off the soup in swirls. Rufus whined again and then curled up next to her feet. Lisa tucked her feet under the dog to keep them warm; the evening was chillier than she had thought. She decided to reward Rufus for his warmth by a slice of the fresh bread when she was done with her Dinner. She took a bite of the creamy, hot soup as she watched the sun begin to set. Orange and magenta streaked across the sky, and the beauty of it cheered her.

As she sat and ate her soup, she noticed the light turn on inside the condo next to her. A few nights back, she noticed that someone had moved in. Each night she wondered if she would get a peek of her new neighbor, but they had yet to reveal themselves. She had kept to the strict stay at home order and only left her apartment to walk Rufus across the street to the park. Normally, she'd expect to run into her new neighbors at this point, but life was different now. As she ate, she thought she saw a shadow move in front of the window. Intrigued, she leaned forward to see if she could get a better glimpse.

Her long chestnut hair dangled in her bowl of soup. When she leaned back in her chair, defeated that she had not gotten a good look at her new neighbor, the soup splattered onto her blouse from her hair. She dipped her napkin into the water glass and dabbed at the soup spatter, grateful it was white. Rufus looked up at her. Taking pity on her dining partner, she broke one of the pieces of bread in half and put one half down for him. He sniffed the bread and then looked towards the neighbor's condo. Lisa watched his ears perk up before she heard the lock on the door of the neighbor's door to their balcony. Rufus stood as the door opened.

A man stepped out in a blue button-down shirt, his sleeves rolled up. Lisa couldn't help but stare. He was gorgeous with his sandy blonde hair and sharp jaw. He was well built, and Lisa licked her lips, not sure what was yummier the soup or the man standing on the balcony next to hers. Rufus stood and growled. The man turned at the noise of the dog.

"Sorry, I didn't see you out here tonight. I didn't mean to disturb you," the man said as he backed towards his door.

"You aren't disturbing me," she said as she turned to her dog, "Rufus, stop that."

The dog laid back down and sulked.

"Are you sure? I've tried to come out after you've finished your Dinner. I know these balconies are close together."

"You aren't bothering me at all." Lisa got up from the table and walked a little closer but still kept a safe distance. Rufus' head picked up as he watched her move closer. She reached out her hand to shake his and instantly withdrew it, remembering that was not a good idea during a pandemic.

"Oh, sorry, I forgot, no contact. I'm Lisa," she waved.

"Hi Lisa," he waved," My name is Harry. It's nice to meet you, neighbor."

"You too. Sorry, I didn't know you had been waiting for me to finish Dinner out here. I can go in and give you some space."

"No way. Please, finish, I barged in on your Dinner."

"We can both be out here. We are distanced far enough apart for health guidelines. I don't mind if you don't."

"Are you sure? The fresh air is nice after being inside all day."

"It is, isn't it?"

Harry leaned against the railing as he looked west towards the last sliver of daylight. The loss of the last of the sunlight turned the air chillier. Lisa pulled the blanket she had draped over the chair around her. Almost simultaneously, Harry cupped his hands and blew into them.

"It's cold tonight," Lisa said, unsure of whether to make conversation or not.

"It is. It's supposed to be in the 40's tonight. I am still getting used to the weather here. I'm from Alabama. We don't do cold like this where I'm from. I moved up here for work."

"Well, Indy is nice. It's normally warmer than this. Cold weather and a quarantine, welcome to town," Lisa joked.

Harry laughed, and Lisa felt it in her knees as heat waved through her. She didn't know how it was possible for him to be even more handsome, but his smile softened his masculine face. That smile, with his perfect teeth, almost took her breath away."

"I am going to guess you're a chef? The smells coming out of your condo always smell amazing."

Lisa laughed. "No way. I decided to learn how to cook during the quarantine. Prior to this, I could make scrambled eggs, and a few other things, but I wasn't very good at it." She laughed.

"Well, it always smells really nice."

"Oh my gosh, where are my manners? Would you like some? It's white bean soup; it turned out pretty good."

"No, I'm good," he said as he put his hands out to signal no.

"Are you sure; I have more than I can eat. I read that you're not supposed to reduce a recipe the first time you make it. So, I'll have bean soup for days."

Harry laughed, "Are you sure you don't mind?"

"Not at all, I'm happy to share. I'm not ill, and I haven't had contact with anyone else since quarantine started. You could always microwave it, just to be safe, though."

"I trust you."

"Let me run in and get a bowl," Lisa stood and walked in to get one before Harry could stop her. She returned a minute later with a bowl, spoon, and cloth napkin for him in her hand. As she stepped out onto the porch, she saw that Harry had brought out a chair and a t.v. table along with an indoor floor lamp. He came back out with a glass of white wine in his hand.

"Can I offer you a glass of wine to go with your soup," he offered?

Normally, she would have never accepted a glass of wine from a man she didn't know. It did sound nice with the wine, so she poured her water into the planter and set it back down onto the table as she dished him a bowl of soup. She set a piece of bread on the wide rim of the bowl and carried it along with the napkin, spoon, and her empty glass over. She held out the bowl, and he took it, setting it down on the small tray. He held up his finger and went inside to fetch the bottle of wine. He held it out for her to see, she nodded, and he poured her a glass of wine.

"Thank you. I was just thinking this Dinner needed wine," she said as she siped it on her way back to her seat.

As she sat, Harry raised his glass, and she raised hers. That night they talked over Dinner, and it dawned on Lisa that this felt more like a first date. She learned that he had moved to Indy for work as a financial manager for a manufacturing company. She also learned that he was single, had never been married, and had moved up three days before the quarantine had started. She shared that she had moved to Indy for work as well. She was originally from Chicago. She had lived in Indy for three years and had grown to really like the city. She was single as well. They moved on to talking about their hobbies and found they had a lot in common. They both liked to be active, play tennis and golf as well as read.

The timer for the cherry pie she had put in the oven before went off, interrupting their conversation. As she went inside, she couldn't believe how much she found herself liking Harry. She brought the small pie out onto the table on the balcony to cool.

"Is that a cherry pie," he asked?

"It is, I sure hope you'll have some. I can't promise it will be as good as the soup. I've never made it before."

"Dinner and dessert, this is a treat! Would you like another glass of wine? I'm going to get one for myself."

"Okay, as long as you don't mind sharing."

Harry refilled her glass, and they both had a slice of the warm cherry pie. It was delicious, the perfect balance of sweet and tart. They sat and talked long after dessert. It was now properly cold, but neither of them wanted to say goodnight. Lisa tried to hide that she was shivering, even with Rufus at her feet, and the blanket pulled around her, she was still cold. They talked well into the night, laughing and getting to know each other. As Rufus began to whine, Lisa took the hint that he needed to be walked again. She stood and began to clean up Dinner, sad that their night was coming to an end.

"If it's okay, I'll wash your bowl and spoon just to be on the safe side. I haven't had contact with anyone, but I'd hate to get you sick," he said.

"Okay. You know where I live to return it. I'm not worried about it," Lisa joked.

"Thank you again for a lovely dinner. It was a nice treat. I really enjoyed getting to know you. Thank you for sharing your Dinner with me."

"Well, thank you for joining me. I enjoyed having someone to dine with, and I'm glad I finally got to meet you."

"It was nice to have a conversation. I'll be honest I only know how to cook like three things, so I've pretty much been eating PB&J sandwiches, scrambled eggs, and cereal since this started."

"I always cook too much, so you're welcome to join me anytime."

"Thanks, that's a kind offer. I had a really nice time tonight. Good night Lisa."

"Night, Harry."

That night as Lisa lay in bed, she thought of Harry next door. She hadn't dated since her last boyfriend, and that had been almost eight months ago. She thought about how well she and Harry hit it off. She fell asleep wondering if he'd join her the next night.

As she walked past her patio doors the next morning with a cup of coffee in her hands, she noticed the bowl Harry had washed sitting on her table with a small bouquet of tulips sitting next to the bowl and a handwritten note. Lisa walked out onto the porch and set her mug down as she picked up the note.

It read:

Dear Lisa,

Thank you again for a delicious dinner. It was to meet you last night. I'd love to have dinner again sometime. The flowers are to say thank you. I picked them from the park across the street. (Shhhh, don't tell anyone). I would have bought some properly, but the shops aren't open.

–Harry

Lisa picked up the tulips, bowl, note, and coffee and brought them back inside. She put the tulips in water and thought about what to cook for Dinner that night. She finally decided on chicken skewers with a satay sauce and jasmine rice. The recipe seemed simple enough. All-day, she wondered if Harry would join her and found it difficult to focus on her work.

Around three in the afternoon, she slipped a note onto Harry's balcony. She put it on the tv tray he had left from the night before and put a small flower pot from her balcony on top of it so it wouldn't blow away.

It said:

Dear Harry,

Thank you for the beautiful tulips. I should let you know I work for the Indy parks department, just kidding. I won't tell anyone you picked the tulips from a public park. I am making chicken satay skewers with jasmine rice and veggies tonight. I'll have plenty if you'd like some.

-Lisa

That night as Lisa set the table on the porch, she noticed that note was gone. She turned on her Christmas lights as she heard Harry's door open. Rufus picked up his head and growled half-heartedly.

"Well, fancy meeting you here, at my new favorite Indian food restaurant," Harry joked.

Lisa laughed, "I see you got my note then. Would you like to join me? I have plenty of food."

"I'd love to, but at least let me pay you for it. Dinner two nights in a row…"

"Nope. It's my treat."

"I must contribute somehow, I don't want to take advantage. I know, how about I provide the alcohol. Wine? Beer?"

"Alright, your pick."

Harry returned with two bottles of beer and set one on the porch, railing for Lisa. She got up and retrieved it, leaving a helping of Dinner on the railing for him in return. She and Harry talked well past Dinner and into the early hours of the morning that night.

Each night of quarantine, they ate dinner together. They both counted down the hours until Dinner each night, and over time, they found waiting for Dinner was a stretch too far. They began to have lunch together too. Lisa fell in love with Harry over the meals she had learned to cook as she shared them with him. He had fallen equally for her. On the last night of quarantine, she finished dressing the salad and set it out on the table, where she found Harry already waiting for her. As she began to plate the food for both of them, Harry climbed over the railings of both balconies. It was the first time he had left his balcony. Both of them had wanted to, desperately, but they had stuck to the social distancing guidelines. Lisa turned to see Harry standing next to her. She sucked in her breath, surprised and excited at the same time. She handed him a plate of roasted chicken, wilted greens, and sautéed potatoes. He took the plate from her and set it down on the table, instead much preferring to hold her. He pulled her into his arms.

"I've been waiting what feels like a lifetime to do this," he said.

He leaned down and kissed Lisa, and she felt it through her whole body. She wrapped her arms around his neck, taking all of him in, the feel of his firm body, the smell of his cologne, the taste of his mouth. It felt like heaven.

Maggie, Greenly, & Abel: Three's a Crowd

Come stay with us," was how it had all started. If I could go back and change things, I would, but I can't. I've made such a mess of things. It all started with Maggie's offer. She and I worked together and watched in fear and apprehension as the global pandemic spread. I was new to the city and was still living in temporary accommodations. You know, one of those long-term hotel places. I had been house hunting and condo hunting when the pandemic changed from happening overseas to something happening here. The thought of living in a hotel scared me, and Maggie saw it. She was my boss, and ten years older than me.

Maggie and her husband Abel, lived on the north side of town, in an old Victorian house. Abel was a writer and worked from home. On a few occasions, I had met him in the six months I had worked for the manufacturing firm, but I didn't know him very well. Able had always kept to himself and seemed the quiet type. Maggie was his opposite, boisterous, outgoing, the life of the party that always seemed to follow her. She had made a generous offer for me to stay, as we sat at the bar across the street from the office one evening. There was a feeling in our office and across the country that something big was coming, and that lockdown was only a matter of time.

"Maggie, are you sure? We don't know how long this lockdown can be. Abel won't mind?"

She swallowed the last of her chardonnay, slamming the glass down on the bar, "It's my house. Besides, he hides in his office most of the time anyway, I doubt he'll even notice you're there."

"It's very generous."

She cut me off, "Nope, you're coming to stay with me. We scoured the country for you and your skillset. We aren't going to lose you now."

"I didn't say I was going anywhere."

The bartender put two more glasses of wine on the bar in front of us and leaned in, "From the two gentlemen across the bar."

Maggie raised her glass in their direction, and I gave a little wave. Maggie was a bigger drinker than I was, and I tried to keep up. She was my boss, after all. She took another large gulp of her wine as she began to dance in her chair at the bar to the music playing as the two men made their way over to us. We all got a table, and I learned that Luke was a loan officer from the local bank branch. He told me he had taken a lot of his cash out of the bank before the shit hit the fan, as he said. I tried to ignore Maggie and the other man in our impromptu party, as they tried to be discrete in fondling each other under the table. While Luke was nice enough, I had no intention of spending the night with him, so as our conversation waned, I made my excuses and left. I had just about reached my car when I heard Maggie call out my name. I turned to see her walking towards me, hand in hand with her date.

"Hey, come by tomorrow morning, around nine. I just got word; the office is officially closed. You can move in then. See ya."

Before I could respond, she and her date snuck off towards her car. I got in my own and wondered if her offer was an invitation or an order. I didn't feel like I had much choice in the matter. As I drove across town towards my hotel, I realized I had forgotten my purse back at the bar. I turned around and went back for it. Luckily Luke had given it to the bartender. Something caught my attention as I walked back to my car, a noise coming from the parking lot. I turned and saw Maggie's car rocking; a tangle of arms and legs were all that was visible from the steamy windows. I stood for a second, wanting to make sure that whatever was going on was consensual. It was hard to tell, and I wasn't sure what exactly was the protocol. I stood for a second longer, just wanting to make sure she wasn't in trouble. I turned to walk back to my car as I caught a glimpse of Maggie as she got on top of her date and began to ride him. I walked away before she spotted me, not that I thought she'd notice me.

The next morning, I packed up my few belongings and loaded up my car. I prayed she remembered our conversation out on the sidewalk in front of the bar from the night before. I wondered about her and the stranger in her car as well. In the two months, I had been with the company, I had heard rumors about her extra-marital activities, but I had left that information there. Maggie was my boss. On my way to her house, I picked up three large coffees and a box of bagels. It was a small way to say thank you for the room. I pulled up in front of the large Victorian house, painted in various shades of blue. The front porch wrapped protectively around the large curved front windows. Maggie's house did not match her personality, and I wondered if the house had been Abel's choice. I walked up the front porch steps, coffee and bagels in hand, and picked up the newspaper that had been left. I rang the bell as I jostled the contents of my arms, praying I would not spill the coffee. Abel came to the door.

"Good morning," I said, "I've brought breakfast."

"Good morning, it's Greenly, right from Maggie's office?"

"Yes."

"Please come in," he said as he moved out of the way to let me in.

I stood in the foyer as he came around me and led me to the dining room.

"I'm afraid Maggie isn't up yet. She had a late-night working. Are those for us?"

I set the box of bagels down and the coffees, praying that my face wouldn't give away Maggie's secret.

"Are you here to work?"

"Um."

I realized that Abel had no clue why I was standing in his dining room. I only prayed that Maggie had not been too wasted to remember her offer from the night before.

"Why don't I go get her?" He said.

I watched him walk out of the room. Normally he'd be my type, a little older, dark hair, brown eyes, a warm face. Abel's hair had thinned considerably on the top of his head, but he wore it well. It gave him a distinguished look. He was taller than me and had broad shoulders. Although he had not shaved, I could see his jawline, which complemented his full lips. I traced the plastic lid on my coffee cup anxiously as I looked up to the floor above me, where I heard raised voices. I hoped that it was not on my account. A minute later, Maggie shuffled into the dining room. She reeked of the bar form the night before.

"Hey," she said as she waved.

"Morning, I brought you coffee."

"Thank Christ," she said as she reached for the cup. She popped the lid off and took a drink of the hot coffee.

"Are you sure it's okay if I stay? I just wanted…"

She cut me off, "Yes. Second door on the left, at the top of the stairs, is yours. You have your own bathroom in that room."

"Thank you. I really appreciate it."

She nodded and walked out of the dining room with her coffee in her hand. She stopped at the foot of the stairs.

"Abel," she shouted, "Come help Greenly with her stuff."

I walked across the living room to where Maggie stood.

"No, there's no need, I don't have much. Really."

"Nah, he can get it, he just sits on his ass all day anyway. Come on, let's go get into those bagels you brought."

"I should help," I said as I watched Abel descend the stairs now dressed in a pair of jeans and a dark sweater.

"Nonsense. Come on," she said as she pushed me into the dining room.

I spent most of my first day getting settled in. There was a mood in the house that day, and I couldn't help but feel that I was the cause of it. Before dinner, I came out of my room. I had just finished a call with my mother, who was worried sick but was glad I was no longer in a hotel. I spotted Abel behind his desk. Our doorways were opposite each other. I knocked gently on the door frame, and he looked up.

"Ah, Greenly. Is everything okay with the room?"

I stepped into the office. The walls had been painted hunter green, and the built-in cherry bookcases and fireplace made the room feel welcoming. There was a large rug that matched a plush couch, and the lighting cast an intimate glow in the room. I imagined long winter nights curled up with a good book in front of the fireplace.

"I just wanted to thank you for your hospitality. It is very kind to let me stay."

"You're welcome," he said as he leaned back in his desk chair.

There was something in his voice that was missing. "You didn't know I was coming to stay, did you?"

"Maggie forgot to mention it."

"I'm sorry. If it's going to be an issue, I can go."

"No, it's not a problem. Besides, if you go, it will only make things crazier with her. It will be nice to have someone else around. I write most of the day, so you won't be bothering me."

"What do you write?"

"Mostly non-fiction. I am working on a book about the occupation of Poland during the war right now."

"That's interesting."

"I think so. It bores Maggie to tears."

I smiled, knowing he was right. There was no way that the topic would interest her.

That evening we all had dinner together in the dining room. Abel roasted a chicken, and it was delicious. I noticed that Maggie did very little to help with dinner. I enjoyed the dinner conversation as I got to know more about my hosts, and they got to know more about me. We talked about our educations, and Abel lit up when he heard I was a history minor in college. From there, the conversation took off between us. Maggie went and got a second bottle of wine. I kept trying to bring her into the conversation, but she didn't seem interested or cared.

Over the next few weeks, I observed Maggie and Abel. I could not understand how or why they were married. They shared very few common interests. What disturbed me most was how Maggie spoke to Able in the time that I had been there. She talked to him more as a servant than a spouse. This situation set me on edge, yet I didn't say anything. Maggie was my boss, and I was a guest in their home. Abel was smart, kind, and funny. I couldn't understand why Maggie treated him with such disdain.

On the morning of my thirtieth birthday, I was awoken by my mother calling to wish me a happy birthday. The weeks of quarantine had begun to grate on me, and I found myself longing for a place of my own. Maggie and Abel had been so kind as to allow me to stay, but I found that the quarantine had brought out a further iciness between the two of them. The more Abel seemed to try, the more Maggie pushed away, it was uncomfortable to witness. I quietly discussed the situation with my mother. She encouraged me to continue looking for a place of my own, stating that the end of a marriage is never pretty.

That evening Able cooked a delicious dinner, and we ate on their back patio. He had grilled steaks, and they had opened a bottle of champagne. I was touched by the kindness. I had not expected any sort of celebration. We sat and drank at the table, soaking up the warmth of the evening. As dusk turned into night, Maggie's phone buzzed. She looked down at it and then announced she was going to the liquor store for another bottle of champagne. Able and I both discouraged her, but she had made up her mind. She was not visibly intoxicated as she left. Abel volunteered to go instead, and Maggie declined. I could not shake the feeling that she was meeting someone.

Abel and I sat on the back deck, with the bistro lights above us twinkling. I ran my finger around the rim of my red wine glass.

"I hope it's okay, I got you a little something for your birthday," Abel said.

"You did?" I asked, completely surprised.

"Yes, but please don't mention it to Maggie, I wouldn't want her to get the wrong idea. I'll be right back."

I watched Abel walk into the house and come back out with a small wrapped gift in his hand. He handed it to me.

"Did you wrap this?"

"I did."

I was touched by how sweet it was. I tore away the paper carefully. He had gifted me the new Cline Fairfield book on the history of the Los Alamos project that we had been discussing over the past few weeks.

"Able, thank you so much. I really wanted to read this. This is such a thoughtful and unexpected gift."

"You're welcome. You'll have to let me borrow it when you're done with it. Do you want cake?"

"There's cake too? Shouldn't we wait for Maggie?"

"She's not coming back tonight."

I looked at him inquisitively. He took a seat across the table.

"I know what this all must look like, her and I."

I put my hand up, "it's none of my business."

Able stood up, "Cake?"

I nodded and watched him walk back into the house. Maggie had just decided she was done with the evening and had not even bothered to pick up her plate. The dismissive act made me angry for Abel. I picked up our plates and walked into the kitchen with them as Abel was walking out with the cake. Not expecting each other, we collided. The chocolate cake smashed into my chest, and the dirty dinner plates in my hand fell to the floor. I stood frozen as lumps of cake fell from my shirt.

"Greenly, I'm so sorry, I didn't see you."

"No, it's my fault. I've ruined the cake."

We both bent down to pick up the mess of cake and glass. I looked across at Abel, who looked up at me. He lent in and kissed me softly. I know that I should have been repulsed by the action, but I wasn't. I'd welcomed it. He pulled away.

"I'm sorry I should not have done that. Greenly, I'm so sorry."

I stood up with pieces of the broken plates in my hand and walked over to the kitchen's garbage can. Abel followed me with what was left of the cake in his hand. I turned on the faucet and ran it as the water warmed to wash the chocolate frosting off me.

"Greenly?" Abel said softly.

I turned to look at him.

"I'm sorry," he said as his deep brown eyes showed concern.

"Can I ask you something I have no right to ask?" I asked as I stopped wiping frosting from my blouse.

He nodded that I could.

"Why are you with Maggie?"

"I thought I could make her happy. I've been waiting for her to leave me. I know I love her more than she loves me, but I've held out hope that someday she'd be in love with me. I think if the pandemic put's things into perspective. If she isn't in love with me through all of this, she won't ever be."

"Abel, that is so sad."

"It is. I know she is out with another man right now."

"Do you still love her?"

"I'll always love her, just not like I once did. We had originally wanted the same things, a simple life, a family. Somewhere down the line, her wants changed. I tried to change with her, but it became clear that the change she wanted did not involve me. I didn't want to hurt her by leaving. Honestly, I don't even recognize the woman I fell in love with and married."

"Have you two tried talking this our, or counseling?"

"Both parties would have to want to fix it."

"Are you sure she doesn't?"

"Yes, she's told me so on several occasions."

"I'm sorry."

"Me too. I'm also sorry if I made you uncomfortable back there. I know I shouldn't say this, but I like you a lot. I feel like you have woken me up as a person. I've been on autopilot for so long. I have wanted to kiss you from the first moment I met you. I think you are the most beautiful woman I've ever seen. Then when you came here, and I got to know you, your intellect, and your kindness. Maggie and I don't... We haven't... It's been almost two years since we were last intimate."

"Two years?" I asked in amazement. "Abel, I know Maggie is my boss and has kindly invited me into your home, but you deserve so much better. You're talented and handsome, and genuinely kind."

Able lent in and kissed me again. This time I wrapped my arms around him and kissed him back. Again, I knew it was wrong, but I wanted to show him what it was like to be desired. He pulled me in closer to his body as he kissed me more strongly.

I pulled away and whispered into his ear, "Not here, let's go upstairs."

I led him upstairs by the hand as if I were having an out of body experience. I had never slept with a married man before and had always had serious issues with such actions. We came down on my bed and made love to each other. We laid in each other's arms afterward as I searched my own conscience for regret.

"You are so beautiful," Able whispered into my ear.

I rolled over, still in his arms.

"Thank you for tonight," he said.

"What about Maggie? Will you tell her about this?"

"No. Will you?"

"No."

Maggie came home in the wee hours of the morning. Abel and I had held me until I fell asleep and then had snuck back to his own bed. I showered the next morning again, trying to erase any trace of his scent from my body. Maggie made an excuse about a flat tire to explain her absence for the night. I saw the hurt on Abel's face as she spoke. It was slight and only visible for a moment until it passed. I did my best to avoid Abel for much of the day. I felt like Maggie could read the infidelity on me.

That night at dinner, we ate outside again. The weather was beautiful. Halfway through dinner Able got up from the table to get another bottle of wine. Maggie sat next to me at the table.

"So did you enjoy fucking my husband last night," she said nonchalantly once Abel was out of sight.

I almost choked on my bite of chicken.

"I really don't care, Greenly. If you want him, he's all yours."

I was absolutely speechless.

"I really didn't think you had it in you. Honestly, sweetie, you can do so much better than boring old Abel. Go get a fun guy, not that geriatric boring old fuck."

Before I could respond, not that I even had the words to do so, Abel walked back out with an open bottle of chardonnay in his hand. Looking at my face, he instantly knew something was wrong.

"What's wrong," he asked?

"Oh, I was just telling Greenly she could fuck you; it makes no difference to me." Abel set the bottle down on the table as Maggie continued. "I really don't care. I didn't think either of you had it in you, though. You want to fuck some thirty-year-old slut, go for it. That has to be some of the most vanilla lamest-ass sex I can think of."

I stood up and quietly pushed my chair in.

"Maggie, you have no right to talk to her like that."

I walked towards the house.

"Greenly, come back," Maggie called out jeeringly.

By the time I made it up to my room, my body was trembling. I could hear Maggie and Abel shouting at each other as I packed my bags. I packed as quickly as I could, tossing everything into my bag, not taking any care what went where. I was almost finished as I heard Maggie come into the house shouting. I started for the door and froze when I heard glass breaking in the kitchen below.

"Leave her alone," Abel screamed at Maggie. "Or so help me God, I will leave you penniless. If you wanted out so badly, you should have just been a fucking grown up and left me a long time ago."

"Who would want you, you old worthless piece of shit. You are a terrible husband, lousy in bed, and boring! Greenly, he's all yours!"

A nervous knot churned in my stomach as I sat trapped in my room. They were fighting at the base of the stairs in front of the front door, my only exit. I heard the front door slam, and Maggie's car peel away down the street. I stood frozen in my room, my bags in my hand, unable to move. I listened as Abel's footsteps ascended the stairs and stopped outside my door. He knocked gently.

"Greenly, can I come in?"

I stood there, silent. He knocked again and called my name before he opened the door. I had not realized it at the time, but I had begun to cry.

"I'm so sorry," I said repeatedly.

Abel walked into the room.

"This was not your fault," he said as he put his arms around me.

I pushed out of his arms and walked out of the house. Knowing I no longer had a job, I got in my car and drove towards my parents' home, sleeping in my car along the way. I was homeless and jobless. It took me two days to get back to their house in the middle of the country. Able called me repeatedly, but I didn't know what to say to him. Maggie called too, shouting at me that I was fired, but I knew that was coming. After I got to my parent's house, I texted Abel that I was safe and turned off my phone. I finished quarantine with them.

As parts of the country started to re-open, I began to look for a new job and started to put my life back together. I thought about Abel a lot, wondering if we had met under different circumstances if we would have been able to be a couple. Despite the dysfunctional circumstances, there had been a genuine connection. I spent a lot of time alone, trying to make sense of what had happened. One morning as my mother and I returned from the grocery store, she spotted a man on the porch.

"Who's that," she asked as we rounded the corner to our block.

"Abel?" I called out

He turned around, with a bouquet of flowers in his hand. My mother squeezed my hand as she took the grocery bags I was carrying and walked around to the back door.

"I have been looking for you everywhere." He said as he walked off of the porch towards me.

"What are you doing here?" I said in disbelief that he was standing in front of me.

"I came to ask you out on a proper date, that is, if you'd like to see me again?"

"You came halfway across the country to ask me out?"

"Yes."

"Why?"

"Because I knew from the first time I met, you would be someone important in my life. I've been lost and so worried about you. I know this sounds crazy, but I haven't been able to stop thinking about you. I want to be with you so bad it hurts. You've been the missing piece in my life, I just didn't know it until I found you."

I looked deep into his eyes, and at that moment, I realized it was what I wanted to. I wanted him in my life. I leaned up and kissed him, knowing that this was the beginning of something big.

Cooper & Anna: A Homeless Tale

I noticed her old, maroon Buick parked at the end of my street. It was a late 90's model but was in remarkably good condition. I noticed the car first because I didn't see many of them left on the road. I drove the same model in high school, except mine was white. I passed by the car on my way to work and back for two days. I kept odd hours as an ICU nurse at University hospital on the West end of town. At first, I thought that someone was visiting one of my neighbors. Until the night I met Anna.

The global pandemic had finally reached our corner of the world, and things were just starting to kick off. I knew that my time laying in my bed for a full eight hours were abruptly coming to an end. As much as I wanted to soak it all in, that glorious sleep, I was restless in my bed. I finally dozed off, and in my half-sleep trance, I thought I heard the spigot on the side of the house turn on. I opened my eyes, staring out into the darkness as I listened for the noise. It was the spigot outside. It was under my bedroom window. I got up silently and walked over to the window as I heard it shut off. I looked out to see a thin woman with shoulder-length hair walk quickly back to the red Buick. She put a jug of water in the trunk and shut it quietly. I watched her climb into the back seat of the car and close the door behind her. Intrigued, I continued to watch her. She looked like she was talking to someone, as the moonlight outside gave just enough light to show her movements in the vehicle.

The next morning, I drove past the Buick and slowed to see inside. The sun had yet to come up, so I wasn't able to see much. Throughout the day, I thought about the woman in the car. Clearly, she was living out of it, but how had my neighbors not noticed. That evening when I came back, I drove slowly past the car but did not notice the woman. I pulled into my driveway and walked out to the mailbox to get my mail. I sorted through it at the box, mostly junk, as I took one last look before I went inside. That night, exhausted from a busy shift, I fell asleep quickly and was woken by the sound of my spigot being turned on again. This time I crept out of bed silently and walked back over to my bedroom window as I watched the woman fill an empty milk jug. She looked out in either direction to see if she was being watched, but ironically, she did not look up, or she would've spotted me. She turned off the spigot and placed the milk jug of water in her trunk liked the night before. I watched her as she walked to the back door of the car. She reached in and pulled out a baby, who looked to be about a year old. The baby wrapped its arms around its mother as she rubbed the baby's back. The child rested its head on the woman's shoulder as she swayed in the street. It looked like she was singing to the baby. I tried to listen for her voice, but I couldn't hear it from where I was. There was something so beautiful, watching the woman sing to the baby. I watched her put the child back into the back seat of the car and shut the door softly. The woman leaned up against the car and buried her head in her hands. I saw her shoulders hitch. She was crying. The plates on the Buick were from Indiana, thousands of miles away.

I put on a pair of pajama pants and a t-shirt and walked outside; I spotted the woman as she was climbing into the back seat of the Buick.

"Excuse me," I said loudly to get her attention but not loud enough to wake my neighbors.

The woman laid flat in the car, so I could not see her. I walked over to the Buick and knocked gently on the back window. I spotted the whites of her eyes first, as her full face came into the lamplight of the streetlamp. She looked scared.

"Can I talk to you?" I asked?

She climbed out of the other car from the other side, over a car-seat where the baby slept. She got out and stood with the car between us. She paused for a second and looked squarely at me before she reached for the driver's side door to get in and flee.

"No, wait," I coaxed. "I live in the house with the spigot, I'm not angry."

"I'm sorry for stealing your water. I've only taken three jugs full; I'll repay you, I promise."

"I'm not worried about the water. Are you living out of this car?"

"I should go," she said as she pulled the door open and the interior light came on.

The light illuminated the inside of the car, which was very full but tidy. The light roused the baby in the car seat behind the driver's seat, and the child woke fully and began to cry.

"No, wait, I have a room," I blurted out.

I wasn't sure where that came from. I did have a spare room, but the woman standing in front of me was a complete stranger. The whole world was turned upside down, and deep down, I knew that this woman and her baby couldn't ride out a global pandemic in a Buick. She paused again and looked at me.

"Look, buddy, I don't know what you're into, but I'm not that kind of woman."

"No, of course not. I wasn't insinuating. I just want to help. I'm a nurse at University Hospital, I'm offering you a room to stay, for you and your baby."

"You're a nurse?"

"We're in the middle of a global pandemic, you can't ride it out in your car. The room is free to you and your baby if you'd like, no strings attached. The only rule is no drugs."

"I'm not a drug user. Can you please look at my daughter? She's been running a fever all night. I'm terrified. She's never been sick before. I would've taken her to the hospital, but with everything going on, I wasn't sure if that was a good idea, I didn't want her to catch the virus."

"Sure, let me get my stethoscope from my truck. Do you want to bring her into the house?"

The woman stared at me and then nodded, judging if I was the sort that would hurt her or her daughter. I turned around and walked towards my truck as I heard the baby begin to wail, and her mother begin to hush her gently. I grabbed my stethoscope from the front seat of my truck and walked inside, leaving the side door open that led into the kitchen. The woman knocked and stepped inside as she spotted me. Her movement gave away her nervousness, and I knew she had to be desperate to ask me for help. In the light, I could see how frail the mother looked. Her clothes made her look heavier than she was, as the gaunt look in her face told another story. The baby, on the other hand, was plump, and both of them looked clean.

"Let's take a look at you, little one," I said as I moved closer.

"Please don't call the police. I'll move on as long as she's okay. I'm sorry again about the water."

"I won't call the police. You said she had a fever?"

The woman nodded, "101 the last time I checked. She was very fussy today, and that's not like her. She wouldn't nurse today either."

I blew on the end of my stethoscope to warm it as I placed it on the back of the thin cotton pajama set the baby was wearing. I could feel the heat radiating from the baby as I listened to her lungs. I took a deep breath, relieved that they sounded clear. I touched the baby's forehead, surprised at how warm she was.

"I gave her some baby Tylenol two hours ago, but it doesn't seem to be helping."

"Why don't we try a Luke-warm bath?"

The mother eyed me nervously.

"It will help bring the fever down quickly. My sister has three kids, and I've done lots of fever duty with them. It will help her."

The baby wailed and bucked backward in her mother's arms. She pulled the baby back in close as the child began to fight in her mother's arms. The mother nodded, and I led them towards the bathroom, internally telling myself how nuts this was that I'd let a complete stranger into my home. I stood outside of the bathroom door and gestured for them to go in, but did not follow them in.

"I'll give you some privacy. There are towels in the cupboard there."

"Please don't call the police. She's never been sick like this before."

"I promise you I won't," I said as I stood outside of the doorway.

"This is a mistake, I shouldn't have come in. Thank you, we'll go," she said as she walked back towards me.

"Look, I will sit right here, where you can see me. I'll stay here the whole time you bathe her. I just want to help. I can tell you're a good mom. She looks well-fed."

We both stood there as the baby put her fingers in her mouth and began to suck on them.

The woman slowly walked back towards the bath and sat on the edge and turned on the water. I sat against the wall opposite the doorway to the bathroom with my hands on my knees so she could see me clearly. I would have preferred to give them privacy, but I understood the mother's hesitation.

I watched as she undressed the baby tenderly.

"You're going to like this, Georgie," she said as she swirled her hand in the water to test it.

She placed the infant in the few inches of water. The baby cried out and reached for her mother. The woman got down on her knees next to the tub to comfort her daughter. The baby stood and reached for her mother as she cried hysterically.

"It's okay, sweetie, it's a bath. Look," she said as she patted her hand on the water. The baby wailed harder.

I got up and took a step into the bathroom and handed the mother a washcloth.

"Here, she might like this," I said before retreating back to my spot in the hallway.

The mother wetted it and handed it to the baby.

"Look, Georgie," she said in a funny voice as she made a puppet with the washcloth.

The baby quieted only, slightly, as her mother made the washrag talk in a funny voice. The baby looked confused and then amused as the washrag continued to talk. The baby began to babble at the washrag, as the mother slowly began to wash and entertain her daughter with it. She encouraged the baby to sit, and that proved too much for the infant who defiantly rose and reached for her mother again. Moving quickly, the mother made the puppet make a funny noise, and the baby giggled.

"Do you want me to grab her diaper bag from your car?" I asked.

231

"Um," I could see her thinking out the logistics.

"I'm not rushing you. I just meant for when she is done."

"Thank you. It's on the back seat, on the passenger's side, the pink bag."

I got up, and I could see that scared look in her eye. I walked into my bedroom and grabbed my cell phone. I stepped into the bathroom and set it on the edge of the sink as both of them watched me.

"That is my only phone. I just didn't want to make you nervous or think I was calling the police," I said before walking out to retrieve the bag from the car.

I stepped out into the humid night air as my inner voice told me that this whole thing was nuts. There was something about the way she cared for her daughter that put me at ease. I opened the car door and spotted the pink bag. It looked expensive. I took a cursory glance around the car, and it was very clean, and the items inside looked well cared for. Whoever the woman in my house was, it was clear that she was not the sort that would normally be living out of her car.

I walked back into the house and back towards the bathroom. The baby was out of the tub and was wrapped in a towel as her mother nursed her. They sat on the edge of the tub, and I tried not to linger as she rubbed the top of the baby's head lovingly. I set the bag down and walked back out. I glanced at the clock on the microwave. It was past 2 am. I knew I'd pay for it the next day, but I didn't feel tired. I sat at the kitchen table and waited for them to emerge.

She came out with the baby in her arms sound asleep, and the bag slung over her shoulder.

"Thank you, Sir. Her fever is gone, the bath worked. I think maybe she has another tooth coming in. This whole thing has not been her usual. I left your phone in the bathroom, where you put it. I didn't touch it."

"Would you like to stay, at least for tonight? I have a spare bedroom; you both are welcome to it. You know if she needs the tub again, or if you'd like to use it, you're both welcome to it and the room."

"I didn't get your name."

"Sorry, I'm Cooper Harish."

"Thank you for your kindness, Cooper. I'm truly grateful. I'm Anna, and this is Georgia, Georgie, for short. We should go, thank you again."

She walked towards the door as I stood up.

"Anna, please take the room. You can't ride out a pandemic in your car. Look, I know you don't know me, but I promise I won't hurt either of you. Please just stay tonight?"

She stopped and turned around and looked at me. I could tell that she wanted to stay but was afraid.

"Stay for her, you can keep my phone with you if you want?"

"Just for tonight, I'm afraid the fever might come back."

"Come on, I'll show you where it is."

I walked out of the kitchen back down the hall, as heard her soft footsteps behind me. I stopped in the doorway again. It sat across from mine and next to the bathroom. I switched on the overhead light. There was a twin bed and a small dresser that was empty, a nightstand, and a lamp. None of the furniture matched, but the room was clean. Anna walked in and put Georgie on the bed. She caressed the child's head as she looked own lovingly at her daughter.

"Thank you, Cooper, for tonight."

"You're welcome. I have to leave for work by 6. You both are welcome to stay. I have plenty of room, and I work twelve-hour shifts, so you pretty much will have the place to yourself tomorrow."

She nodded, and I could see tears behind her deep blue eyes. I took that as my sign to leave and shut the door quietly behind me as I walked out back into the kitchen. My stomach rumbled, and I grabbed a granola bar and walked back towards my own bed when I realized that perhaps Anna was hungry. She was so thin. I walked back towards the kitchen and made a peanut butter sandwich for her. I knocked gently on her door, and I heard her get up. She cracked the door, and out of the corner of my eye, I could see she had made a bed for herself on the floor and had given Georgie the bed.

"I thought you might be hungry. I was having a snack, so I made one for you if you'd like?"

"Thank you," she whispered as she glanced back at Georgie, who slept peacefully.

I handed her the plate with the sandwich and a bottle of water.

"If you're still hungry, please help yourself to anything in the kitchen. I mean it."

She took the plate and water bottle from me as I turned and walked towards my own bedroom. She stepped out into the hallway.

"Why are you so nice to me?" She said quietly.

I turned around and looked at her. "It isn't hard to be nice."

"It is for some."

"Not me. Good night Anna."

The next morning, I woke, feeling like I had been hit by a truck. My body ached, and I shivered under my blankets. I was sick. I remembered the baby from last night and wondered if I had caught the virus going around from her. Although the medical part of my brain knew that wasn't possible. I knew the symptoms would take a few days to show. I also knew I couldn't go into work sick.

I looked for my phone and remembered I had left it with Anna. I needed to call work to let them know I was ill. I heard a soft knock on my bedroom door, and I sat upright, causing my head spin. I wondered how I was so sick so quickly. The knock came again, and I heard Anna call my name through the door.

"Come in," I croaked.

She cracked the door.

"I just wanted to say thank you and goodbye. We're going to be going. I left your phone in the kitchen."

I cradled my head in my hands as the dizziness turned into a sharp ache. I heard the door creak as she opened it further. I looked up to see that she had showered. Her dark brown hair was still damp and rested softly on her shoulders. Her blue eyes sparkled in the sunlight streaming into my room.

"Cooper, are you okay? You look awful. I'm sorry, I mean, you don't look like you are well."

"Sorry, I woke up with a bug, I think. You don't have to go; you and your daughter can stay as long as you'd like."

"Thank you, I appreciate that. I truly do. I'll never forget your kindness."

I went to step out of bed as the room began to spin again. I grabbed onto the metal footboard for stability. Anna came across the room to help me.

"You need to get back in bed, you're not well." She said as she grabbed onto me. She was close enough to really see her face. She was stunning. "I need to get my phone to call work. I was supposed to be

234

in at 6. Do you know what time it is?"

"It's almost 10 am."

I walked away from the bed to get my phone from the kitchen. I was so late and had not called off. I took two steps before the world went black.

I woke up tucked safely into my bed. The sunlight had shifted, and by the light of the room, I knew it was late afternoon. I sat up again, and the same dizzy feeling came. I looked over on the nightstand and saw a glass of water and my phone. I knew Anna had left it. I had hoped she had not left too. I picked up my phone and saw three missed calls from work. I called them back to let them know I was out sick. Concerned, my nurse supervisor asked me to track my symptoms carefully. As I hung up the phone, I heard a soft knock on my door and saw it open as Anna looked in.

"You're awake," she said softly. "How are you feeling?"

"You're still here."

"Sorry, I didn't want to leave, with you being so ill. You passed out," she said as she took a few steps into the room. "I just wanted to make sure you're okay. I can go now."

"No, I didn't mean it like that. How did I get back into bed?"

"I put you there."

"How? I'm twice your size."

"I'm stronger than I look. You should have some more fever reducer. I also made you some chicken soup."

"Wait, I'm so confused. When did I have fever reducer?"

"After I got you into bed, you were lucid enough to take some. I asked you if you wanted me to call an ambulance, and you said no."

She walked closer to the bed, and I held my hand out to stop her. "No, don't come any closer. I might have the virus."

She stopped walking towards me and nodded in agreement. "Well, if you do, I do too at this point. You helped me yesterday when Georgie was sick. I am not afraid to help you in return. Now, fever reducer and some soup."

She walked over and opened the bottle shaking out two tablets into her delicate hand. She held them out to me and the glass of water. I was speechless. I knew she was right, but it was still an incredible act of bravery. As I swallowed the tablets, she took the glass from me and propped the pillows behind me to sit up. I watched her walk out, and she returned with a bowl of chicken soup. I looked at the soft yellow color of the broth and realized she had cooked it from scratch.

Over the next ten days, Anna nursed me back to health. She kept me hydrated, fed, and looked after me better than I looked after my own patients, and I was a damn good nurse. On the eighth day of my illness, I noticed Anna started to look unwell. She came down with the virus two days later.

I looked after her as diligently as she had looked after me. As sick as we both were, we got to know each other. I helped look after her daughter Georgie, who was adorable, bubbly, and so sweet. After a full three weeks, both Anna and I were finally both well. I had fallen for her hard, and I knew I wanted to spend the rest of my life with them both, as a dad to Georgie, and a husband to Anna.

Anna ended up staying for a few months as the virus raged. In the meantime, she made plans to get back on her feet once it was safe for her to venture out and set up a life out on her own. One night as we were having a cookout in the back yard, we watched Georgie toddle in the grass. Georgie had begun to walk, and when she took her first full steps, it had been me she had walked to.

"Anna, I want to ask you something," I said as I put my hand over hers.

She looked over at me, her blue eyes sparkled, and her face had filled out, and she had gained some weight. She no longer looked malnourished.

"I want you to stay."

"I'm going to stay tonight, Coop." She said as she smiled.

"No, forever. I want you and Georgie to stay forever."

The smile faded from her face.

"What are you asking me, Cooper?"

"I am asking you both to stay. You and I have been through hell and back over these past few weeks. I'd say I've gotten to know you very well. You mean a lot to me, Anna, please stay, please continue to be a part of my life, for always."

I saw the tears in her eyes, and I moved closer to comfort her.

"Cooper, my last relationship, I had to flee with my baby. I…"

"Anna, I will never hurt you or Georgie. You two have become my whole world."

I wiped a tear from her cheek.

"Cooper, you've never even kissed me."

I softly pulled her lips to mine and caressed them gently with my tongue. I felt the tension in her body ease. Her kiss deepened, and the world fell away. I knew in that movement I was kissing my soulmate. She pulled away first as she nodded yes.

"Yes," she said softly.

"Yes, to what?"

"To forever."

I pulled her into my arms and truly kissed her. That moment was the beginning of forever. While the pandemic was catastrophic, it had brought me my soulmate. We married three months later. It seemed within weeks of tying the knot, we found out Georgie was going to have a sibling.

Georgia & Tom: A Tale of Forgiveness

I felt the landing gear dislodge from the bottom of the plane for landing. This was a mistake, what the hell was I doing. I promised I would not come back. The day I walked out, it was for good, forever. Now I was getting ready to see my husband and my three kids, who I had not seen in almost three years. I was toxic, a bad person. I had walked out of my life one day without warning. Good people didn't do that.

I looked out the window and spotted the skyline of Chicago. We'd be on the ground in a few short minutes. I would have never even considered coming back, but the worry in Tom's voice scared me. I loved Tom, and I loved our children. He had been the model husband, sexy, a good provider, sociable, a great dad. He did not deserve what I had done to him, none of them did.

We were the model couple with three beautiful children, Megan, Matthew, and Louis. I had wanted each of them. I had a comfortable life full of playdates, PTA meetings, coffee dates, and book clubs. My social calendar was packed with other women who had once been working professionals like myself but had come home as families grew and the realization that the nanny was raising their kids came into focus. I quit my job, willingly after Matthew was born, I had two kids under three, and I felt like I was missing too much. Two years later, Louis came along unexpectedly, but Tom and I were still thrilled.

Louis was not like Megan and Matthew, who had been happy, easy babies. Louis had colic and cried constantly. I didn't know it at the time, but I was suffering from postpartum depression. The morning I left, I dropped my older two children at school and drove Louis to my best friend's house, Elaine's. I asked her to watch Louis because I had a doctor's appointment, I lied. Elaine, always a great friend, was just relieved I was seeing a doctor, she said as she took the diaper bag off my shoulder. Everyone had become worried about my mental state after Louis was born. I kissed my baby and told Elaine there was extra breast milk in my freezer if she needed it, then I walked out. I got into my black BMW SUV and headed west, away from my life.

My heart was in my throat as I crossed Illinois. By the time I reached the Mississippi River, terror radiated through me. I pulled over at a lookout point, stopping on the Iowa side. I knew if I stopped on the Illinois side, I would turn around go home. I got out of my SUV; the early fall air was chilly. I looked down at my cellphone in my hand that trembled, and I chucked it as hard as I could into the river. With the gravity of what I was doing, sinking in, like my phone in the river, I continued to drive west. I stopped in Des Moines and pulled money out of my private account. It would be enough to start a new life. I had always kept this account for this reason, not that I ever thought I'd run out on my husband and kids.

The next night as I stopped at a small roadside hotel in Nevada, I picked up the phone. The last thing I wanted was anyone to suspect foul play. Elaine picked up my house line, the fear in her voice hurt. Tom grabbed the phone from her and pleaded with me to come home. I hated how scared the people in my life were, and that I was the cause of it. I told Tom I wanted a divorce on that phone call.

I eventually made it to California. I took a job at a farmstead, doing their marketing for them and set up a new life, but I couldn't hold the job. My life was a mess. Tom spoke to me several times, begging me to come home. When that didn't work, he flew out to California. I never met him at the airport. After that, things between us changed, not that I could blame him. I ended up seeing a therapist and was diagnosed with severe postpartum depression. In the meantime, I divorced Tom and gave him full custody. What judge would give me rights to see my kids after I had walked out? I was an unfit mother, and I knew it.

My memory jogged back to the present as I pulled up to my house, on the Northshore. It had been a full three years since I had left. Nothing had changed, except for the car in the driveway, a new Volvo. Tom had called two days earlier and asked me to come to stay as the pandemic took its hold on the U.S. I reluctantly agreed. The cab came to a stop at the curb, and the bile in my stomach rose up into my throat as I got out. I grabbed my bag from the trunk and paid the cab driver. I turned towards the door to see Tom standing in the open doorway.

I stepped up onto the brick walkway that led to the front door. It had been so charming when we bought the house.

"Thank you for coming, Georgia," Tom said as he reached out to hug me.

I took a step backward. Tom touching me was something I had not been ready for.

"Sorry," he said, "Can I take your bag?"

"No, I'm sorry. It's a lot, being back here. This was a mistake; I shouldn't have come."

Tom stepped out onto the front patio step. "Georgia, I am so grateful you came. Please stay. I know how difficult this must be for you for all of us, but we want you here. Our children want you here, please."

I could hear my therapist's voice, in my head, you are a good mother, Georgia. You love your children, and you left because you thought you needed to protect them. I gave a little nod, and Tom's face softened as I stepped forward. He reached his hand out for my bag, and I let him take it off my shoulder. I followed him into what had been our home. Nothing had changed. It was still pretty much as I had left it, just cleaner. He set my bag on the bench in the entryway.

"Doing okay?" His voice was tender.

I nodded.

"They've been waiting all day to see you. Are you ready?" He held his hand out, and I grabbed it as my body trembled.

Together we walked into the living room where Megan sat with her phone, and Matthew was playing a racing video game, Louis was

241

eating a bowl of goldfish crackers. They had changed so much.

"Guys," Tom said gently.

Megan noticed me first and leaped from the couch. She slammed into me as we both began to cry. She was so big. Matthew got up and from his game and came over and hugged me too. I held my sweet babies, and it wasn't until I held them in my arms that the reality of how much I had truly missed them slammed into me. Tom scooped up Louis and brought him over. I wiped the tears from my eyes as I looked at the baby I had left. He was a toddler, the most beautiful little boy I had ever seen.

"Mommy?"

"Yep, buddy, that's mommy," Tom said.

The little boy reached out for me, and I took him into my arms. He still smelled the same as he had when he was a baby. I sobbed with him in my arms.

That night we had dinner together, and the kids told me all about their lives, what they did for fun, and showed me their rooms. I sat in my own room, the guest room that had been decorated to my mother-in-law's exact specifications. It had to be perfect for their annual visit. I sat on the edge of the bed, not sure how to come to terms with the fact that I had not allowed myself to truly feel the love I had for my own children for so long. There was no way to make up for what I had done to them.

I woke in the night my sheets soaked in sweat. I had learned that my body gave signs of distress when I was highly stressed. My therapist had worked with me to notice them, night-sweats were one of them. I got up and showered in the en-suite bathroom. My hands still shook, despite being fully awake and showered. I redressed in new pajamas. I stared up at the ceiling as the tree outside my window cast a shadow across it. My head turned towards the door as I heard a soft knock. The door opened, and Tom peeked in.

"Are you all right? I heard the shower?"

I sat up in bed.

"Come in."

He stepped into the bedroom, and I patted the top of the covers next to me. I wasn't inviting him in for sex. I wouldn't do that to him, hurt and confuse him. He came and sat on the other side of the bed and stayed on top of the covers. I turned to see him, only the moonlight showed his features.

"Tom, they're incredible. You've done such a good job with them."

"They are. Half of that is you, too, you know?"

"Will they be okay? I mean, with me coming back for this virus? I don't want to confuse them."

"They'll be okay if we're okay. Please know you can talk to me. I am here if you need me."

Over the next few weeks, the virus worsened, and the kid's school closed. As time went on, I began to take on more responsibilities with the kids and Tom's work transition to home. We began to settle into a routine, but I was still hesitant to fully commit. I was terrified of hurting everyone I loved again. Megan and Louis climbed into bed with me each night, and I never put them out. They were so beautiful, I often laid awake unable to take my eyes off of their little faces.

Matthew turned out to be a little more skittish than his siblings, not that I could blame him. It took him a while to warm up to me.

Tom came in one morning while the kids were eating breakfast. I had planned a trip to a local strawberry farm for all of us. I had taken the kids every year before I left.

"I'm sorry I can't go strawberry picking. I have to go into our offices. I have to collect some files. You are more than welcome to still take them; I don't want to ruin the fun."

I held onto my coffee cup, "You'd let me take them by myself?"

"Georgia, you're their mother, the past is the past. Besides, I do not have a single doubt in my mind that they aren't safe with you."

I bit down on my bottom lip nervously.

"I can go picking tomorrow if you want me to come along, I just didn't want to mess everything up. I know you had to make an appointment for us and all."

"No, I can take them," I heard myself say like an out of body experience.

We dropped Tom at the commuter train, and the kids and I headed off for an afternoon of strawberry picking. The kids and I had a blast. Louis ate more than he picked, the red ring around his little mouth and pink stain down his shirt. After we got home, the kids and I played in the pool in the back yard. It felt wonderful to be a mom to my beautiful children.

Tom arrived home in the late afternoon, and we cooked out for dinner. After dinner, Tom and I stayed out on the back deck, sipping the wine that Tom had opened. We had spent the past ten weeks in total lockdown and the last month in a stepped re-opening. It seemed as if this stolen bit of time was quickly coming to an end.

"A penny for your thoughts," he asked.

I swirled the rosé in my glass.

"Tom, thank you for inviting me out here. Thank you for trusting me today. It was," I stopped finding emotion welling up. "Thank you," I said as I wiped the tears that had escaped my eyes.

He reached over and put his hand over mine. "I did it for them too. Thank you for being so brave to come back and be with them through this. It has meant the world to us, to me."

I nodded as I wiped another tear away. Tom moved over and pulled me into his arms and held me.

I pulled out of his arms, "I don't understand, why are you so good to me? I fucked you over, hard. I don't understand, and I'll never be able to thank you for how kind you've been."

"Because Georgia, I love you. I know through my own therapy that the day that you left, you were ill. I wish I had seen it before it had gotten to that point, where you felt leaving was your only way out. Can I ask you something, you don't have to answer if you don't want to?"

I nodded that he could.

"Was it me? I have spent the past three years wondering what I did wrong? My therapist said I didn't do anything, that it was your choice, but I just have to ask?"

My heart sank.

"Tom, it wasn't you. Your therapist is right. If I could take it all back and do it differently, I would. I am so sorry I hurt you, and I hurt them."

"There hasn't been anyone since you. I haven't dated, not a one-night-stand, nothing."

"Me neither I got close, but it just felt wrong. I know I could have; we are divorced, but I haven't been anywhere near ready for something like that with a stranger."

Tom brought his lips to mine and kissed me gently. At the first sign of tension, he pulled back.

"I'm sorry. I.."

I pulled his lips back to mine. He felt like home, like salve on a painful open wound. Why the hell had I ever been crazy enough to walk away from this wonderful, kind man, I wondered to myself. The world around me began to spin, and I clung to Tom tighter. I needed to cling to him. I felt like he was my lifeline to sanity at that moment. I climbed into his lap, both of us shedding clothes, like horny teenagers. We had sex right there on the back porch, as our children slept in their beds upstairs. It was the best feeling, more than pleasure, it came with love, and I felt almost drunk with it.

That night I slept in Tom's bed. We made love again, and I fell asleep in his arms. I woke with a jolt in the early hours of the morning. Panic washed over me. What had I done last night? I was terrified. I had made a colossal mistake. What if I left, what if I ran again? My mind raced. What would life look like now that we had slept together? Did he want me to move back in and be wife and mommy? Did I want that, really want that?

I got out of bed, my body trembling, and walked into the bathroom. I saw my reflection in the mirror, and I looked away. What had I done? I walked to my room and dressed quietly. I grabbed my wallet and walked out of the house as the sun began to rise. I needed to clear my head and think I couldn't do it in Tom's arms, or with my children sleeping down the hall. If I came back, it was for good. I would not return until I was sure I would not repeat the mistake I had made three years ago. I could not hurt the ones I loved most again.

I walked the eight blocks into town and saw that the bakery was open. I bought a dozen donuts, knowing no matter what, my choice was that I would not run off without saying goodbye properly. I wouldn't hurt them again. As I came around the corner, I spotted Tom standing in the driveway. He jogged up to me.

"Where did you go?"

"I needed to clear my head, I went for a walk, and I got donuts."

Tom looked down at his bare feet, "When I woke up and saw that you weren't there, I worried that I had scared you away."

I set the box of donuts on the sidewalk and put my arms around him. He embraced me tightly and kissed the top of my head.

"I love you, Georgia."

"I love you too. I don't know what the future holds for us. Please just make me one promise?"

"Name it."

"Can we please take this slow and without expectations?"

Tom tipped my chin up, "Yes, and will you promise me one thing in return? Please don't run off again, never. Talk to me, if you don't want to stay, we'll deal with that. Please don't ever stop talking to me and letting me know where you are with all of this. I love you; I will always love you."

I leaned up and kissed him right there for all of the world to see, in front of our home.

Amelia & Ian: The Small Town Hero

I moved to Baker's Ridge, the flattest stretch of land in Indiana. I'm not sure why the town had the name ridge in it. There was a hill, bluff of Ridge, to be seen for miles. I moved from New York in late January. Ever move across the country in the middle of winter, to the middle of nowhere? Oh, and I forgot the most crucial factor at the beginning of a global pandemic? Of course, at the time, I didn't know it was a pandemic or just how big it would be.

My company, once headquartered in New York, had picked Baker's Ridge, Indiana, to set up our new global headquarters. Yeah, you read that right, Indiana. But truth be told, there was a lot of emerging tech happening in Northern Indiana. A lot of the once-industrial cities of the Midwest were undergoing a renewal with a new tech scene. Rent was cheap, workers were plentiful, the air was clean... It just made sense.

I moved into the top floor apartment of an old Victorian house in town. The apartment was a massive three-bedroom apartment, with all of the original fixtures, hardwood floors, and a working fireplace. I would've gone broke even trying to get close to renting something like this back east, and that's if I could find it. Below me, the landlord lived, a pretty woman who worked for the city. I had been struck by Amelia's beauty the first time I saw her. She wore her dark brown hair in soft curls in a timeless cut that looked ladylike and elegant. She was petite but curvy. Normally she was my type, but it was her eyes; they were beautiful and sad at the same time. It was her eyes that I noticed most. They were greenest eyes I'd ever seen, the color of emeralds. I'd never seen anyone with eyes her color before, so much so that after our first meeting, I thought that maybe she wore contacts.

Her boyfriend, Billy, was a Baker's Ridge police officer, and a real asshole. He lived with Amelia, and they fought a lot. It was heated, but I'd never seen or heard signs of violence. I settled into my new life, going to work, coming home, and doing it all over again. Honestly, I was so busy getting the office up and running that I paid very little attention to the coming storm that the pandemic would bring.

One morning in early March, I got an email saying that everyone would be working remotely for the foreseeable future due to the virus that was spreading across the country. While everyone else would work from home, that meant my next week would be a living hell as I helped get everyone and our technology equipped for remote work. I lived at the office for that first week of quarantine and only returned home to change clothes.

Finally, after the longest week of my life, I shuffled into my apartment in clothes I'd been wearing for two days and drenched from the slushy wet snow that fell outside. Being March, the perception was somewhere between snow, ice, and rain, and it just soaked everything in cold water that would be sure to ice up after dark. I threw my keys in the dish that sat on the ledge by my door and kicked my shoes off. I needed food, a shower, and my bed in that order.

I microwaved a frozen lasagna and went through the stack of mail that had piled up while I was gone. The lasagna finished, and I ate it so quickly I burnt the hell out of my mouth. I looked outside as the wet snow had fully transitioned to sleet. If it kept up, I knew we'd lose power, and all of the work for the past week would be for naught. People couldn't work without power.

Showered, I collapsed in my bed and fell asleep before my head even hit the pillow. I awoke in my dark apartment to a noise that it took me a minute to recognize was my front door. No one ever came to my door. I looked over at my phone, and the time said 2:35 a.m. I reached over to click on the lamp on the nightstand, but the light didn't come on.

I got out of bed and stumbled through my dark apartment. I looked through the peephole of the door, I saw Amelia's silhouette walking down the stairs, her flashlight held out in front of her. I opened it, and she turned at the noise.

"Sorry to wake you, I didn't know if you were home or not. I wanted to offer some extra blankets and a flashlight or two if you needed them."

"Thanks, is it the ice storm?"

"Yes. I also wanted to apologize for earlier with Billy and me."

"Sorry, I'm not following."

She pulled the quilt she had wrapped around her shoulders tighter. I wanted to pick her up off of the stairs and carry her to my bed. She was gorgeous in the dark stairwell.

"Oh, just that we were loud earlier, things got out of hand. I'm sorry for the noise."

"I didn't hear anything. I came home and went to bed."

"Are you ill?"

"No, thankfully, I've just been working like crazy. I'll be here now working from home like the rest of my company. I had to get everyone set up to be remote."

"Well, that's good, I'll grab the flashlights and blankets, I don't know how long we'll be out. I guess lines are down all over town. I'll be right back."

I watched her walk down the stairs before I walked back to my own room and put on a sweatshirt. I had answered the door in a pair of pajama pants and nothing else. The apartment seemed to grow chiller by the minute. I waited for her to return, and after twenty minutes, I went down to her apartment. She'd left her door ajar, and I knocked as I called out her name. The room was dark, but her apartment had mirrored mine in layout from what I could tell. It was very dark, but it looked like furniture was out of place, like it had been tipped over.

"Amelia?" I called out.

I walked towards the back of the apartment and tripped over a kitchen chair. Her apartment was a mess. I saw the glow of the flashlight under the bedroom door, and she opened it at the noise of my falling.

"Ian, is that you?"

She found me as I got up. In the beam of light, I could see that the apartment was a wreck. I wondered if this was the noise she had meant earlier.

"Sorry, I wondered if you needed any help with the flashlights or blankets?" I noticed I could see my breath in her apartment. "Does your fireplace work?"

"It does. Yours does upstairs too."

"Would you like some help starting a fire? Do you have any firewood?"

"I do. I'll get it. Are you okay, did you trip?"

"I'm alright."

"Sorry about the state of the place. Billy isn't normally like this, he's just. I think it's the stress of all of this, you know."

I wanted to nod that I agreed, but from what I could see from the light of the flashlight, her place was a wreck. I wondered how'd I'd managed to sleep through all of the noise of him wrecking her place. I wanted to tell her so much that Billy was an asshole before this, and she could do better and that I was afraid for her, but I kept my mouth shut.

"I have a stack of blankets on the bed and two extra flashlights. I can bring some wood up from the backyard if you'll take the blankets."

I got to my feet and followed her into her bedroom. She reached down to scoop the blankets up and froze as she looked towards the doorway. I turned to see what she was looking at.

"What the hell is going on in here?" Billy said, standing in the doorway, in full uniform.

The look on Amelia's face broke my heart. She was terrified. I turned around.

"Hi Billy, nasty night, huh? Amelia was just lending me a few extra blankets and a flashlight. I was unprepared for the ice storm."

He let out a huff, "yeah, your city boys ain't prepared for shit. Don't you have blankets at your own house?"

"Billy, please." Amelia choked out. "It's..." She stopped talking mid-sentence as he glared through her.

"Get your blanket, then city boy, and get the hell out of my bedroom."

Amelia handed me the blankets and with a flashlight on top of the pile.

"Come on, let's go, city boy."

I know that Amelia registered the flash of anger in my face, and her eyes silently pleaded with me not to engage with Billy. I slid my hands under the blanket, and for some reason, I squeezed her hand as I took the blankets from her. It was only a split second, but it was the first time I had physically touched her. I didn't want to let go. I turned and walked out without saying anything.

After I deposited the blankets in my apartment, I went out back and grabbed two armfuls of firewood. I left one by Amelia's door and took the other armful up to my apartment. With the power out, the whole house was very quiet. I heard muffled arguing, but I couldn't make out what was said. I sat up until they quieted downstairs. I fell asleep on my couch, with a fire going for warmth.

After that night, Amelia kept her distance. I watched Billy come and go, and the lockdown intensified, and the virus took hold. Work dragged on, and I felt like the four walls of my apartment were closing in. Desperate for a new scene, I grabbed my laundry basket and took it down to the basement. There was a small laundry room that both units shared. I opened the door and saw Amelia folding a towel.

"Oh, sorry," I said, standing in the doorway.

I couldn't help but notice how thin she looked, almost frail.

"I'll be done in a minute." Her body language tensed at the sight of me. "Actually, I'll finish folding these upstairs," she said as she chucked the folded laundry on top of the unfolded laundry."

"There's no need to rush on my account, take your time, I'm not in a hurry."

"No, I'm sorry. I should go."

"I'll come back, you finish up."

She picked the laundry basket up and walked towards the door. As she approached, she caught her foot on the leg of the table and tripped, sending the basket and it's contents flying. I reached out to catch her, and she landed in my arms. I had ahold of her by her t-shirt, which exposed her upper arms because it was pulled tight. There were dotted bruises, and it took me a second to realize they had to be Billy's fingers. She stumbled out of my arms and bent down to pick up the laundry.

251

"Amelia, your arms."

"It's nothing, I'm so clumsy."

I knelt down. That's not clumsiness. Those are Billy's fingerprints."

She nodded that they weren't as she began to tremble. I'd never heard him hit her, but I'd heard him rage again and again. Without thinking, I pulled her into my arms. She was so small in them, and she froze, yet I didn't let go. She looked up at me, her green eyes piercing through me. I was in love with this woman, and no one would ever hurt her again. She didn't have to return the love, but I'd protect her just the same, I knew it at that moment. She leaned up, and I looked down at her as our lips met. It was a gentle kiss, but it packed a punch in my gut.

She pulled away suddenly, "I'm sorry I don't know why I did that. I'm so sorry."

Frantically she started to pick up the clothes off of the floor. I didn't know what to do, and my heart overrode my brain, and I pulled her back into my arms. This time she wrapped her arms around me. She buried her head in my chest. I felt her cry before I heard her. The sound of her soft crying practically ripped my insides out. I held her for a long time, just giving her somewhere safe to work through her thoughts.

"Amelia," I said softly.

She looked up and wiped her eyes. I didn't know it was even possible for her to be more gorgeous, but her eyes sparkled from crying, and her face was flush. I knew at that moment I was in deep; I was in love.

"Tell me how to help," I said.

She shook her head. "You can't. He's a cop, I work for the city. You're new here, you don't get it."

I moved off of my knees and sat on the cold cement floor. "Explain it to me."

She fingered the edge of the towel still in her hand.

"Billy and I grew up here. He was the quarterback, a war hero, the town's son. There is no wrong he can do. He was there for me when my parents died."

"He's abusive, look at your arms."

She looked away and brought the back of her hand up to her mouth as she nodded. Tears ran down her cheeks, and she wiped them away.

"You don't understand, I reported him once. The first time he got rough with me, I kicked him out, and I went to the staff sergeant and reported him."

"What happened?"

"It just pissed him off more, and my boss came into to see me. It was suggested that I not make trouble for Billy, who was a vet trying to get on his feet."

"Are you serious?"

"Like I said, you're not from here. Baker's Ridge is a small town."

"So, what's the plan then?"

"For what?"

"To leave him."

"No, you're still not getting this. If I leave Billy, I lose my job, my house, probably my life."

"I won't let that happen."

She threw the towel down in the basket that she held. "Are you nuts? Billy owns this town. You make a move against him, and you wreck your life too. Seriously the best thing you can do is just forget about this. Forget we ever had this conversation."

She got to her feet and picked up the basket. I stood.

"Amelia, wait, please."

She stopped in front of the basement door and turned around.

"If you want out, I'll help you. It doesn't mean you have to be with me. I'll help you, no matter what. You say the word, and we're out of here. I'll help you in any way I can, help you set up a new life."

"You're a good man Ian. I wish life was different. I wish we'd met in another time and place."

She walked out of the basement before I could reply.

The next day I watched for Billy's squad car to pull away and went downstairs. I wanted to finish the conversation we started the day before. I knocked on the door, but Amelia didn't answer. I heard noise from the back yard and walked out of the back door from the common hallway. Amelia was sitting on her back porch with a mug of coffee in her hands. The morning sun cast a warm glow across the back yard. It felt like the first warm spring morning. Without saying anything, I came and sat next to her. She reached out and grabbed my hand and interlaced her fingers in mine. I looked down at her, and I couldn't help myself. I brought my lips over hers and kissed her. She kissed me back, and it was like my whole world exploded.

I pulled her close, spilling her coffee over my leg. Thankfully it was lukewarm. She tasted like coffee and vanilla, and cinnamon. I couldn't get enough of her, I needed more than a kiss, but I'd be damned if I'd be another man in her life who would hurt her.

She pulled her lips from mine and whispered in my ear," follow me."

Like a lost puppy, I followed her back through the house up to my apartment. She opened the door and stepped inside before she turned around back towards me. I pulled her back into my arms and kissed her, desperate for the connection with her again. She pulled at her mint-green sweater to remove it. It was physically painful how much I wanted her, but not like this. She pulled her lips away to remove her shirt. I saw the fresh and faded bruises from Billy. My face must have shown my surprise and horror as she realized my reaction. She put the shirt over her torso.

"I... I'm... I should go." She said.

I grabbed her hand gently, "wait, please. I want this so much it hurts; I want you so much it hurts. From the first movement I saw you, I've been in love with you. I stayed up all night last night listening to make sure you were safe."

"What?"

"You don't know me. I realized yesterday in the basement that I haven't been me for a long time. The real me wants you. I want a new life. I don't want to be some tragic statistic."

I crossed the distance between us.

"What is your full name?" I asked as I pulled her back into my arms.

"Amelia Ann Purdy."

"Hi, Amelia Ann Purdy. I am Ian Jacob Green. I'm from Wisconsin, and I've lived in New York for the past ten years before coming here."

She giggled, "I know this, I'm your landlord, remember."

"True."

"Tell me something else, something no one else knows about you."

"My favorite food is cheese sandwiches with pickles on them."

She laughed, and I just about melted to see her smile. I hadn't had the chance to see her smile. I was a goner for this woman.

"My favorite food is homemade apple pie. I used to make it with my mom and grandma every year. They owned a farm just outside of town, and we'd harvest the apples each September. I miss all of them so much."

"That's a nice memory. I grew up in the country too. I used to ice-skate on a pond behind my house in the winters."

"Really? Me too!"

I lent down and kissed her.

"Please make love to me, Ian. It's been so long since I've felt what real love is."

I made love to her right there in my bed, and it was love. Her body felt like home. We connected like I had never connected with another woman. She was it, the one. I knew it.

Each day after Billy would leave, we'd spend the afternoon in each other's arms. In our own little quarantine bubble. It seemed that with each day we spent in each other's arms, that Amelia grew stronger, happier. One afternoon as we lay in my bed naked in each other's arms, she looked up at me.

"I'm going to leave Billy today. I want off of this sick rollercoaster with him."

I felt relief. Each night that she returned to her apartment with him there, I was a nervous wreck. I knew she needed to find her own way out. It was important o her. I also knew that all she needed to do was say the word, and we'd be gone together to start a new life.

That night when Billy returned from work, I'd be ready for him. I set up a few extra cameras I had from our office around the property with Amelia's permission. If things went south, I wanted proof. I also invited over a few security guys from the office. I told them the whole story, and they knew they were there to be witnesses and protect Amelia. I could deal with getting hit, but I didn't want anything to happen to her. Phillip, our head of security, insisted on being there as well.

We all waited awkwardly for Billy to come home. Amelia came up and stood alongside me. She grabbed my hand, and I squeezed it. I felt her hand tremble in mine, and I'd follow her lead. She insisted on being the one to break things off. The three guys from the office and I were there to back her off. She glanced and me nervously as he pulled up in his squad car. I prayed she wouldn't get cold feet.

"What's all this?" Billy said as he walked up to the front porch. "Amelia, you're entertaining half the men in town on my porch. What the hell? Get your ass in the house."

Phillip stood up. He towered over Billy in size and stature.

"No. No, I won't follow you inside so you can beat the crap out of me. No, you can't come inside my house. I want you to leave and never come back. We're through."

I was so proud of her. Her body trembled.

"What the hell did you just say to me?"

He moved towards her, and she took a step back. I came up alongside her.

"This is none of your business, city boy. You don't want any trouble," he said as he rested his hand on his firearm.

"You heard her get the hell out of here."

He took another step towards me as I said it, we were about the same height, and I didn't cower. I gently pushed Amelia, so I stood between her and Billy. Phillip came to the front edge of the porch. He'd been destined for the NFL when he tore a ligament in his knee. Now he worked security. I'd seen some of the nastiest looking people scurry away at a stare from Phillip. Billy stopped.

"Amelia, this isn't over. I'll be back later, and we will discuss this."

Phillip stepped off the porch and came up and stood next to me. Amelia came from around both of us.

"No, you won't. Don't come back here ever again."

"Don't tell me what to do. This is outrageous. You've lost your damn mind. This is my house, I live here."

"You have a house of your own, go live there." She said.

I looked at the woman I loved in perhaps her bravest moment of life. Billy grabbed her arm and pulled her close before anyone could do anything.

"Get your ass in the damn house. I'm done with this shit."

"Let go of me."

Everything happened so quickly as I moved towards Amelia, and Phillip moved towards me. I felt a fist collide with my face, but I couldn't tell you who hit me. The other two guys came down as they took Billy down to the ground, and Phillip called the police.

"No, they'll arrest you guys, he's a cop," Amelia said as she stood up.

I looked up at her, blood pouring from her nose. Terrified, I took off my t-shirt and held it up to her nose. I only prayed we had him on camera hitting her. I knew I had not thrown the first punch, and I also knew none of the security guys had either. The cameras I had put up earlier would come into play. Phillip came over and looked at Amelia and then me.

"You two make quite the pair." He said as he shook his head. "Her with a broken nose and you with a split brow."

The police showed up, and it turned out that with the camera footage and the weight of being one of the biggest new employees in town, Billy was put on administrative leave, pending investigation. In the meantime, Amelia and I had the chance to see where things could go in our relationship.

Every day with her got better and better. She had quickly become my best friend, my soulmate, and the light of my life. In August, I suggested a road trip to see my parents. Things weren't completely open, and quarantine restrictions were lifted, but there were still restrictions in place. As we drove through the country roads, I looked over at her and shifted the contents of my pockets. I only prayed she would notice the ring box I had in there. I was going to ask her to marry me on the lake while we were there.

Taylor & Greg: The Nanny and the Man

Greg was a great dad to his three daughters. That's what attracted me most to him. I met him and Kailey, Ellie, and Annie when I replied to an ad on social media for a nanny. I graduated from college mid-year, and I figured it wouldn't hurt to put some money away while I was job hunting. I talked to Greg first on the phone, and there was something about his voice that put me at ease. He explained that he occasionally traveled for work and would need someone to stay with his girls. He gave me a few days to think about it before we set up a meeting after that first interview over the phone. In the call, he didn't mention the girls' mother, and it didn't feel like the time to ask.

I met Greg in person on Valentine's Day. The large brick townhouse sat on a corner with a black wrought-iron fence around it. The townhouse wasn't overly large, but it was grand in the sense that it was old and stood proudly on the corner since the day it had been built. I turned the handle on the gate and walked up the front steps as it started to snow again. We were due for a big storm, but the worst of it wasn't expected to hit until much later in the day. This snow was just the beginning. I knocked on the large black set of doors and turned around to watch the snow fall. I turned back around at the noise of the door opening and finally saw Greg face to face. He was older than I had imagined on the phone, but he wore it well. I would have guessed he was in his thirties by his voice, but by his looks, he looked closer to mid-forties. It was his eyes that caught my attention. First, they were icy blue, but it was more than the color. If the eyes are the window to the soul, Greg's eyes said he was sad, hurting, and searching for something I did not know. He wore a beard, cut short, and it complemented his chocolate brown wavy hair. Standing about a foot and a half taller than me, he had a slim but muscular build, that I got the hint of by the way his clothes fit.

"Hi, you must be Lucy," he said as he held his hand out to shake mine.

"I am, you're Greg," I asked, taking his and into mine.

His handshake was firm, but I noticed the warmth of his hand and his skin on mine, but it was the warmth more than the grip that I noticed. He moved out of the doorway and gestured for me to enter. I walked in, pulling my hand away from his, and felt a flutter from deep in my stomach. I couldn't take the job, I knew it then, I was supremely attracted to Greg. He came around me and let me into the front sitting room. The house was tastefully decorated, not like a bachelor would have done it, or he had hired a decorator. Whoever had done the room knew what they were doing, it was gorgeous with the two white couches that sat opposite each other, and a fireplace with a small fire going. I instinctively walked over to it and put my hands out to warm them.

"It's cold out there, isn't it? Can I take your coat," Greg asked as he followed me into the room.

"It is, we're supposed to get a snowstorm tonight. You'd think it would be too cold to snow," I replied as I took off my coat and handed it to him.

He took my coat and walked out of the room as I looked at the pictures on the mantel. His three daughters, with their bright red hair, freckles, and smiles, were in almost every picture. I finally spotted a picture of the woman who had to be their mother, her dark auburn hair with its soft wave, fell softly around her shoulders as her blue eyes radiated happiness. I wondered why she wasn't here to interview me. I looked in the mirror that sat above the fireplace, and my reflection

260

showed my cheeks bright pink from the cold. The natural pink hue complimented my dark brown hair and green eyes. I couldn't see much more of my face, as I was too short, and the mantle was tall. I heard Greg walk back into the room, and I turned around at his entrance to the room.

"Would you like something to drink, perhaps something warm, coffee, cocoa, tea?"

"No, thank you. This lovely fire has done the trick," I replied as I walked over and sat on one of the couches at Greg's urging.

Greg walked in and sat opposite. I folded my hands in my lap and waited for him to begin. I had so many questions, but so far, I had liked what I had saw.

"So, you've graduated early then?"

"Yes, I took an extra course each semester."

"What did you study?"

"Journalism."

Greg nodded, "Good major, so what is your ultimate occupation and why nannying right now?"

I let out a nervous laugh, I always did that when I was nervous, and I hated it, but I couldn't help it. I wasn't sure if it was sitting opposite to a man as handsome as Greg or actually wanting the position, but my nerves kicked into overdrive.

"I want to take some time to figure out what I want to really do in journalism. This position would give me some time to assess where I want to be."

"That makes sense. So it is just the girls and me. We've had a lot of change in the past year and a half, so I want whoever I hire to be around for a while. Does that sound like something you could do?"

"How long is a while?"

"Maybe the next year or so. I have to be honest, with you just starting a career, this seems unfair to ask."

"I can't commit to a year, but a solid few months. I understand if that won't work for you and the girls. Can I ask?"

He put his hand up before I could finish my question and took a deep breath.

"I'm a widower. My wife passed away almost a year and a half ago. She slipped and fell onto the El tracks, hit her head, and never woke up."

"I am so sorry for your loss. I understand why stability would be so important right now."

"Thank you. I've hired a few nannies through agencies, but it has not been a great experience. I just need someone who will look after my girls, keep them safe, and be a friend to them. It sounds simple enough, but I've had a string of bad luck finding the right person."

"You said they were, 9, 7, and 5, is that right?"

"Yes. They're in school, and so on weekdays, they'd be there. The job would most getting them ready in the mornings for school and picking them up from school and then evenings until I got home. I've tried to cut back on my travel for work, but I still occasionally have to go. I've been leaving them with my sister, but she lives out in the burbs and has kids of her own, it just gets tricky."

"I understand."

"They've been through a lot, my girls, and I have to get this right for them. I can't be everywhere, here for them, and working the hours I need to."

"What do you do for a living?"

"I'm a private equity attorney. Does this position still interest you, even if you can't commit to the long term?"

"It does. I might work well. I'd be willing to give it a try."

"Really? There's a room for you too, so you wouldn't have to pay rent somewhere if you didn't want to, and that is included in your compensation. You'd pretty much have run of the house. You said you had experience working with children?"

"Yes, I come from a large family and babysat all through my teen years."

"Your family, are they here in the city?"

"No, they're all back east. I went to Northwestern and fell in love with Chicago. I'd like to stay here and make a career here if I can."

"It's a good news city. Would you be willing to meet their girls?"

"Of course. They have to feel comfortable with me."

"I'm relieved to hear you say that." He said as he looked down at his watch. "They'll be home in a few hours. Would you like to see the house in the meantime?"

"Okay. I just wanted to clarify or ask, would it be okay for me to only stay when you are out of town? I have a place of my own not far from here, and I'd feel more comfortable that way."

"It's not what I had in mind, but it can work. I'd like for the girls to stay here if I'm away on business. It's important to me that they're in their own beds each night."

"I understand."

He stood up, and I followed his lead as he took me through the townhouse. There were four large bedrooms upstairs. Each of the girls had their own and were the sweetest rooms I had ever saw. One thing was clear that Greg loved his daughters deeply. His face lit each time he spoke of them. We wound our way through the house, down the back stairs, and into the large kitchen at the back of the townhouse. I was surprised to see that the original cabinets, tiles, and stove sat, like a time capsule. It was charming.

"My wife wouldn't let me touch this room when we moved in. She loved the vintage look of the kitchen," he said as if he had read my mind.

"She was right, It's charming."

"That's exactly what she said, I'll be honest, I don't get it."

We rounded a corner and passed through his office, with its dark wood panels and bookcases on either side of the room. The next room was the master, with its en-suite bathroom. We wound back out to the foyer.

"So that's the house. I have a cleaning lady that comes twice a week, so I wouldn't expect you to do that. What do you think? Still want to meet the girls?"

"Yes."

"You could have the free room upstairs when you stayed if that would be okay?"

"Yes, it will work. When would you like me to meet them?"

"Are you busy this evening?"

"I don't have plans tonight."

"On Valentine's Day?"

I laughed nervously again. "Not this year."

That night I came back and met his daughters, who were adorable and charming. I also knew I was going to have to be careful to keep my attraction in check. Greg's looks had disarmed me when we met and set me on edge. Seeing him with his daughters, so kind and gentle, about made me melt. I stayed for dinner, as we ate spaghetti from Inga's Tatorttoria down the street. Greg went and picked it up, giving the girls and I a few minutes alone to get to know each other. I was smitten with their freckles and red hair. They were adorable balls of girly energy. I adored them instantly. We laughed through dinner as the girls grilled me on every aspect of my life. I found it adorable, and Greg seemed pleased. After dinner, the girls went up to their rooms to play and finish homework, leaving Greg and I alone in the dining room.

"What do you think? Still interested in the position?"

"Absolutely, they're wonderful."

"You have no idea how glad I am to hear you say that. I haven't seen them that excited in a really long time. They genuinely like you."

"I like them."

We agreed that I'd start the following Tuesday, which gave me three days before I started. The first week I spent getting the girls to and from school. I helped them each evening with their homework and made them dinner. Greg usually arrived home between 7:30 and 8 pm each night. I admired how, when he came in the door, his girls were his immediate and only focus. He was a great dad.

After a month, one night, as I put my coat on to leave, Greg told me that he'd have to go to Seoul, Korea for a week for work. I felt ready to take the girls full-time. Honestly, caring for them did not feel like a job. I was having a blast. I also loved that I got to see Greg each day. I was crushing hard on him and tried to keep my feelings hidden, but tension was growing between us, it seemed. I hoped it wasn't in my head, but I reassured myself that it couldn't be. I had caught him looking at me in the way one looks at someone they're interested in.

I came over the following Sunday to get the rundown for what I needed to know while Greg was out of the country. He had dropped the girls off at his sister's for their cousin's birthday party, leaving us alone in the house. I walked into the front door and announced my entrance as my greeting echoed through the empty house. Greg's office door was shut, and I pressed my ear up against the door before I knocked. I could hear him on the phone, so I put my coat over the chair that sat opposite so he would see that I was there when his call was over. I walked through the house, it felt empty without the girls, as I continued into the kitchen to make a cup of tea. I was frozen solid from being outside. I filled the kettle and put it on, then grabbed a mug and a teabag. I ignited the gas burner as Greg walked in.

"Hi, I thought I heard you in here. Sorry, my call went long. Thanks for coming by today."

"Do you want a cup of tea? I boiled enough water for two. I hope you don't mind that I helped myself, I was so cold."

"Not at all, as of tomorrow, this will practically be your house. Do you feel ready?"

"Yes. I'm excited. I adore the girls. Are you ready for your flight and all of that?"

"I am. I hate leaving them."

"In general?" I asked as I realized he might have meant he was nervous about leaving them with me.

"Yes, of course, I have full confidence in you, Taylor. I wouldn't leave if I didn't. I must confess, the girls adore you too. They talk about you constantly when you aren't here."

I smiled as the kettle began to whistle ever so softly.

"I'm sorry, did you say if you wanted a cup of tea?" I asked as I walked over to remove the kettle.

"Sure."

I reached up into the cupboard and grabbed a teacup out. The cup slipped from my hand and fell, hitting the counter, cracking, and then shattering as it hit the floor.

"Oh no," I said as I tried to catch it. I watched as it shattered, sending glass shooting out in all directions from the impact point. "Oh, Greg, I'm so sorry."

I bent down to pick up the shards of broken glass as Greg came over to help.

"No worries, it was only a teacup. I've broken quite a few of these in the exact same way. I think it's the glaze on them that makes them so slippery."

He bent down to help me pick up the glass, and I looked him in the eye. His deep blue eyes, I felt like I could get lost in them. I tried to look away as he kept my gaze. A piece of the teacup dug into my finger and pulled my gaze away instantly.

"Ouch!"

I pulled my finger away, and blood started to drip from the wound. The cut was small but deep.

"Here, let me see."

Before I could protest, he pulled my hand gently towards him and

265

pulled a kitchen towel off of the counter at the same time. I leaned in to examine my finger in his hands as he did the same. He gently pulled the small shard of glass out of my finger and wrapped the towel around my hand. He looked up at me, and I wanted to kiss him, his soft pink lips. I imagined what it would be like to kiss him, what he tasted like. Without warning, he leaned in and kissed me. Like the ignition on the gas burner on the stove, his kiss sparked a flame deep inside my belly. His kiss was soft and gentle. I could smell his cologne and the natural scent of his body as he slid his free hand along my cheek. Abruptly he pulled away.

"Shit, Taylor. I'm so sorry. I…" he trailed off.

I looked away, embarrassed at my own actions. Usually, from anyone else, I would take the admission of guilt as a lie, but I could read it on his face. He knew he had crossed a line. He let go of my hand and stood up.

"I'm sorry. I should not have done that."

I stood up and met his gaze, leaving the broken teacup on the floor for the moment.

"I'm not offended."

"I just don't want you to think I am this sort of guy, I'm not."

"I don't think you are."

"Let me get you your tea and a band-aid. Please sit, I'll clean this up."

I put my hand on his arm, I could tell that he felt awful.

"Greg, it's okay."

"I haven't kissed anyone since my wife. I haven't even been interested in anyone since Maggie. I don't know if it has been seeing you with the girls or what. I promise you I will keep my hands to myself. That will never happen again. I don't want to make you uncomfortable in any way."

"You didn't. Please don't be so hard on yourself."

The way he looked back at me as I moved away and took a seat at the kitchen table told me he needed some space. There was so much hurt and pain in his eyes. He poured the hot water into my teacup and let it brew as he began to pick up the glass from his teacup. I pulled the kitchen towel away from my finger and saw that it had already stopped bleeding. I watched him as he walked out of the kitchen, and I wondered where he had gone. He came back into the room with a first aid kit and stopped to grab my tea. He set it down on the table, and the kit too as he sat down next to me. I reached over for the kit and grabbed a band-aid. As I tried to pull the wrapper open, my cut began to bleed again.

"Here, let me help." He said as he reached for the band-aid in my hand.

I held out my hand for him to put it on, his touch on my skin was wonderful, and I looked up at him again. I saw him start to move in towards me again, but he stopped. I leaned in instead and kissed him gently. He welcomed my kiss as his tongue met mine. I pulled away first, just enough to talk.

"I know that this is not a good idea, but I wanted to kiss you too."

He looked at me and slid his hand along my cheek again, bringing my lips back to his. We kissed until my lips tingled, we were both out of breath. For as eager as we both were, there was a gentleness to his touch. He pulled me towards him, and I felt as if I would spontaneously combust. He pulled his lips away but still held me in his arms.

"I wasn't lying; I haven't done this since Maggie. Are you sure this is what you want?"

I searched his face, unsure if he was looking for me to be the stronger one, to pull back for the both of us. Before I could answer, he spoke up.

"We can't do this, it isn't right. I'm sorry, Taylor. I want to, but it just isn't right."

He gently released me from his embrace as I reached up and stroked the side of his cheek before I sat back in my seat. Before I could say anything else, he had put on a professional face and began to give me the rundown on caring for the girls while he was away. I found it difficult to concentrate, not that there was anything that he said that was unexpected.

"Lastly," he said, "I don't know if you've been following the news about this virus going around. I prefer you keep the girls out of large crowds."

"Of course, it's pretty scary. Do you think it will come here, and will you have any issues traveling to Asia?"

"I shouldn't, it is a quick trip, so hopefully I'll be home before anything kicks off. I think it will come here, but we have some time yet, and it won't be widespread, but I don't know."

The next morning, I arrived before the sun rose. The girls were still asleep in beds. Greg met me in the foyer.

"Good morning, coffee is on if you want a cup." He said as I took off my coat and set my bag down.

"Yes, please."

"Please help yourself, I am going to go grab the cash I have for you while I'm away."

I walked into the kitchen as he walked into his office. I tried to shrug off the awkwardness that hung in the air. Although I agreed with and respected his decision to not sleep together yesterday, the desire was still there. I poured myself a cup of coffee, and I could not help but think of yesterday afternoon, being in his arms. I heard a knock at the front door and hurried to open it so the noise wouldn't wake the girls. The driver for Greg's car had arrived. I told the driver he'd be right out and shut the door. I walked into Greg's office, knocking first.

"Your car is here."

He stood behind his desk. I could see there was concern on his face.

"Don't worry, I will take good care of the girls, we'll have a blast."

"I have no doubt you'll take great care of them. I forgot to mention that I'd like to call them each evening."

"Of course. What time?"

"Will 8 pm work?"

"Yes. We are going to stick pretty close to home. Did you see the paper this morning? The virus seems to be spreading in New York now."

"I saw, I am wondering if this is a good idea to travel right now. I'll be in and out," he reassured himself.

He walked up to me, and I couldn't help myself. I leaned up and kissed his cheek.

"Safe travels," I said gently as I leaned back down.

"I couldn't sleep last night. I kept thinking about yesterday afternoon."

"Me too."

He placed his hand on my cheek, and I turned and kissed the inside of his palm, holding his hand against my face. He leaned in and placed a soft kiss on my lips and then leaned his forehead on mine.

"Please take good care of my girls, they're my whole world."

"I will. Go before you miss your flight."

He pulled away, his hand still in mine, and squeezed it as he walked out of the front door.

Three days after he left, all travel from Asia ceased. Greg frantically tried to get back home to The States. It scared me to see him so afraid. I made sure to keep the news off, to not scare the girls. Greg and I talked each night privately and texted back and forth. The more we talked, the more I knew I'd completely fallen for him.

Two weeks later, when the lockdown started in Chicago, Greg told me I could take the girls to his sisters if I wanted. I declined, wanting to keep them home. We made the best of a terrifying situation, and I did my best to keep them entertained. The girls yearned for their father, and I wanted Greg to be home too. School for the girls canceled, and it seemed as if life ground to a halt. That night when the girls went to bed, I called Greg to give him the daily update. I Facetimed him from the living room. The screen came on, and I noticed he looked distressed.

"Hello," I said.

"How was today?"

"Good, we played nail salon and built forts in the living room. The girls are in good spirits. How are you doing?"

"I'm going out of my mind here. I want to be there with you guys. I'm not allowed to leave my room, and it feels like I will never get home."

"You will. In the meantime, I am keeping the girls safe. We are shut-ins too."

"Thank you for that. You don't know what it means to see them so happy while all of this is going on."

"You look stressed."

"I am. This is so hard."

"It is, but we'll get through it."

"Taylor, I don't just miss the girls, I miss you too. I'm sorry if that makes you uncomfortable."

"If I'm being honest, I miss you too."

"I can't stop thinking about that afternoon in the kitchen."

"Me neither."

"Does this make you uncomfortable? Please tell me if I'm out of line here?"

"You're not."

"I know I keep asking about the girls, but how are you doing? Are you okay?"

I smiled; his concern touched my heart.

"I'm all right. I'm scared like everyone else but doing my best to not show it to the girls. My family is upset that I didn't come home, but I explained the situation to them, and they understood the importance of me being here for you and the girls."

"Thank you, I know how difficult this situation is for you too."

Each night Greg called, and we talked. We got to know each other over Facetime. I learned about where he went to school and how his career had started. He also talked a little about losing Maggie and how they had met. It was clear that he was still very much in love with her, not that I minded. She was the mother of his three beautiful daughters. Greg also got to know me, too, about my goals, and dreams, and ambitions. I told him about my family and growing up. As the days turned into weeks, the girls missed him terribly, and I had to admit, as silly as it was, I did too.

Finally, Greg was told that he would be able to fly home in four days. We debated whether or not to tell the girls. We didn't want them to be disappointed if it didn't work out for some reason. The night he booked his ticket, he called me. We sat in talked as usual, as the migraine I had all day roared furiously. I tried to push the pain aside as he showed me his ticket. He was so excited to be home, to hug all of us. He could tell I was in pain, and he offered to have his sister come to look after the girls if I needed help. I declined, hoping I would feel better in the morning.

The next morning, I woke feeling awful, and I knew that this was more than a headache. I was scared. I took my temperature, and it was high. I didn't know if I had caught the virus somehow, even though we had isolated ourselves. Scared, I called my mother, who offered to fly to Chicago. I declined. If I had the virus, the last thing I wanted was to pass it to her. The girls woke and saw how sick I was. I could tell that Kailey, the oldest, was scared too. I reassured her and told her we'd just have a movie day and take it easy. All three girls tried their best to help take care of me, and I could not believe how sweet they were. Greg and Maggie had raised wonderful children. That night I fell asleep on the couch, too sick and sore to move to my bed. I heard my phone ring off in the distance, but I didn't have the strength to go search for it. I knew it had to be Greg, but I'd have to miss tonight's call.

I struggled through the next day, sicker than I had ever been. I seriously considered calling my mother or Greg's sister to look after the girls. They were terrific and so self-reliant, but I feared what would happen if I didn't make it past this illness. There was nowhere for me to get tested, and I couldn't leave the girls alone to go do it. If I had the flu and not the virus, I didn't want to expose all of us either. That night Greg called, and I barely had the energy to speak to him. I read the alarm on his face when I answered the Facetime call. We talked briefly before I fell asleep, forgetting to hang up the call. I woke the next afternoon, still feeling rotten. Panicked, I managed to get myself off of the couch and check on the girls. Kailey had made them all cereal, and the three of them were playing in her room. I laid down in my bed and tried to listen for them. I fell back asleep, too weak and winded from the climb up the stairs.

That night I didn't hear my phone ring from Greg's call. I rolled over around 3 am and saw a soggy bowl of cereal that one of the girls had left for me. By sheer will power, I managed to get out of bed and went and checked on them. They were tucked into Greg's bed down in his room. I made my way back to the couch to try to stay on the same floor as them, so I could hear them better. I felt like I had abandoned my post to look after them. It was unfair that this was all falling on Kailey's shoulders, but the way she soldiered on, it was clear she had been in the role before, looking after her younger sisters.

When I woke again, daylight streamed through the front windows, as I laid on the couch I had sat and been interviewed on. I felt something wet across my forehead and turned to look. Greg stood above me, wetting my brow with a cool washcloth. I tried to sit up.

"Shhh, just stay still, help is on the way." He said, trying to soothe me.

"Are you really here," I croaked.

"I am."

"The girls?"

"They're upstairs."

"No, I don't want you to get this, stay away."

"Too late, I'm exposed."

I heard sirens approaching and wondered if they were coming for me. In my fever-induced haze, I was afraid he had called the police because I had not cared for his girls over the past few days. Too weak, I couldn't move. I tried not to cry, but I couldn't help it.

"It's okay, you'll be okay."

I closed my eyes.

When I opened them again, I was in a hospital room with an iv in my arm. I didn't remember the ambulance ride or going through the emergency room. The doctor came in a while later to let me know that I had caught the virus but that I was doing very well. His comment surprised me, as I felt as close to death as I ever had. I could only imagine what a bad case of this would have been like. A nurse came in with a small blue gift bag.

"This was left by a very handsome, very concerned friend of yours. He can't come up and visit, but he asked me to give it to you."

I reached out for it, and she handed it to me. Inside there was a blue stuffed bunny and handmade cards from the girls. I smiled as I read them.

"Are those from your girls," she asked?

I smiled and nodded even though they were exactly mine. Going through all of this, I felt like they were now in a weird way. I looked into the bottom of the bag and saw an envelope with my name on it. I pulled it out and opened it. It was a letter from Greg. The letter said:

Dear Taylor,

I have no words to convey my level of gratitude to you for keeping my girls safe. When I got home and saw you on the couch, I have only been that afraid one other time in my life, the night Maggie died. I didn't get a chance to tell her how much I loved her one last time. I don't want to miss my chance again. I pray that you get better soon because all I want to do is hold you in my arms. Over these past few weeks, I have fallen for you. I know how crazy that sounds, not even being on the same content, but I love you, Taylor. Please fight with everything you have in you. The girls and I need you.

Yours,

Greg

I held onto the letter tightly. I felt like it gave me strength, the will of the girls, and the love from Greg to fight off the virus. I was in the hospital for ten days, and each day fresh roses arrived to my room from Greg. My mother had once again offered to fly in to care for me when I got home, but the doctor advised against it. Although I was better, I could still be infectious. The hospital arranged transport back to my apartment, where I would be isolated for two weeks. It felt wonderful to be in my own place, although the only place I wanted to be was with Greg and the girls. That evening, as I sat on my couch, I heard the girls' familiar squeals and giggles.

"Taylor," they called up at my window on the third floor.

I got up and walked out to the balcony to see Greg and the girls down on the sidewalk. The girls cheered as I stepped out of my apartment. I could see relief wash over Greg's face to see me up and about. We had continued to talk each night on the phone while I was in the hospital, and I swear that it was the promise of being able to be with him and the girls that gave me the strength to heal. I waved down at them.

"We wanted to come by to see you," he shouted up.

We had our distanced visit for a couple minutes before I got winded trying to shout, and seeing that I was getting tired, Greg took the girls home. That night he called and told me that being so close but not being able to hold me had been difficult. Together we counted down the days until my isolation period was over.

While I was in isolation, he had himself tested for immunity. We wanted to be extra careful, the test came back positive, and we were thrilled. He had contracted the virus but had been asymptomatic. The morning that my isolation period was over, I woke thinking about Greg. We had decided that they'd come over for a short visit so the girls could see me, and we'd go from there. Sunlight shone through the open windows of my apartment, as the early June air blew in. I rolled over in bed, grateful that I had made it through the worst, and so far did not have any long-lasting effects.

My doorbell rang, and I rolled over in the direction of the door. My stomach did a little flip as I hoped it was Greg. I got out of bed, and I pulled my bathrobe around me as I made my way to my front door. I opened it and saw Greg standing on the landing with a massive bouquet of roses.

"I couldn't wait any longer to see you in person."

I smiled as he stepped into my apartment. He set the roses down on my table in the hallway and pulled me into his arms. My body felt small in his grip, and I loved the feeling. I felt safe for the first time since I could remember. I put my arms around him and held him. We stood in my living room with the sunlight around us, happy to be able to have each other. We stayed like that for a long time, as I listened to his breath and smelled the scent of him. The moment felt surreal, he was actually here, and I was in his arms. Emotion got the better of me, and tears streamed down my face. Noticing my breath hitch, Greg tipped my chin up towards him.

"Honey, what's wrong?"

"I just can't believe you're actually here."

He leaned down and kissed me softly.

"I will always be here."